THE BOOK OF THE RIVER

B6 ᴋᴀᴀ

THE BOOK OF THE RIVER

by

IAN WATSON

LONDON
VICTOR GOLLANCZ LTD
1984

This novel was first published in four parts in *The Magazine of Fantasy and Science Fiction*.

British Library Cataloguing in Publication Data
Watson, Ian, *1943–*
  The book of the river.
  I. Title
  823'.914[F]   PR6073.A683

  ISBN 0-575-03396-7

Printed in Great Britain by
St Edmundsbury Press, Bury St Edmunds, Suffolk

To Ed Ferman
for encouragement

Contents

		page
Part One:	THE BLACK CURRENT	9
Part Two:	NEW YEAR'S EVE AT TAMBIMATU	53
Part Three:	A WALK TO MANHOME, AND AWAY	103
Part Four:	THE WORM'S HEAD	155

Part One

THE BLACK CURRENT

From time immemorial no boat had crossed the river on account of the black current. Yet of course that did not stop us from plying our trade up and down the eastern shoreline all the way from Ajelobo in the south down to Umdala in the north where the river fattens out vastly, becoming salt not fresh, and storm-tossed. And it had always been my ambition as a little girl in dusty Pecawar—almost midway along the axis of our navigation—to join the boating guild and be a riverwoman.

And why not? reasoned my parents. At least that's the brave face they put on my decision (or so I thought at the time). I wouldn't remain on the river forever, but would be bound to find myself a man sooner or later somewhere along those seven hundred leagues of shore between north and south and bring him home to Pecawar to settle him there to raise our family, and probably settle with him—just as other girls took passage in the spring and returned in the autumn with a newly-claimed husband. In my case it might simply take a little longer, but surely I would tire of wanderlust. The river, though richly varied from the southern jungles to the cold northern marshes, is hardly infinite. So after five or six years of sailing up and down it I ought to be all too familiar with change for its own sake.

My twin brother Capsi, as though perversely determined to play west to my north and south, had set his heart on joining the tiny monkish fraternity of observers down in the town of Verrino fifty leagues to the north; about whom we knew little enough in Pecawar, apart from the mere fact of their existence—but this was enough for Capsi. From an early age he had peered through a succession of home-made spy-glasses over the league-and-a-half of river—beyond the black current that streams midway—at the western shore, even though this is quite blank and barren opposite Pecawar.

I myself had no interest at all in the western shore. Nor did anyone else that I knew of, apart from brother Capsi and those obsessives in Verrino. Why should we be interested in what was unattainable and incommunicative, and which had no effect whatever on our lives, nor had for as far back as records went?

But all this changed subtly when, at seventeen, the very minimum age, I applied for membership of the River Guild, and so learned their first guarded secret, the very existence of which I was sworn, upon *The Book of the River*, to keep secret. Namely, that one did not merely sign on, but must be initiated.

"But what *sort* of initiation is it?" I asked the quaymistress in her clapboard office down on the waterfront, after I had sworn and been told. For I associated the word initiation with strange painful rituals up in the Ajelobo tropics.

"Child, do you wish to travel as passenger, or crew?"

"Crew, of course."

"Then you must be initiated, whatever form this takes." The quaymistress laughed, and tossed her sun-bleached hair. She was a handsome, weather-beaten woman of late middle age. She held up her hands, palms out. "See, we don't chop off fingers. Nor do we keelhaul you, or toss you to the stingers, or anything savage like that! We don't really even haze you, or terrify you. I assure you my hair didn't go white from fear."

I nodded, and she rightly took my silence for consent.

"There's a lateen-rig due in tomorrow afternoon. Be here at sunset." With that she dismissed me, and delved back into her manifests.

So the following evening I duly presented myself and was taken by the quaymistress on board the *Ruby Piglet*, and down below deck to the boatmistress's poky cabin, lit by a single oil lantern; and by now I wasn't so much worried as to the nature of the initiation—which in this setting, it seemed to me, could hardly be spectacular or exotic—as that I might somehow be committing myself to sail the river on board *this* cramped tub. I'd had grander visions in mind, of two masts or three. A brig or a schooner.

When we knocked and entered, the boatmistress was wearing a fish-mask, such as we see at the regatta once a year; nothing particularly daunting in that, even if the lantern light did lend more credence to the illusion of a woman with a piscine head,

12

than whenever I'd seen such a mask by daylight. On a little table before her lay a much-thumbed copy of *The Book of the River*, with a smaller chapbook perched upon it. The boatmistress opened this smaller volume and flicked through it in a desultory way as though to refresh her memory; then she suddenly snapped out at me, giving me quite a start.

"Candidate rivergirl, say what the black current is!"

I suppose I gaped.

"Say!"

"It's, well, it's the current that stops us from crossing the river."

"What is its nature?"

"Black?" I suggested.

"Is it water? Is it oil? Is it thin, is it thick? Is it fast, is it slow? Is it living, is it dead?"

"Anyone who tries to cross it dies," said I boldly. "But first they go mad. They're swept away, they're dragged down, swallowed. . . ."

The boatmistress read out of her chapbook. "It isn't water, and it isn't oil. It is more like blood, but not our red blood. It is more like a nerve, but not our nerves. It is more like a spinal column, but not our bony spines. It is all of these, and none.

"The body of the river lives its life from south to north, and the black current is its secret soul; but not like our souls, if we have souls. The black current is its mind; but not like our minds.

"For the river is a creature, and an entity. We are parasites upon her flesh, and the black current is the life-vein of that flesh. Enter it, and she drinks us, drowns us. But first she makes us mad.

"For all the water on this world is alive; it is all one whole, joined to itself. The river is the flexing tail of the dreaming ocean, ever rippling downstream, ever replacing itself."

Suddenly I was terrified, for to us in Pecawar, ever since I had learned to lisp and point and ask questions, the river had simply been the river: a body of water, something to gaze up and down as boats sailed by (though not to swim in because of the stingers), a supply route, a signpost both ways to different cities, different landscapes.

13

Certainly we blessed the river as provider of irrigation (the stingers never surviving in still water), of trade and mobility, and of rain and thus of our habitable zone itself—for the baking deserts commenced quite soon inland, even up south in jungled Ajelobo. But *The Book of the River* was no more, really, than a gazeteer and guidebook to everything that lay along the eastern shore: a manual for living in our world. Nowhere did it claim that the river was alive, and maybe malevolent; that it cared about us approximately as a dog cares for the fleas on its back—which seemed to be the implication here, with the added rider "let sleeping dogs lie".

The black current, in so far as I'd ever bothered about it, was simply an obstacle equivalent to whirlpools, though much worse; and what it was an obstacle to—namely the western shore and whoever might live there—was uninteresting except to monkish oddities, since there was no way of reaching it. And what's more, whoever was over there, if there was anyone at all, was as uninterested in us as we were in them.

But if the river was alive . . . Well, we all drank the water, didn't we? And human bodies are almost entirely made up of water. So we were built of river: heart and lungs, blood and brains.

"Women are of the river," I quoted; and the boatmistress snapped back at me:

"But she is not of us!"

Surely this was all some masquerade, precisely equivalent to hazing me or making me walk a plank, blindfolded, to tumble into the midst of stingers: something to bind me emotionally to the sorority of the river and the guild. So that perhaps I might remain loyal to river life and never choose to settle down with my imported husband? There were a few such shore-husbands, though not very many, living in Pecawar—but naturally I had hardly ever even seen their wives, who remained afloat, only returning for holidays. But just then the fortunes of husbands were hardly very much on my mind.

Still, if this was all just an emotional bonding thing, I was convinced! Though it was a warm evening, particularly in the stuffy cabin, I shivered.

"Yaleen," the boatmistress said to me. "If something isn't to notice that you're foreign to it, then it must think that you're part of itself. That's how a parasite survives in the flesh of its host. Every New Year's Eve, from Tambimatu in the south. . . ." She paused.

"Where the river rises, beyond Ajelobo."

"The river doesn't rise, Yaleen. It doesn't come from a little spring or bubbling fountain."

"I know. It flows out from under the Far Precipices. So it must come through an underground channel from beyond."

"And it has the same girth at its Tambimatu source as it does at Umdala, where it spreads into the wild ocean. It emerges from under the Precipices the same way as a worm emerges from the earth, oozing solidly out."

"It has to come through a channel."

"But what is behind the Precipices? We don't know. They're unscalable. They rise into air too thin to breathe, in any case. Maybe they're ten leagues thick, or a hundred; or maybe they're as thin as a sheet of paper. Filter paper. They filter the salts from the sea as it squeezes through to become the river—drawn along by the muscle of the river. And maybe if they filter salt water into fresh, the way our kidneys filter our blood, then deposits of salt are massed up and up within and behind the Precipices. Salt islands like iceberg slabs may calve vertically from time to time and crash back into the hidden ocean, to float away, break up and dissolve somewhere far away. Maybe in time you'll see far Tambimatu, where the jungles reek around the base of the Precipices, and where the whole river oozes out at once into the open; then you can guess, as well as anyone. But, Yaleen. . . ."

"Ah yes. Every New Year's Eve?"

"Right. At midnight when the world sleeps, a guild boat sets sail from Tambimatu across the river to the edge of the black current."

"To try to cross over between one year and the next—as though it mightn't be noticed? As though the river is midway between breathing one year in, and the next out?"

The fish-mask shook in denial. "No, to bring back several buckets full of the blackness. Presumably, since it has always

15

been this way, midnight at year's end is something like the metabolic low point of awareness of the river. Still, that journey out to midstream isn't without its risks to the volunteers so honoured. Occasionally it happens that a crew-woman loses her sanity and throws herself overboard."

"You bring samples of the black current back to analyse?" I asked, perplexed.

The woman shook as though laughing silently; naturally I couldn't see her expression.

"What apothecary has the tools to analyse anything as alien as that? No, that isn't why. But *this* is." And from a shelf the boatmistress snatched a stoppered phial with wet darkness inside it. "Do you still wish to be a riverwoman?"

I hardly faltered, reasoning that the contents of that phial were surely simply ink-stained water. Or something similar.

"Yes, boatmistress. I do."

She unstoppered the phial and held it out to me.

"Then drink. Drink of the black current."

"And what will happen?" For maybe, after all, the liquid wasn't simple and innocuous. Maybe it was exactly what she said it was.

"Why, I'm still alive and of sound mind, aren't I, child?" murmured the quaymistress, at my shoulder.

"What will it do to me?"

"It will make you a riverwoman. Drink it quickly—all in one gulp."

Accepting the phial in my hand, I sniffed it, detecting hardly anything at all: a smell of . . . dankness, perhaps—and I drank.

The sensation wasn't so much that of liquid flowing down my throat, as of swallowing a fat garden slug whole. Or a blob of jelly. One moment it was blocking my throat entirely; the next, and it was gone.

I held the phial up to the lantern light. The glass looked perfectly clean, with no dregs or droplets clinging inside.

Laying the empty phial down on the table before me I awaited . . . I knew not what. A sudden sunburst of light and understanding? A plunge into terror or ecstasy? Creeping clammy cold? Delirium? Menstrual cramps? I sat and waited; and my two witnesses—or assessors?—waited too.

16

Finally the boatmistress nodded. "You're safe. The black current doesn't heed you. You don't offend it."

"What if I had?"

"Then you would have run up on deck, leapt over the side and done your best to swim oblivious of stingers all the way to the current to join it. In other words you would be dead."

"I've never heard of anyone doing such a thing."

"It doesn't happen to female applicants very often. Once in a thousand times, if that. And then we have to put it about that they signed on and sailed away without telling friends or family, and had an accident, or else that they stowed away and jumped the boat in a distant port."

"So I wasn't very worried," put in the quaymistress mildly.

I laughed nervously. "You said 'female applicants', as though there could be such a thing as a *male* applicant!"

"Poor choice of words. Men may only sail once in their lives, with their wife-to-be; thus our genes are mixed."

I knew this, of course; it was laid down in the preface to *The Book of the River* (though I'm sure this boatmistress had no more notion than I, exactly what "genes" were). "But what if men *do* sail twice? Or try to?"

"Ah, there we have it. The black current calls them, and drowns them. The river is a jealous female entity, I suppose. Once, she permits a man to sail, so that we may thrive. Twice, and she kills."

"I thought," said I, "that she simply ignored us?"

The fish-mask dipped, as if in prayer. "Strange are the ways of the river. But one thing's for sure: if you're a woman who's really a man, she'll cull you out."

"A woman who's really a man?"

"You know! Well, you're young yet, so perhaps you don't. . . ."

I was sure (or at least halfway sure) that all this rigmarole was simply guild lore that had bloomed in the misty dark age after our arrival on this world, as a way of authenticating social patterns that had proved so stable and self-perpetuating: with women being the travellers and traders, with men marrying into their woman's household. Matrilineal descent, and so on and so

17

forth. It was really all gloss on the privileges of the guild; and I reminded myself that any man who was so inclined, and sufficiently energetic, could walk all the way back to his home town away from a wife he had grown to hate, or anywhere else for that matter. But obviously out of self-interest in the status quo no boat would ease his passage.

The boatmistress lifted her mask; she was a sharp-faced freckled redhead, perhaps forty years old.

"That's all over," she said. "Not a word, mind. Now you can forget about it." She reached for a flask from the shelf containing a different kind of liquid—ginger spirit—and brought down three glasses, too. "So: welcome to the river and the guild, apprentice boatwoman." She poured. "Here's to faraway places, and unfamiliar shores."

The spirit was strong, and rushed to my inexperienced head.

"The most unfamiliar shore," I heard myself saying presently, "is just a league and a half away, right over there." Nudging the glass westward.

The boatmistress looked angry, and I hastened to add, "I only mention it on account of my twin brother. He wants to watch from Verrino."

"Verrino, eh? That's a long walk, for a young fellow." In the boatmistress's voice I caught a hint of vindictiveness, as though Verrino was some bastion of rebellion against the rightful way, the way of the river. If Capsi wished to get to Verrino he would have to hike the fifty leagues; unless by some wild chance a husband-hunting girl from Verrino decided to visit us in Pecawar, fell madly in love with young Capsi and carried him back home with her to wed. I didn't think that Capsi quite qualified yet as a noteworthy catch. Maybe in another couple of years he would. But equally, why should some girl marry him just to provide him with an easy journey downstream to that watchful fraternity of his?

"When do I join a boat?" I asked, in more practical vein. Wishing, a moment later, that I hadn't—since I had no particular wish to bunk down on the *Ruby Piglet* (named, perhaps, in sardonic honour of its red-headed boatmistress?). But I needn't have worried.

18

Said the quaymistress. "There's a brig due in, day after tomorrow, with two empty berths; bound for Gangee, carrying grain. They heliographed ahead, wanting crew. Then they're running back all the way down to Umdala. Far enough for you, first-timer?"

I got home at nine o'clock, quite tipsy, and went up to Capsi's room; he was in, playing around with his latest reconstruction of the original spyglass, adding an extra lens or something. For all the good that would do. Perhaps my face was flushed: Capsi gave me much more than a second glance.

"I've joined the guild," I said proudly.

"Which guild?" he asked with mock innocence, as though there was any other guild for me.

"I'm sailing out. Thursday. Bound for Gangee, then Umdala. On the brig the *Sally Argent*." As though the name of the brig would mean anything to him. *He* hadn't spent years hanging about the quayside, sniffing around the ropes and bollards, and getting in the way of the gangers unloading.

"Well, Sis, if you're going to Gangee, you'll be back here in about three weeks."

I advanced on him. "That's the last time you're going to call me Sis! I'm older than you, anyway."

"By two minutes. Fancy some rough and tumble, eh?"

I halted. "Not especially."

"Some sublimated eroticism? Grope and squeeze?"

"How dare you!"

"Well, what do they get up to when you join the guild? Strip you naked and prod you with a windlass handle? Splice your mainbrace, whatever that means?"

"What makes you think they get up to anything? Well, they don't. So there."

"And pigs can fly." Had he slunk down to the quayside, and spied on me? Or had he just happened to notice that the *Ruby Piglet* was in town? Or neither—since it's often said that twins are empathic? Well, there was precious little empathy going on right now! At first I couldn't understand it.

He pointed his spyglass at me. "Seriously, Sis, you need a

19

tumble. You'll probably have to learn to fight with knives, if you're going on a boat."

"Oh, I see. I *see*. You're bloody jealous—because after I've been to Gangee and back, in another week or two I'll be sailing smoothly into Verrino, while you'll still be stuck here burning your eyes out staring at sweet all. Don't worry, Capsi: when I'm home, from Umdala, in six months or so, I'll tell you what your darling Verrino's all about."

His lips whitened. "Don't *you* worry. I'll be there by then."

"In that case," and I peeled off one shoe, then the other, "you'll be needing these, and more!"

The first shoe missed him, bouncing off the wall where he had his pen-and-ink panorama of nowhere-land, the opposite shore, tacked up. But the second crashed into his spyglass, spinning it from his hand, with a subsequent tinkle of glass. Curiously, he disregarded its fate. At first, anyway; what happened after, I don't know, for I was already fleeing from the room. No, I wasn't fleeing. I was withdrawing in haughty dudgeon.

During my hastily organized going-away party the following evening Capsi hardly spoke to me at all. Then, when I was on the point of leaving the house the morning after, with my duffle bag over my shoulder—which wasn't too traumatic a parting, from Mother and Father's point of view, since the run to Gangee and back was short—he winked at me, and whispered, "See you in Verrino."

"I'm sailing upstream first," I reminded him. "See you back here in three weeks."

"Don't be too sure of that, Sis." And he dealt me a playful punch on the shoulder.

Learning the ropes on the *Sally Argent* was no less—and no more—strenuous, muscle-forming, et cetera, than I'd expected; and of course there were no knife fights among the crew, or any other such garbage. Being a riverwoman was just work, with free time sandwiched in between.

The spring winds were blowing leisurely downstream, so our course—allowing for the long slow curves of the river one way, then the other—was basically west of south away from shore for a stretch till we were just over a third of a league out, then east of south back inshore again; repeat *ad infinitum*. Downstream river traffic at this season kept to a narrower sailing corridor nearer midstream, though always shunning by at least a sixth of a league the vicinity of the black current.

The dusty complexion of the country did not change markedly till we were almost at Gangee itself; then quite suddenly green hills bunched up, and foliage proliferated, and the semi-arid land disappeared—not to be seen again should we sail on as far as Ajelobo. For the Pecawar section marks the closest approach to civilization of the eastern deserts that parallel the whole course of the river from tropics to cooler north, generally at from ten to fifteen leagues' distance.

What was beyond the eastern deserts, further to the east? There was no way of knowing. Some expeditions had gone into the deep desert, in the past. One or two disappeared; one or two returned with the hard-won but unexciting news that the desert just went on and on.

Gangee, anyway, is on the very edge of the southern tropics, and is rather a fly-blown town, of sandstone buildings and rank weeds. It has neither the scoured dry neatness of Pecawar—with its shady arcades and secluded retreats of courtyards and fountains—nor the luxuriant bloom-bright tangle of cities further south. It's neither one nor the other; so it's weedy rather than lush, and stony without bothering to beautify. Still, I visited the bazaar, and the rather clammy river-aquarium with all its exotic southern species—frills and teeth and blobs of paint—next to its collection of dourer northern specimens.

Then it was time to sail back down midchannel to Pecawar again.

The *Sally Argent* carried a complement of twenty, with one berth still empty; and on the whole my riversisters treated this apprentice in a brisk and friendly way. The boatswain, Zolanda, was a bit of a sod at times, usually in the mornings, as though she always woke up with a headache (and perhaps she did); but my special friend was a rigger, Hali, a dumpy but energetic twenty-year-old with curly black hair and milky opal eyes: depending upon the light these either looked enchanting, or else slightly diseased with incipient cataracts.

The voyage downstream was straighter sailing than all the tacking upstream had been, and swifter with the tail wind. And less than a third of a league to port flowed the black current—which was the closest I had ever seen it, though it wasn't close enough for it to seem anything other than a thin strip of crêpe ribbon laid along the entire midriff of the water. Actually, the current was about a hundred spans wide.

Remarkably, now that I thought of it—for it wasn't something that one generally wondered about in Pecawar, with only one sample of barren shore opposite—there was no river traffic at all discernible across the water to the west, not even the smallest inshore fishing craft, so far as I could see. What's more, there seemed to be no villages on that other bank—let alone towns— yet the land was obviously inhabited, judging by the occasional wisp of smoke and, once, a tower on a hilltop way inland. Didn't they know what boats were, over there? Or that there were tasty fish in the river? (And who *were* "they", anyway?)

I was relaxing on deck, soaking up the spring sunshine with Hali during a slack time two days out of Gangee, and staring vaguely at the black current—which was so much a natural part of the river that it was hard to remember that it meant: *madness*, and *death*—when the events of my secret initiation popped back into my mind, prompting a question that I hoped was discreetly phrased, so that it didn't violate my oath on *The Book*.

"Did you ever eat a black slug, Hali, before you joined the guild?" I asked quite lazily and casually.

And no sooner had I asked the question than I felt as sick as though I had indeed just crammed a garden slug, fresh from a bed of lettuce, into my mouth and was trying to swallow the slimy thing. I had to scramble up, rush to the rail and vomit over the side.

Hali was behind me, steadying my shoulders. "All of us," she whispered, "ask the question once. I was wondering when you would, Yaleen. You see, we are of the river now; and we obey its rules—we break them at our peril."

The convulsions in my guts were easing.

"Riversick?" asked a familiarly abrasive voice. It was Zolanda, of course. "What, on this titchy little swell?"

22

She stared at me coolly, as I wiped my mouth; and I realized that she was offering me an excuse—because she must have known.

"I'm all right," I mumbled.

"Too much basking in the sun, that's your trouble. Get some work done." And she set me a whole heap of tasks.

Of course, my vomiting was probably all psychological. To violate an oath, or try to circumvent one—particularly one taken on *The Book of the River*, which is our whole life, and all there is for us—is a pretty slimy thing; and essentially in such situations one punishes oneself, and sharpish too. So that night in my bunk, as we rode at anchor, I experienced an awful dream in which the black current reared up high out of the river like a serpent, developed a gaping mouth, full of void, and descended on me blindly.

I woke up with a cry, convinced that I'd been about to die. Soon a scantily-clad Hali was comforting me; and presently she was doing so a little too intimately for my taste—or for my depths of inexperience—so that I cooled off from her somewhat for a few days, though we still remained friends. And the dream did not recur; because it didn't need to. I worked at being a good boatwoman.

And so back to Pecawar, to pick up a load of spices.

And home for one night. I even invited Hali home, reasoning that if she liked me, she might like my twin brother too.

And Capsi had gone. Quit the nest. Trekked off northward, leaving his panorama of the further shore and his home-made spyglass behind as though they were but childish toys.

I had to spend some time consoling and reassuring Mother and Father—not so much because Capsi had absconded (a man eventually ought to leave home), nor even because he had departed unwed, as because of the double desertion within such a short span of time. True, *I* would be returning home, but the voyage down to Umdala and back was a matter of months, not weeks. And who knew whether I would be returning on the *Sally Argent* at all? Or if I did stay with the boat, whether it would be sailing as far upriver as Pecawar the next time?

23

I told Father that I would try to look out for Capsi in Verrino, though this was a fairly vain undertaking since we would be sailing into and out of Verrino before Capsi could possibly have reached the town on foot. I was careful not to *promise* to find him, even on the return trip.

So the overnight stay was a rather muted affair, even though Hali did her best to sparkle. I was only too glad to say goodbye the next morning.

You can spot Verrino from a long way upriver on account of its Spire, the natural rocky column rising from a particularly steep hill behind the town. On top of the Spire, up hundreds of steps with only a guiderope to stop you falling off, was where the little band of observers lived in presumably spartan circumstances, staring across at the further shore through telescopes till their eyes grew dim. From the town itself one couldn't see anything of their activities, and the steep steps were quite a disincentive to further investigation. I did climb up as far as the base of the Spire itself, then gave up, feeling obscurely that I had done my duty. In any case it was quite impossible that Capsi could be up there yet.

So I turned my attention, instead, to exploring the town proper: a pleasant bustling twisty up-and-down place, with sudden arbours and piazzas, wooden footbridges hung with clemato and cisca-vine crossing over alleys, which in turn tunnelled through rock or under buildings, themselves to emerge unexpectedly at rooftop height: rooftops crammed with terra-cotta urns of fuchsias. After the flatness of Pecawar, I adored Verrino, though the place made my calves and ankles ache. The people scampered everywhere, chattering like monkeys, many of the men with laden baskets balanced on their heads, the further to defy gravity—though no one that I saw ever went so far as to shin down vines as a short cut from one level to the next.

Yet scamper about though they might, it certainly wasn't fast enough for boatmistress Karil, who by the second day was grumbling about demurrage charges, and by the third was inveighing that we would have to spend the whole damn week here, the way things were going.

24

What was holding us up was a large consignment of spectacle lenses from the glassworks and grindery inland—another reason, by the by, in addition to the towering vantage point of the Spire, why the observers congregated above Verrino—and since lenses are such a costly item compared with their size, and since they were bound all the way to Umdala, Karil was loth to sail off and leave the freighting to a subsequent boat, thus losing a handsome percentage.

So the crew were free to roam—one or two to go looking, speculatively, for possible husbands; those older women such as Zolanda, who were already married with a husband ensconced in some far port, to go hunting discreetly for a spot of carnal appeasement and amorous intrigue with married men; and some of the younger women with whoever took their fancy.

Naturally, married men whose wives were absent were bound to be the husbands of other riverwomen; and you might have thought it was rather poor form for one riverwoman to have fun with another riversister's man while she was away. But actually this was something of a game and generally winked at; and when I came to think of it, it made sense. Some women might be away for months, even as long as a year, and during this time obviously they nursed desires—as did their spouses back home. Better, much better, that there should be a kind of covert swap arrangement, all within the embrace of the guild, even if nobody admitted it publicly.

But besides these stranded husbands, there were always a number of adventurous and available young men—who could hardly look to the girls of their own town to marry; and this firm custom cast a risky pall over seducing those girls, or even flirting too boisterously.

So the next secret of the guild that I learned—from Hali, who else?—was how to avoid getting pregnant in foreign ports, a skill without which these shore-leave adventures could have proved bothersome. A drug, which in river argot was simply called "Safe"—thus keeping it our own preserve, should shore ears be wagging—could be extracted by boiling up the entrails of the barbel-fish.

Not that it was any crime to become pregnant, though given

the exertions of our work this could end up by "beaching" a riversister for quite a while; and you would sometimes see girl children on passing boats, though generally all kids were left at home in the husband's care.

Girl children: that was the real problem. Boy children could no more sail the river repeatedly than could youths or grown men—which would mean that boys born or wombed on the river would, when they grew up, have to walk all the way to a future wife's town, should she care to put up with this inconvenience for the sake of love; and sometimes the river might even take exception to a male foetus well before its term, making the mother miscarry; and who was to know whether a foetus was male or female? So a riverwoman contemplating pregnancy generally arranged this with some care, and beached herself for the full term. Many riverwomen played it Safe permanently; and would only consider adopting a family. And many never bothered marrying at all.

So, on what was to be our penultimate evening in Verrino, Hali winked at me. "Let's try the night life out," she said, and handed me a little blue phial of fish juice.

I accepted it laughingly, only partly out of bravado.

"Why not?" I winked back, and drank it down.

A couple of hours later we were in a busy wine-arbour lit by fairy candles, bantering with a pair of slim handsome brothers with coppery skin, lambent eyes and pert turned-up noses—with the banter gradually becoming more serious, though of course destined to remain a game; whatever happened, a game. I was a little tipsy, and my partner, with whom I danced a few turns, said that he was called Hasso—and maybe he really was called that. I kissed him, and when I next paid attention, Hali had vanished from the arbour along with her new friend.

Hasso murmured sweetly, "I know somewhere."

"I know lots of places," I said, rather wickedly. "Pecawar, Gangee. . . ."

But he took my repartee in good part; as indeed he would, since he was anxious to please me.

And not so many hours later we were at that somewhere, the

26

two of us—it was an attic room, window choked with night-scented clemato, reached by a long thin bridge—and I was discovering that I didn't know everything, though I was quick to learn.

Nor did he know everything; though the gaps in his knowledge were other than mine.

"Must be marvellous, river travel," he nuzzled in my ear. Or something to that effect; I was on the point of swinging round to approach him by another route.

"Must see all sorts of things on the far bank, while sailing." He was leaving out the personal pronouns, perhaps without realizing he was doing so. As I surmised presently, he thus drew back from actual spoken breach of faith.

"Cities and such—"

At this stage I wasn't offended; I simply thought that since the aura of the river was about me, this was turning him on as much as my young charms.

"Ah, beyond the black current—"

I thought, capriciously, of telling him what that current *tasted* like, but I had no particular desire to test whether I would vomit as readily on shore as I had on the boat. Besides, I already had my mouth full, being otherwise occupied.

He relaxed with a groan.

"Tell me *something* that's seen over there, eh? Something wild and wonderful. Anything at all."

I broke off abruptly, squirmed aside and found my clothes. I *knew* now. It was no coincidence that Hali and I had fallen in with these two personable brothers at the wine-arbour. They'd been looking for such as us. Or rather, for such as me: someone new and naive, freshly filled with all the wonders of the river and its sights, and probably boastful. No doubt the other brother was simply keeping the more experienced Hali suitably occupied, while Hasso set out to pump me on behalf of the observers up there on the Spire. . . .

I didn't cry or make a fuss or accuse him, consoling myself with the thought that *I* had pumped him. Dry.

"Have to get back," I lied. "I'm on nightwatch."

Why any boatmistress should order nightwatch kept in a

27

harbour, I had no idea; but it was the first thing I thought of.

Hasso propped himself on his elbow, grinning. "Are you *sure* you have to get back to your ship, little Yaleen?"

"My *boat*," I corrected him hotly. "Shorelubber!"

And in another moment I fled past the veils of clemato, whose smell seemed cloying now, and over the high slim wooden bridge, alone.

I'd wondered whether or not to tell Hali of my suspicions; however it was the wee hours before she returned on board and by then it had occurred to me that she might imagine I was rationalizing some sort of sexual disaster; which I was not, by any means. So in the end I pretended to be asleep, and said nothing at all.

And early in the morning the padded boxes of spectacle lenses arrived. Almost immediately afterwards we cast off and set sail downstream, for all points north to furthest Umdala.

I didn't return to up-and-down Verrino for a whole year, by which time I was no longer just an apprentice but newly held my guild ticket; nor was I on the *Sally Argent* any more.

In their first year or two, young riverwomen are encouraged to work a variety of craft, and I was no exception. Besides, I think that subconsciously I chose to hop boats in the way I did so as to delay my return to Verrino (and Pecawar) for quite a while. What I told myself was that I ought to see as much of downriver as I could, while I was still freshly impressionable.

So I had sailed with that first boat of mine all the way down to cool, misty Umdala, calling *en route* at Sarjoy, Aladalia, Port Firsthome, Melonby and Firelight. At Umdala I'd skiffed across the marshes, and I'd wandered the geometrical streets of blockhouses with their steeply pitched roofs, like rows of wedges set to cut whatever weight of snow might settle from the sky in deep winter; and I'd seen the enormous widening of the river where fresh water became salt, a prelude to the angry ocean—with the black current ribboning out and out. And I had wondered whether Umdala was built as it was entirely to defeat white winters, or whether there might not have been another hidden thought in the ancient builders' minds—for this was an outpost city: outpost, not against human enemies, but against what the river became as it broadened out, the unnavigable dire sea.

I returned on the *Sally Argent*, still with Hali, as far upstream as the soft green grazing hills of Port Firsthome, where I wondered at the time-worn Obelisk of the Ship—a "ship", as all but shorelubbers know, being something quite distinct from a boat, which plies water and not the star-void.

At Port Firsthome I hopped off, with a good endorsement on my papers from boatmistress Karil, and signed on the three-mast schooner *Speedy Snail,* a lumbering heavy-duty boat which only cruised from Aladalia to Firelight and back; and through the summer and autumn I stayed with her till I'd won my ticket. Then, as the winds blowing from the north became quite chilly, it was goodbye to the *Speedy Snail* and hullo to the caravel *Abracadabra* and local hauls in the Aladalia region, which distanced me from the worst excesses of deep winter. Not that I was scared of catching cold! Still, I did hail from Pecawar where the desert keeps us dry and where the winter only brings a few ground frosts before dawn. Somehow I didn't yet feel like sailing further south, up Verrino way.

So for a while artistic Aladalia was my home, with its weavers and jewellers and potters and its orchestra, almost as much as the *Abracadabra* herself; and I even got involved in something of a relationship (casual but warm: I needed to keep warm) with one Tam; and because this was a sweet experience I think I'll say less about it than about my first time, with Hasso. Just in case I find any little flaws in this affair, too? No. It remained quite innocent of any reference to what went on or didn't go on over the water.

But came spring, and a letter from my mother, and a concerned note from my father; so from the caravel I hopped to the brig *Blue Sunlight* bound for Sarjoy and Verrino; and who should be waiting on the quayside as the *Blue Sunlight* tied up at its destination, but Capsi.

I waved and waved, and as soon as I was free of my duties I rushed ashore and hugged him.

"How did you *know*?"

He laughed delightedly. "Well, I knew you'd have to pass this way sometime. After all, there aren't two rivers! I simply paid the quaymistress a little retainer to keep an eye on the Guild Register for me."

"You're lucky, then. I only just joined *Blue Sunlight* in Aladalia."

"Lucky, indeed! Fine thing to say about your own guild, Sis. Oops, apologies, Yaleen. But surely you mean 'efficient'? One boat got here ahead of you, with the latest crewlists *ex* Aladalia. And before *Blue Sunlight* it was *Abracadabra*; and before that—"

"You seem quite efficient too. Obviously you know everything about me." (But he didn't know *all*, I added inwardly. I was a girl when last we met; but now I was a woman, and a riverwoman too.)

Arm in arm we strolled up the steep cobbled street to the nearest wine-arbour, to toast our re-encounter.

"So how's it with you?" I asked him, as we sat on a bench beneath familiar garlands of clemato.

"Oh, I sits up the Spire, and I stares," said he jocularly.

"Seen anything amusing?"

His voice quietened. "There's a little town about two leagues inland over there. Just a little one, but we have Big Eye trained on it. That's our newest telescope, with lenses right at the limits of the grinders' art. You must come up and visit me at work."

"Must I?"

"You'd be interested—who wouldn't be?"

"Maybe I wouldn't. I've seen Aladalia and Port Firsthome and Umdala. Why should I want to squint at a nameless *little* town? I bet what you see's all wavery and blurred—and so far away."

"It isn't as blurred as you'd think. We're high up."

"So what do you see?"

"People."

"Surprise, surprise. I expected dragons."

"Very tiny people, of course."

"What, dwarfs?"

"Cut the sarcasm, Sis. This is important."

"More important than our first meeting in a year?"

With a perceptible effort he untensed, and chuckled. "'Course not. Let's drown that year, eh?" And he drained his glass. "I know a marvellous little spot to eat. Afterwards. When we need something to soak it all up. Fancy some spiced sweet-rice and kebabs?"

And he punched me softly on the shoulder. Somehow though, that particular patch of my flesh seemed sore, from way way back.

After his first over-anxious little outburst, which had been like a premature ejaculation of something long pent up, Capsi played me carefully; I'll give him all credit for that. He kept off the subject and showed me the town, which I already knew, but hardly as well as he knew it. I'd signed off the *Blue Sunlight* and taken a small rooftop room for a while, after writing ahead to Mother and Father to announce that I'd be arriving soonish, a letter which I left with the quaymistress to forward by the next upriver boat.

Credit, yes . . . though there was the genuine happiness to see me, too, and brotherly affection; which rather confused the matter for me emotionally, otherwise I might never have fallen for his suggestions. But my actions seemed correct and brave at the time; and in defence of my own sex, even.

Indeed, Capsi managed to keep off the topic of his own obsession so well that after a couple of days I relented, and asked him, "Well, what about the tiny people over there?"

"Tiny, because they're at the range of the Big Eye's powers of resolution."

"Oh, I *know* that."

He frowned. "But on a clear day, when the atmosphere's still, you can tell the men from the women. They're dressed differently: the women all wear black."

"How can you tell they're women?"

"Babies. Sometimes they take babies with them, into the fields."

"Could as easily be the menfolk."

"*Feeding* a baby? That's how it looked to our keenest-eyed watcher." He hesitated before naming him: "Hasso."

31

"Ah," I said; I was *almost* prepared for this.

"He sends you his affectionate apologies, Yaleen."

I flushed; did my brother know all about that first night? I was angry, ready to walk away; but instead I shrugged, and said, "It seems to me that you people base a whole lot of inference on one man's voyeuring of something leagues away!"

He waved his hand dismissively. "Maybe, maybe not. The people over there don't go anywhere near the river. They don't sail so much as a plank on it. They don't net any fish. They don't even have a single shack that we know of, anywhere near the water. Why?"

"Because . . . only women can sail the river—"

"And no woman is allowed within a league of it. As I said, it's only a little town—so where are their cities, if they have them? Presumably they do. They're inland; right inland, as far away into the habitable zone as they can get."

"Assuming there are deserts beyond. Same as this side."

"Fair assumption."

"So they don't like the river; that was always obvious. What else is new?"

"What else is new, Yaleen, is that they *burn* women over there."

". . . What?"

"About six months ago, when Big Eye was first commissioned—"

"Only boats are commissioned, brother dear."

"Well, whatever word. Through Big Eye we saw a crowd gather outside the town. Then a litle cart was pulled through the crowd, to what looked like a pile of wood. One of the tiny black figures—we couldn't be sure they were women then—was dragged off the cart . . . and soon the flames crackled and the smoke curled up."

"Is this true?"

"I swear on *The Book* it is."

"But why should they do anything so cruel?"

"Because they hate and fear the river. And woman is of the river. And fire is the foe of water."

I gripped Capsi's wrist. "Water," I said, "*quenches* fire."

32

And this was the beginning of my undoing. Well, perhaps not of *my* undoing personally; but certainly the start of a fateful sequence of events for my brave if wayward brother.

The very next day I was toiling up that damned never-ending stone staircase. Capsi climbed behind me; thus at least I could set the pace.

The stairs wound round the Spire at least thrice before we finally entered an upward tunnel with subsidiary stairways and chambers leading off it, cut in the naked rock; and thus arrived at last back in the open air up on the top stone platform. This was wider than I'd expected from down below: about seventy spans across, with a safety rail around the exposed parts of the rim. On the eastern side a stone wall acted as a windbreak—not that the wind would blow from the east for more than thirty days in the whole year (unless high wind was different from river wind), but up on this exposed eminence a windbreak of any kind was probably better than none. Set on the western edge of the platform, blocking my immediate view of the far shore, was a low observatory building of brick, roofed in slate.

The platform was an austere, breezy place, strangely blank and untenanted—yet at the same time worn smooth by habitation.

"Where is everyone? Where do you live?"

Capsi jerked his thumb below. "Underneath in the rock. There are lots of rooms."

How weird and contrary to my expectations that Capsi, so high up in the air, should be leading what amounted to a troglodyte life!

High, yes: far higher than any mast I had ever shinned up. Walking over to the guard-rail I stared downriver, away and away in the direction of Sarjoy, though even so Sarjoy itself must have been quite some distance beyond the horizon. I picked out familiar landmarks on the eastern shore, and at least half a dozen boats which might almost have been motionless (but weren't); and I missed something. My whole body missed it, so that I gripped the rail for balance. It was movement that was absent: the slight rocking to and fro that I'd known any other time I had been up a height, upon the river, the gentle tilt back and forth of a masthead.

Yet the clouds above looked to be as high in the sky as ever; and the river, strangely, seemed wider rather than narrower now that I was seeing its span entire from bank to bank, the way a bird sees it. The river—with the band of the black current dividing it midway like the loading line along a beached hull.. . .

I scanned the far shore for Capsi's reputed town, somewhere inland amidst the rolling, wooded hills and little valleys, but couldn't pick it out unaided—nor any other landmarks but those of nature. Highways? No, I could see none . . . Unless . . . was that one, far far off, winding inland?

And directly below me was bustling, hither and thither Verrino: half a league of activity and variety, with its orchards and vineyards beyond, and off to the east some sandy hills hiding the glassworks.

"What a sad life up here, Capsi!"

"Sad? What's that got to do with it? Come on, I'll show you Big Eye." He pulled me away from the railing and all its grand vistas, towards the brick building; and it seemed to me that none of the sights were quite real to him unless he spied at them from out of the dark indoors, through a glass like a voyeur.

A wooden door, studded with rusty iron bolts: he pushed it open, and I was prepared to find myself in gloom reminiscent of the river-aquarium in Gangee.

But no: it was light and airy. A whole strip of exposed scenery cut a welcome swathe several spans high through the whole length of the westerly wall; for the midriff of this wall was all hinged windows, with most of the panes hoisted up and out to form a canopy, ventilating the observatory and sheltering the instruments from rain, unless a shower was scudding from due west.

Several ancient telescopes were retired to corners, but three principal instruments poked their barrels through different windows, two of these in use—the westward gazers seated on wooden chairs with straight backs, and cushions as a concession to comfort. There was no doubt at all which of the instruments was Big Eye: it was fully nine spans long, and my arm would hardly have gone around the tube.

34

The northern wall was shelved, with what I took to be logbooks filed on it, and sketching material: while the whole south wall was taken up by a huge panorama which quite dwarfed the one that Capsi had made for his bedroom wall back home. Quite what use the panorama was, with the reality in plain view, I thought I would forbear to ask—though doubtless it was easier to examine details (such as individual trees?) upon that great scroll of paper, and measure the distances from place to place. (And doubtless too, trees grew . . . so that the panorama must always be inaccurate.)

The man seated at the smaller instrument glanced round. Dressed in worn brown trousers and a tight jerkin, with his shirtsleeves rolled up for business, he was white-haired with a wrinkled impish face. He simply registered our presence, nodded, then got back to his observations—which struck me as something of a waste of time, since surely his aged eyes were feebler than the young man's next to him, and the telescope he was using was less powerful too.

The young man next to him . . . Wearing jauntier attire: boots, flared trousers tucked in, and an unforgettable shirt, striped scarlet and black.

"Hasso," said Capsi; and as though the watcher at Big Eye had awaited this signal, he looked round; and sprang up. Hasso was just as handsome as I remembered.

"See all sorts of things on the far bank," he remarked merrily and unselfconsciously. "Welcome back, Yaleen."

"And sometimes," said I, "you have to go fishing for hints. How's your brother?"

"Oh, he's a townsman at heart. Never comes up here. We just go around together . . . on occasion."

"Okay, okay, I don't mind." (But I did mind, quite a bit.) "That's so much water down the river."

Fortunately he did not attempt anything as crass as to advance and peck me on the cheek; he simply motioned me politely to his chair, and the vacant eye-piece of Big Eye. I sat down, and shut one eye to stare.

The telescope was trained on the little town—no more than a large village, really, nestling in the gradients of the land; and for me the weirdest thing of all in looking upon it was that the place was nameless. Nowhere in *The Book of the River* was its name inscribed; which meant that it did not exist—and yet it did.

Compared with Verrino, or even the smallest settlement on our shore, even to my unpractised eye it looked impoverished and primitive. Straw thatch? Apparently. Walls of dried mud? Some, perhaps, of wood. There was nothing of architecture or adornment about the settlement, except for one central building of stone, with an onion dome at one end. I felt not so much that I was gazing across a few leagues of space, as back hundreds or even thousands of years through time. Perhaps Capsi was right in his obsession, after all, and here was a more curious sight than any to be seen from Ajelobo to Umdala . . . I found myself itching to peel away the hills, step up the power of the telescope and discover what *did* lie further to the west; yet this wasn't a particularly pleasant sort of itch, not the kind that it's satisfying to scratch.

"Do you see a black patch, on the green outside the town?" Hasso whispered in my ear, as though the folk I was spying upon might hear him if he spoke too loudly. "That's where they burned her. Alive. In flames."

I broke off my viewing, not desiring this kind of covert closeness.

"How do you get all this stuff up here, and your food and water and everything?" I directed my question at Capsi, though he was hanging back as if he had arranged for Hasso to be here especially to please me; which it didn't. "Up all those wretched stairs?"

"We hoist heavy supplies. Winch 'em up in buckets."

"And how do you pay for them?"

"Oh, donations," he said vaguely. "And some of us work part-time down in Verrino."

"How many of you are there, anyway?"

"About twenty. Some young, some old. Come and see— we've nothing to hide. It's that lot over there who are hiding. They're hiding from the river. And they make women wear black. And they burn them."

"But you're all *men* up here, aren't you?"

36

Hasso chuckled. "We aren't misogynists exactly. . . ." He had the good grace not to add: *As you surely noticed.* "I hope Capsi passed on my affectionate apologies?"

"He did. Verbatim. It seems to me that the men over there must be the kingpins, who decide what women do—and *you* aren't above using women, if it suits you! Could there perhaps be a certain element of envy in your activities up here?"

"There could be, but there isn't." It was the old imp who spoke up; so he must have been listening, instead of looking. "Sister Yaleen, knowledge is our goal; that's all. The knowledge of what on earth is going on over there, with the whole other half of our human community. They who share this world with us."

So he already knew my name. Which meant that they had all discussed my coming. I was as much part of a plan now as ever I had been—in a more casual, extempore way—when Hasso lovingly deflowered me that evening a year ago.

"You feel . . . threatened, perhaps?" said the old fellow gently. "Please don't. It's the women over there who are under threat. Your sisters, not you."

Yes. But the observers hadn't known of this threat till recently, when they had acquired Big Eye. And yet maybe they had guessed for a long time that the west bank was opposed to everything that our river society stood for. . . .

"Well, that's Big Eye," said Capsi lightly. "Come on and we'll show you around, below."

"*You* can show me around, brother dear. I'm sure Hasso has lots more peeping to attend to."

Hasso pursed his lips; he seemed more amused than offended.

So Capsi proceeded to give me the guided tour of their eyrie and citadel—carved into cell rooms, kitchen, refectory, store rooms and such, and culminating in the "map room" where was filed or displayed every iota of information, supposition or hearsay that they had ever gleaned about the west bank all the way from Ajelobo to Umdala, a labour of goodness knows how many years. A hundred? Two hundred? More? I saw panor-

37

amas and sketches and even maps of the immediate hinter-land, though the maps themselves must have been beset with flaws due to foreshortening, given the perspectives they were drawn from.

Such dusty patience. Such dedicated . . . waiting. Capsi confessed to me offhandedly that he, and they, rather regretted that he had not brought his own pen-and-ink panorama of the shore opposite Pecawar with him from home. But when I offered to collect it from our house and drop it in at Verrino next time I was passing by, he didn't seem quite as glad of my offer as I should have expected. Perhaps he had already promised his colleagues something better?

Then, the tour at an end (if I had indeed seen everything: the place was a bit of a maze), Capsi escorted me back down those ankle-aching stairs to real life and bustle, and a bottle of wine and spicy lamb couscous with minted yoghurt.

If he had further schemes in mind for me, he didn't go into them. Though what they might be, I was hard put to imagine—so much so that I was almost on the point of asking him outright.

Two days later, in the afternoon, just after I'd come back to my little rooftop room after a visit to the quaymistress's office enquiring of a boat with an empty berth to carry me back to Pecawar in another week or so, Capsi burst in upon me, panting with exertion, his face flushed.

"They're at it again," he panted. "Crowd outside the town. Bonfire piled up. Come on!" Strangely, he seemed glad. Almost radiant.

I wondered briefly if this was a trick; but obviously something that happened six months ago can always repeat itself six months later. I raced with him.

It only took us about twenty minutes—with Capsi ducking up and down short-cuts that would have lost me—to snake through the town and out to the Spire, and spiral our way up till, almost heart-burst, we emerged on to the platform.

As soon as we entered the observatory, which was crowded, a path opened for me to Big Eye, where Hasso jumped out of his seat to make room. I was shaking and panting so much from the sprint that I let him steady my shoulders as I sat there.

I peered: at a tiny crowd on a greensward, half of the people robed in black; and an empty cart, and a bonfire burning. With a stake set in the centre of the flames, and something fastened to the stake.

I watched a long while, till the crowd began to troop back towards the wretched village, dragging the cart along with them, leaving a smoking ruin behind.

Then I ran out, around to the guard-rail. Sure enough, away to the west hung a tiny faint smudge.

I returned; the observers, young and old, all watched me expectantly.

"What do you want me to do?" I asked them.

Capsi answered quietly, "We want to send an observer over. To find out."

"Over there? But that's impossible. The black current's in the way. You haven't learnt to fly, by any chance?"

"Our ancestors must have known how to fly," remarked the old imp, whose name I knew now as Yosef. "A lost skill, eh? Perhaps deliberately so. Still, I've had a few ideas on the subject. . . ."

I quoted the preface to *The Book of the River* at him. "Man is of the shore, woman is of the water, only birds are of the sky. . . ."

He stared at me fixedly. "Yes, precisely. So there's no point in my entertaining such thoughts, is there, boatwoman? Or we would threaten the balance of the applecart. Something that no self-respecting guild would ever allow. . . ."

"River society *works*," said I. "And nicely, too. Obviously things don't work very well over there."

"Oh, I wasn't suggesting that this particular applecart is in any danger of overturning. None whatever! I've ruled out any fancy, speculative notions of flying. It's a somewhat visible thing to attempt. Meanwhile, girls like you are burning over there. Twice now, in that one miserable little town."

What I'd seen had been far away, tiny and silent; yet just for a moment I felt an intuition of the fear, the awful fear, and the agony, and was nearly sick from it. Flames licking round my feet, crisping my skin to pig's crackling then burning through to the bone, while I screamed and screamed. . . .

39

"Somebody has to cross the river and report back," said Capsi. "You do see that, don't you?"

"Men can only sail the river once. Cross, and report back? That's twice. You aren't suggesting that *I* make the crossing? It's ridiculous: the current's in the way, in any case."

"No, Yaleen, I wasn't suggesting you. Obviously a man is safer over there than a woman. It's *me* who'll go. Just once. One way. And I'll report back by heliograph."

"But how could you get through the current? It's madness— and death. That isn't just some rumour that we women put around!"

"Oh, it's true, and no denying," said old Yosef. "The river has a mind of its own, and senses things, and reacts to them. Or rather, let's say that the black current acts this way. So it's a creature: a very long creature that lives in the river, anchored to the Precipice Mountains at one end like a tapeworm, floating all the way along it and spilling out into the sea at its other end. And it can smell what happens in the water. It can scent one man's odour and remember it, and distinguish it from half a million others; and it can put thoughts into his brain, of despair and death, if it smells him twice. Whereas women it favours. No doubt because they pose no threat to it."

His speculations seemed dangerously close to some of the secrets of my initiation ceremony; though plainly the black current couldn't be a creature such as he envisaged—not if it was possible to scoop out parts of it and bottle these in phials. It had to be of a different nature, and much larger than their concept of it: larger than our whole country, and perhaps much more powerful, in its apparently quiescent, unrevealing way, than any of them supposed.

I said nothing at all to confirm or deny to what extent the guild might have reached the same conclusions—which of course had precious little to do with the business of everyday life.

"So," I said simply, "there's no way through. However crazy you are."

"Not through," replied Capsi. "Under."

"*Under*?"

Old Yosef stuck his oar in again. "Based on the reasonable

40

presumption that the black current doesn't extend all the way to the bottom. Why should it, when it floats? There must be clear water beneath. Maybe the current is only a few spans thick."

"Ah, I *see*. And it's only a hundred spans wide. So Capsi is just going to hold his breath for five or ten minutes, plunge into water infested with stingers, and . . . It's preposterous. Since when, Capsi, could you swim like a fish?"

"I've been practising." he said defensively. "Down at the Verrino baths."

"And is that also where you've been practising holding your breath, till you turn blue?"

"You misunderstand," said Yosef. "Come, and we'll show you how."

Down below, we entered a stone chamber with mullion windows cut in the rock wall facing east. I'd certainly not been admitted here two days before, during Capsi's guided tour.

A long wooden table was piled with curious gear: a large glass globe, a leather suit, boots with lead weights attached and flipper-like protuberances, various flexible tubes sewn out of river-snake skin, bladders, thick glass bottles, satchels—and unmistakably, a dismantled heliograph. So these Observers had mastered our river code, presumably.

"That," announced Capsi proudly, "is my diving suit. Enough air can be bottled under pressure to let me breathe inside the glass helmet for nearly twenty minutes. The helmet and other glass parts are by a special commision from the grindery. The weights and the gear I'm carrying slung about me will counteract the buoyancy of all the air. And here," and he picked up what was plainly a lamp, though of curious design, "is my underwater light supply, if I have to dive deep and need light, fuelled with magnesium."

"It'll explode."

"No, it won't," Yosef assured me. "Been tested."

"Then I float up, discard the bowl, and my head is protected from stingers by this leather cap and wire mask."

I turned to Yosef, who had obviously dreamed up all this apparatus. "You seem to have thought of everything—except for one little detail: what Capsi is going to *do* for the whole of the rest of his life over there."

My brother grinned at me wolfishly. "Explore, that's what. I'd say that there's quite enough *terra incognita* to occupy a lifetime. And I'll report back, of course. At intervals."

"So where do I come into all this?" As though I hadn't already guessed.

"You have access to boats, sister dear. You know the ropes and the routines. We only need a very small craft. Sufficient for me and one other helper, who'll surrender his once-in-a-lifetime chance on the river to assist."

"And I suppose that brave volunteer is Hasso?"

Capsi nodded, unabashed.

"I'm not sure if I can handle even a cutter or a sloop on my own. . . ." But I thought that I could. *Whether* I should was quite another matter.

"We were on the verge of appealing to your better nature," explained Yosef, in an old wise way. "But now—you have seen what you have seen."

Yes. The bonfire. The burning woman. The smoke rising up.

Unsure whether I was championing my sex, or betraying it, I too nodded.

After this, events achieved a momentum of their own. The very next midnight, starlit and clear, saw me—or rather failed to see me, since I had "borrowed" the little cutter discreetly, though with my heart in my mouth—rocking far out upon the river on dark water, within a stone's throw of the deeper darkness of the current.

Masked and helmeted in his preposterous fish-bowl, his suit hung with gear, Capsi was assisted over the side by Hasso. And my brother sank.

We didn't hang around; we were drifting closer to the current. I set sail, grabbed the tiller and we fled back to the shore, where I let Hasso off somewhere upstream of the quay before sneaking the cutter back to its berth. Without being noticed. Though I expected at any moment that somebody would stroll up on deck for a breath of air, or reel back from a very late night on the town.

Returning to my room, I tried to sleep but couldn't. By earliest dawn I was toiling up the hundreds of steps of the Spire.

Almost all of the observers were up on the platform, spread out along the guard-rail, keeping silent vigil upon the western shore—with two men even watching the southerly stretch, though it seemed unlikely that Capsi could have forged upstream against the flow. With the exception of Big Eye, all of the telescopes, even the ancient ones, had been pressed into service—brought out into the open, mounted on swivel tripods; though no one was using these to scan just at the moment. One's ordinary field of view, including peripheral vision, was more likely to catch the tiny blink of reflected light when it came; if indeed it ever came. Hasso and Yosef were inside the observatory; so I stayed outdoors.

An hour went by—and meanwhile the sun rose behind us.

Then suddenly, when I was really beginning to fret, a man cried out and pointed—quite far to the north.

Other observers hastily swung telescopes about and clapped an eye to them; but even at that distance I could spell out the winks of the helio-mirror.

"S-A-F-E. *Safe*," I called out.

The rest of the brief message was: *Tired. Must sleep, then move south.* "Tired" was no doubt a considerable understatement.

No sun-signal was sent in acknowledgement, not merely because the sun was at our backs, but in case anyone on the opposite shore might see it, and be able to interpret. However a smoky billowing fire was lit briefly in a brazier; and after a couple of minutes, quenched.

Since it seemed ridiculous, after that, to keep returning to my room down in the town I accepted Yosef's offer of a little bed-chamber in the Spire; and by midday I had stored some of my gear at the quaymistress's office and humped the bare essentials aloft, declining Hasso's assistance.

Yet once ensconced up top, I had nothing to do, and within a few hours I was feeling bored and restless.

And anxious? Where was the use of anxiety for someone

whom I could never see again—except maybe briefly through Big Eye?

I ought to have been feeling intensely curious about what Capsi would report, as pre-arranged, at dawn the next day. Yet when it was a question of why women were being burned alive, "curiosity" hardly seemed the right description of my feelings. I . . . dreaded to know the answer. And as to the facts of life on the west bank, well of course I felt some superficial curiosity—but how much of it could Capsi satisfy effectively within the first few days? I was leaving. Soon. And I had no wish to sail away and yet remain in mental thrall to these observers forever more, impelled to dash back constantly to hear the latest. If I acted in that style, why, Capsi would have made me a slave of his for life, on a chain as long as the river!

Selfish little Yaleen? No, not really. Only sensible, I'd have said. . . .

Sensible? Hardly! I soon began fretting that by taking up temporary residence on the Spire I might have identified myself too visibly with the observer men, prompting some busybody in Verrino to ask the question: why?

I realize now that I was in a very confused emotional state, about what I'd done and what Capsi had undertaken. I wished to flee, but had to stay—and *vice versa*! By six o'clock I found myself hesitating at the top of the stairs, craving a drink in town and ordinary chatter around me. I had to pull myself up sharpish and retrace my steps to my room, because actually I was almost ready to keel over in exhaustion and tumble all the way down into town.

So back to my chamber I crept. Then, without my quite knowing how it happened, Hasso was standing by my bedside—where I lay fully dressed.

"No!" I cried, blinking at him.

And he chuckled, indicating the faint grey light beyond the mullion.

"Dawn's breaking, Yaleen."

"What?"

"I thought I'd best come and fetch you—just in case you slept right through. I'm sure you'd never have forgiven me for *that*."

* * *

44

When the light of the heliograph blinked out, half an hour later, it came from almost opposite Verrino. But we could be fairly sure that no one else would see it. It was very low, and we were high; and besides, who else would be looking out for a signal light from that direction?

Today's message was longer.

Went inland. Avoided contact. Hid near town. All females wear black, confirmed. Town is shabby, poor, dirt-agric. Plus pigs, chickens, goats. Mining activity south side hills, thus reason for location. Male and female workers. Overheard passers-by on track. Same language, few strange words, accent thick but imitable. Diving suit worked a dream. Black current fifteen spans deep approx. Same time tomorrow. End.

So there was nothing whatever to do till then. Unless I wished to pore over panoramas and grub through records of past observations and hearsay from Ajelobo to Umdala; which I did not.

I could just as easily have stayed in town, and climbed up every day before dawn!

Perhaps. Perhaps that mightn't have been quite so easy in poor light. . . .

After a breakfast of black bread, raw fish and pickles in the refectory I decided that I should certainly spend the day in town, and slipped quietly away.

Not quietly enough, however. Hasso caught up with me halfway down the spiralling steps.

"Yaleen, would you let me treat you to lunch? Please."

"Lunch," I pointed out, "is four or five hours away."

"Well, I don't mind waiting, if you don't."

"Did they send you along to keep an eye on me?"

"Of course not. What possible harm could you intend us? And what harm could you possibly do, without harming yourself into the bargain?"

"You've lost me my brother," said I. "You've lost him for my parents. Forever."

"I think, Yaleen, that you and they lost him a long time ago. But don't think of him as vanished. Don't count on his not being hailed as a hero, one of these days."

"A hero—of what?"

"Of the knowledge of why things are as they are."

"And of how to alter them?"

Hasso remained silent.

"He'll be so alone," I went on. "Utter strangers, different customs, always having to sneak around and pretend. . . ."

"Not necessarily. He *is* a man, after all. Who's to say that they won't welcome him over there? Just as soon as he's checked out the lie of the land. And as to loneliness, maybe he was always alienated . . . But you know, where one man can cross, another man can cross too."

"Is that what it's really all about, then? Emigration?"

"Oh, come off it! Diving suits don't exactly come cheap or easily. Will you stop pulling such gloomy faces? We should be celebrating. For the first time in history something new has happened. We even know the depth of the black current now. I'll bet that's something your own guild doesn't know."

"No comment, Hasso."

"No comment asked for, either. Let's stop fencing, shall we? I *like* you, Yaleen. Those few little queries I raised a year ago were very much the second thing on my mind then. If not the tenth! And it was *you*, I'll remind you, who came looking. . . ."

"Hmm."

And presently we did continue on down the stairs together. Though both down in the town itself and later on when we returned up the Spire, I was careful not to seem to be sailing in the direction of *his* personal harbour. However, by then the real truth was that I hadn't drunk any Safe recently.

The next day again dawned bright, as usual at this time of the year; though perhaps it would cloud over later.

And the light winked from the same location.

The message went:

Made contact. Woman alone gathering wood. Pretended am traveller from afar. Asked reason for black patch outside town. River worshippers burnt recently. Mother caught bathing nude in river. Burnt. Later daughter went mad. Questioned. Burnt too. Who by? Brotherhood. Query? Sons of Adam. Why? Incompre-

hension. Repeated query. River quote Satan unquote. Satan query? Woman alarmed. Tried to flee. Overtook. Tell her am Son of Adam. On mission. Keep mouth shut. Same time tomorrow. End.

"So what's Satan?" asked Hasso, expressing the general puzzlement. "And who's Adam?"

"Maybe Satan is 'sanity', mixed up?" I suggested. "Because the black current drives men mad. . . ."

Yosef nodded. "Possibly. And possibly the word Adam has a negative prefix, as in words like 'abort' and 'apathy'—and dam is a female parent? Thus: 'sons without a mother'."

"There are quite a few of those on this side of the river," commented Hasso, somewhat acidly.

"Were you one of those?" I asked him sharply. "Was your mother a riverwoman?"

"Uh? Oh no. Not at all. Please don't leap to so many conclusions about me, will you not? I thought we'd made it all up yesterday. Well, maybe not *all*. . . ."

"Okay, okay. Sorry. So where does this Satan and Adam business leave us?"

"The answer to that," said Yosef, "is: considerably more knowledgeable than ever before. Plus, we know that some women over there worship the river, as though it's a God."

"Out of despair at their lot, presumably."

"Maybe," he went on, "it *is* a God. In the sense of a very powerful, though rather torpid being. Or perhaps a being which has other, more interesting things to think about than us. . . ." He leaned against the guard-rail, surveying the landscape around Verrino. "Fertile place, isn't it, our habitable zone? With a desert barrier bordering all of it, and precipices to seal off one end, and the wild ocean the other end. Rather like," and he smiled, "an ant colony in a very long trough. How illuminating it might be to watch how two separate ant colonies developed, supposing they were separated by a glass wall midway . . . Granting, of course, the vast difference between ants and humans."

"What are you getting at?" I asked him.

"Just that, if there's a God—or Goddess—around, she

47

doesn't seem particularly worried whether her worshippers are burned alive . . . But maybe if she interfered, that would break the rules of her game?" Yosef hesitated. "And of course, if there were a higher being involved, humans could hardly hope to understand it—or perhaps even to prove that it *was* a higher being. No more than an ant can hope to understand a man, however much time it spends crawling along him from head to foot. In which case, our particular tragedy would be to *suspect* that this was so—because an ant could never suspect anything of the sort in a million years."

Hasso looked impatient, and tried to interrupt.

Yosef simply raised his voice. "Yes, we would be conscious of the existence of a mystery—whenever we bothered to pay attention to it—without ever being able to solve it. Rather like the mystery of the whole universe of space and stars, itself. *Why* is it? *How* is it? We're in it, and of it; and so we've no idea. Perhaps if we could solve the mystery of the river, the mystery of existence might well come next?"

"One thing at a time, for goodness sake!" broke in Hasso. "It's the other shore we're exploring."

"And why is there another shore, so very separated from us? I do sometimes wonder whether there can be men, who act as Gods to other men—without scruple?"

"You mean those Sons of Adam? That Brotherhood?"

"No, not at all. I was wondering: is the black current entirely natural?"

I just had to laugh. None of these men had any concept of the sheer scope of the river. It might well be a creature, or at least part of one, a tendril—its spine or bloodstream or whatever—but that it could be a *made* thing? Oh no.

The old imp smiled at me, unoffended, and bobbed his head. "Quite!" he cried. "Quite! You're right to be amused. Far, far better that the river is an alien goddess, than the handiwork of men like Gods. Or of *women* like Gods."

And so we went below to the refectory, for a breakfast of boiled eggs, bread and hot spiced milk.

"Perhaps Yosef's right," said Hasso, intercepting me on my way

48

to the head of the stairs. "I'm going out to the glassworks and grindery today. Want to come?"

"Why there?"

"The first helmet worked a treat, didn't it? So it's only sensible to have another one on hand. Just in case."

"Maybe Yosef was right about what?" I asked him.

"About women like Gods . . . Supposing that was so, mightn't some wise old guildmistress have an inkling of the truth?"

So she might. If. And supposing. But recalling my initiation on board the *Ruby Piglet*, I suspected not. Unless the boatmistress of the *Ruby Piglet* knew little and cared less. . . .

"Why ask me?" said I, lightly. "I'm hardly a guildmistress."

"Who knows? Some day, Yaleen, some day. . . ."

Rain showered down on our way to the glassworks, settling all the dust which had been oozing out of the cracks of the world, and soaking us both; however this hardly mattered once we arrived at the sand pits with their sheds housing tank furnaces. Before long we were both dried as crisp as biscuits. While Hasso conducted the business of ordering a new diving helmet to specifications—with no particular appearance of furtiveness on his part—I wandered about the sheds, peering at the furnace pots and moulds, the drawing hearths, and the bare-chested glassblowers playing their tubes like fanfare trumpets, arriving eventually at the grindery where much more delicate work was carried on. The time passed quickly.

We returned to town by one o'clock under a clear sky, for the rain clouds had passed away upriver and the sun come out again; and slaked our thirst and filled our bellies with savoury pancakes at a wine-arbour new to me.

Later, as drowsy and replete as if we had made love, we toiled back up the spiralling stairs, pausing every fifty steps or so. I didn't know what was on Hasso's mind, but personally my heart was set on a siesta.

And as we rounded the Spire for the second time, already high above the roofs of Verrino, I saw the tiny winks of light from the far side of the river. Even as I pointed, the signal ceased.

"Something's wrong. Come on!"

We ran all the rest of the way; and I arrived with a stitch in my side.

The platform was buzzing.

Immediately Yosef saw us he hurried over, brandishing the copied message, his face grave. He thrust the sheet of paper into my hand.

"That's all there is. He broke off in mid-word."

I read:

Men hunting me. Surrounded. Wom—

Without thinking, I crumpled up the sheet as though the message would go away. Gently Yosef retrieved the paper from my fist, smoothed it out and handed it to someone else for safe keeping. To be filed in the archives, of course. Then he put his arm around my shoulder.

Three days passed, and they were days of silly hope for me: hope that another message would soon blink, boasting how well in Capsi was—as thick as thieves—with the men over there.

And on the evening of the third day, on that twice-burnt sward outside the settlement, a crowd of tiny figures gathered once more, and a cart was hauled through their midst, and something black was dragged from the back of the tumbril as though it had no more bones or volition than a sack of corn; and presently a bonfire blazed, and smoke rose greasily.

It *could* have been a woman; could have been. . . .

But I knew that it wasn't.

And what could they have been doing during the three previous days, those Sons of Adam, but tormenting Capsi terribly, for information?

The very next evening I signed on a brig, the *Darling Dog*, bound for Pecawar and home. I had no idea at all what I was going to tell Mother and Father. And I still hadn't decided this as I walked up the familiar dusty lane to our door. Contrary to expectation, in spite of all my travels this lane seemed no shorter or narrower or even dustier than it ever had before. Pecawar was just as it had always been. The world no more changes than the river changes; it flows on, and yet stays the same.

I banged the door knocker instead of just pushing on in and calling out, "I'm back." And by this choice I made myself a stranger.

Mother opened the door, and I stared at her in bewilderment, for she was a stranger too. Her body had changed shape: she was visibly pregnant.

My first fleeting thought was: so she's replaced Capsi already! And my second thought: she's replaced *both* of us. My third sad, frightened thought was: she's forty, she'll die, it's too late to have another baby!

But there she stood, young and glowing, with the false bloom of pregnancy about her. . . .

How could anybody turn back the clock like this? Way back nearly twenty years to another bout with infancy and toddlerhood and school days? But the truth about a clock is that its hour hand moves on and on inexorably—until suddenly it's back at the very same hour it was, once in the past.

"Hullo, Mother." I embraced her cautiously, though she seemed to have no such reservation about squeezing me, almost to death. (Had the Sons of Adam crushed Capsi with heavy weights? Had they used red-hot pincers, and ropes to rack his bones out of joint?)

And I had my answer to the problem of how to tell her. Was it a coward's answer—or a brave one, because it left me with all the weight to bear myself?

Now that she was pregnant I couldn't possibly tell her that Capsi had just been burnt alive over on the other shore. Not now. The shock would make her miscarry; then there would be two deaths on my conscience, double grief for them. I *would* tell Mother, of course; but not just yet—not till my next visit home, which I would make sure I timed well after the baby was born. Nor could I load this weight upon Father alone.

And one part of me was asking, all this while: how much *had* Capsi and Yaleen ever really meant to her, or even to both of them? Or did Mother only really care about herself?

How strange, this second late motherhood of hers. I felt lost and alone because of it.

51

"I visited Capsi in Verrino," I said brightly. "I've just spent a week with him."

"Really? You must tell me all his news." Mother laughed. "Young rascal, running off like that! Almost as bad as you . . . So what are we standing here at the door for, like a pair of strangers?"

Thus after a year away I entered my home, which wasn't *my* home any longer but the home of a child unborn who would never regard me as a sister but only as another adult member of the family, a sort of aunt or third parent mostly absent.

I left after less than a week spent brooding around Pecawar, and signed on to sail south upon the schooner *Spry Goose*, determined to remain with this same boat for at least a year or two, as though its crew were my real family; and determined also to become an impeccable riverwoman upon it, thus somehow to compensate for my dereliction at Verrino.

And I suppose I must have succeeded in my aim, all too soon, for by the end of that same year, far to the south in the steamy tropics I was invited by my guild to volunteer for the New Year' Eve journey out to the black current.

Part Two

NEW YEAR'S EVE AT
TAMBIMATU

Was I glad when the *Spry Goose* got to Jangali! Boatmistress Marcialla was actually going to allow her crew a few days' holiday. Imagine that. A rest.

Of course, nothing is ever as simple as it seems. By the time we were to resume our voyage again, a few score hours later, I would feel distinctly relieved to be back on board. When we arrived on that sultry late autumn afternoon, however, I wasn't to know this. A somewhat weary Yaleen was just looking forward innocently to the Junglejack Festival.

The problem with the *Spry Goose* wasn't that Marcialla was a martinet, a disciplinarian. Nor her boatswain Credence, either. It was simply that Marcialla was boat-proud; and the *Spry Goose* being a three-mast schooner, there was quite a lot of boat to be proud of. So when we picked up a load of paint at Guineamoy, and Marcialla had said casually, "Let's give the *Goose* a lick of paint," I didn't know what we were in for.

I soon found that painting isn't a matter of slapping on a fresh coat, then sitting back to admire it. First there's the rubbing down of the old paint, often to the wood. Next, any knots in the exposed timber have to be sealed with knotting juice, and any cracks filled with resin-gum. After that there's priming, and then there's undercoating . . . and a long, long time later you actually get to doing the painting itself—twice over.

The less said the better, I think, about all the laborious hours that I and several others spent while we sailed south with the autumn winds behind us! Three times over we plied from Guineamoy to Spanglestream and back again. Then from Spanglestream to Croakers' Bayou four times there and back. Rubbing, knotting, priming, painting. And on each of the return trips, as we tacked against the prevailing wind, I had rope and canvas to occupy my idle hands. I think Marcialla deliberately timetabled the loading and delivery of cargoes just so as to build in optimum drying times.

Yet at least this kept my body and mind occupied. Thus it was *almost* "innocently" that I arrived eventually in Jangali, anticipating a little holiday.

Innocent, though, I was not. Not deep in my heart. For had I not helped my own brother to go to a horrible death on the far side of the river, where they burn women alive? Had I not watched through a telescope, while they burned him?

And I had not dared tell my mother or my father, rationalizing this failure of courage on my part as a responsible decision—since anguish at the news of Capsi's fate might make my mother miscarry. (Though what she imagined she was up to by having another baby, was beyond my comprehension!)

All the labour of painting seemed to have laid a coat of paint over these scars in my soul. Yet it hadn't really done so. I hadn't knotted and gummed and primed those scars. When the paint dried, they would soon show through again as dark shadows. The fresh skin of paint would crack and peel.

Also, while busy painting—and reefing and luffing, belaying and shinning up rigging—I had kept my eyes fixed on the tasks in hand. Even so, the black current was always there. No amount of paint, no spread of sails, was going to hide it or erase it.

Was it really a living creature six hundred leagues long and more? A powerful, sensitive yet generally comatose being which for its own purposes allowed women to ply the river, but not men? Was it some kind of alien goddess? Or was it, as old Yosef had implied, something artificially created to separate us from the "Sons of Adam" on the west bank, that mysterious brotherhood of men who turned their backs superstitiously and savagely upon the river; about whom almost all we knew was the little that Capsi had been able to heliograph back before they caught him?

I had drunk of the current, and it knew me; but it I did not know.

Maybe it was impossible ever to know what the black current really was. In which case how much more sensible it was to ignore it, and get on painting a boat, and enjoy the journey as much as possible.

And really—hard labour and scars of the heart apart—there were so many new sights for me to soak in. Even when seen twice and thrice over they still remained quite exciting, by and large.

South of Gangee, that scruffy town which I'd visited on my first voyage aboard the *Sally Argent*, was Gate of the South.

The tropics put in their first hesitant appearance there—with the townsfolk doing their best to encourage the show. Butter-blooms cascaded from balconies, and biscus trees were kept well watered by a network of tiny cobbled streams, although the red trumpet flowers were smaller than those I was to see further south.

Just as my own home town of Pecawar made a virtue of being on the verge of the desert, so did Gate of the South rejoice in its own position—more so than some towns of the deep south which were tropical through and through. At Gate of the South it was still possible to "garden" the vegetation. There was even a ceremonial stone arch which spanned the road from north to south, with a signpost by it listing all the distances to furthest Tambimatu 280 leagues away. What practical use this was I couldn't say, except perhaps as a disincentive to the local men to set out on foot! My new friend Jambi, with whom I went ashore for a few hours, was a six-year veteran of these southern reaches, and she pointed out in high amusement that no road actually ran all the way from Gate of the South to Tambimatu. The swamps around Croakers' Bayou were obstacle number one. Further south than that, the jungle increasingly had its own way with roads.

Jambi was dark-skinned and jolly, with long black hair which she generally wore in a bun so as not to get tangled, thus hoisting her up the main mast inadvertently. She hailed from Spangle-stream, and the only time I mentioned the black current to her she merely glanced and wrinkled her nose, and that was the whole of her interest in it. This made me suppose that she was rather a good choice as a friend. She wouldn't remind me of anything painful. Jambi had a shore-husband and a baby boy at Spanglestream, though she didn't seem to bother about them unduly, except to the extent that she stayed in southern waters.

After leaving Gate of the South, we called at Guineamoy—

source of that wretched load of paint. At Guineamoy you could also have gardened the tropics. But the people didn't bother, perhaps because Gate of the South had stolen their thunder. Guineamoy preferred to wear an ugly face and hide everything in grime. The people seemed to make a virtue of this, as though foul air and the stink of chemicals were their way of dealing with the burgeoning extravagance of nature. Smoke and steam belched out of lots of little workshops. There were kilns and smelters and smithies. There were warehouses and rubbish dumps; and outside of the town, half a league inland, was an artificial lake of filth. Inland, yes. Whatever stenches they pumped into the air, obviously they had no desire to risk polluting the river itself. If they had, I suppose the river guild might have banned their cargoes. What the black current itself would have done about such pollution, if anything, I had no idea. Just then, I didn't wish to wonder.

I suppose grime is comparative. If Guineamoy seemed a filthy place to me, maybe to its inhabitants it seemed a paragon of virtue and energy, and everywhere else excessively rustic. Maybe I was unduly sensitive to it, like a green leaf vulnerable to blight—because I was already a little blighted in my soul.

After Guineamoy came Spanglestream, which was renowned for its tasty fish and its dozens of lug-sailed fishing smacks decorated with painted eyes on hulls and sails. It was equally famous for the phosphorescent streamers which snaked across the river at night in bright silver, transforming the river into one of stars. These streamers only occurred for a couple of leagues to the north and south of the town, and looked like bubbly exhalations of breath from the midstream current. I suppose they must have been made up of myriads of tiny organisms which fed on minerals or whatever was abundant in the water there—providing in their turn a non-stop meal for the shoals of larger fish.

I stayed ashore overnight at Jambi's house. Her husband I found obliging and amiable. Obviously he adored Jambi—which relieved her of the need to adore him unduly in return. But otherwise he was just a little bit of a zero. I foresaw trouble if Jambi ever had to quit the river; and I could only wonder quite how she had put up with being beached during the course of her pregnancy. I played with her little boy, too. Alas, this reminded me of the infant stranger my own mother was cooking up. . . .

Jambi, husband and myself visited a raw fish restaurant that evening, where we filled ourselves with thin slices of madder-coloured hoke and yellow pollfish and velvety ajil dipped in mild mustard sauce. And we drank ginger spirit. Afterwards we strolled down to the promenade to view the spangling phosphorescence, which put on a particularly fine display for my benefit; which was the only time that I mentioned the current to Jambi.

"Maybe," I said, "all the tiny silver things feed on something the black current jettisons here? A sort of excrement from it?" I'd asked earlier, and it turned out that no one really knew. The glassmaker's art, à la Verrino, had never produced any lenses powerful enough to plumb the really microscopic.

That was when she glanced, and wrinkled her nose. Perhaps this wasn't surprising—in view of the fact that she had just treated me to wonderful fish. Here was I suggesting that the black current used the neighbourhood as a toilet! This may have seemed an unholy slur on her native town.

More likely my remark seemed like tipsy nonsense. Jambi was a bustling, practical person who probably dismissed her own Guild initiation quite soon after it occurred as merely a metaphorical masquerade—as something mystical, in which she had no interest.

As soon as I asked her this, to my alarm I felt a queasiness in my guts. Was this because of the presence of a male, her husband? Pleasantly fired by all the ginger spirit, I might have been on the verge of saying too much. Remembering how sick I had been when I was indiscreet about a Guild secret that one time on board the *Sally Argent*, I promptly shut up and enjoyed the silvery show.

Jambi couldn't have minded my comment, since she invited me back to her home on our subsequent calls at Spanglestream during the next few weeks. I accepted her invitation the second time. That night she was throwing a party for some local fisherwomen she had been at school with—at Spanglestream the call of the river did not necessarily call you very far from home. Yet on the third occasion I made an excuse. These invitations, kind as they were, reminded me of how I myself had invited a friend, Hali, home to Pecawar, only to discover that brother Capsi had decamped. To his doom. And then there was the presence of the little boy. The child seemed, by proxy, to dispossess me of all possible homes except those afloat.

After Spanglestream we came to Croakers' Bayou where the river spilled slackly inland into a maze of hot dank swamps. Here stilt-trees meandered in long winding colonnades, forming vaults and corridors and tunnels. Mudbanks emerged and submerged at whim. Puffballs and great white fungus domes studded the exposed mud. The big froggy croakers squatted and hopped and played their ventriloquists' tricks, voices echoing off the water and the arched tree trunks.

And I thought fancifully that if the anus of the black current was located off Spanglestream, then here at Croakers' Bayou was the mouldy decaying appendix of the river. The grating croaks were a sort of flatulence, a shifting of gases in the bowels.

Once out of Croakers' Bayou forests cloaked the shore. The western bank, far away, was likewise a ribbon of green. It occurred to me that the Sons of Adam might not rule the roost everywhere along the far side. How could they, when they denied themselves the advantages of river transport? Maybe *their* southern reaches were uninhabited. Or perhaps those who dwelled there were savages, without even the dubious level of culture of the Sons.

Savages! Ah, yet gentler perhaps than the Sons in their treatment of women. . . .

And maybe they were even worse than the Sons. I spotted no canoes; no smoke plumes from campfires near the shore. If anyone lived over there, they too shunned the river.

But this was the least of my worries, compared with the unending paint-job. Whenever it rained, which it did with a vengeance now and then, we had to rig tarpaulins.

Gradually the forest knotted and tangled itself with vines and moss-mats, epiphytes and parasites, moving towards true jungle. Which, by the time we reached Jangali, it was.

We carried two young lovers as passengers on our journey to Jangali: Lalo and Kish. Kish was a boy from Spanglestream who was a friend of Jambi's family on her mother's side. Lalo had decided that she loved him and was now escorting him back home to Jangali, on the one river trip of his life, to wed him.

It struck me as a slight shame that Kish's horizons should thus be limited to the small stretch of land between two nearly adjacent towns. Well, granted that Spanglestream and Jangali were 80 leagues apart! But a riverwoman usually thinks big, and I imagined in a rather snobbish way that it was a teeny bit unenterprising of Lalo to seek her husband from a town which was comparatively close to home, rather than from far Sarjoy (say) or Melonby.

We were chatting below decks one day, the four of us, getting better acquainted. Lalo was holding hands with Kish, while I was trying to pumice some paint off my fingers.

Like Jambi, Lalo was dark-skinned, though her hair was short and curly. She had an unusually loud voice and always spoke with particular emphasis. At one point she happened to mention that some trees deep in the Jangali jungles were "quite as high as the Spire at Verrino". She just mentioned this in passing, but so assertively did she voice it that I almost tore a nail off on the pumice stone.

"Ouch!" That Spire, and its observatory, were all too fresh in my memory.

"Oh, so you got as far as Verrino?" asked Jambi innocently. This was indeed a singularly innocent question coming from a riverwoman, since there are half a dozen major towns further north than that. But Jambi, as I say, was a devoted Southerner.

"Why yes," said Lalo. "I didn't waste my time. I just didn't find anybody suitable. Not till Spanglestream on the way back." And she squeezed Kish's hand affectionately.

"It's often that way." Jambi sounded smug.

I couldn't help wondering whether Lalo had not been growing anxious by the time she got as close to home as Spanglestream.

61

But maybe she had been especially choosy on her travels; which meant that she had made a sensible choice. The marriage would last, and last well.

I guess from Kish's point of view there was a whole world of difference between Spanglestream and Jangali. Judging from his questions it was plain that Kish was a little apprehensive at the prospect of becoming a junglejack—if indeed he *would* become one. Lalo teased him with this prospect intermittently. Just about as often, she corrected his misapprehensions. . . .

"It seems to me," I said, and I suppose I spoke thoughtlessly in the circumstances, "that a woman could find her ideal partner in almost any town chosen at random. It's all a bit of an accident, isn't it? I mean, which street you happen to walk down. Which winehouse you pop into. Who you sit next to at a concert. You turn left here, rather than right, and it's this fellow who'll spend the rest of his life with you, while another fellow walks on by. It could so easily have been the other one instead."

"Oh no!" Lalo protested. "A feeling guides you. A kind of extra sense that you only use once. You *know* you should turn left instead of right. You *know* you ought to carry on to the next town, because the scent's gone dead in this one. You're operating by a sort of special instinct during your wander-weeks. Honestly, Yaleen, you'll know this if it happens to you. It's a heightened, thrilling feeling."

"You're a romantic," said Jambi. "Kish is lucky. I tend to agree with Yaleen myself. Anyone can settle down with anyone else." (That wasn't quite what I'd said.) "But then," she added, "I also have the river as my first love."

And lovers in different ports as well, I wondered? Jambi hadn't spoken of this to me. One didn't gossip about one's harmless amorous adventures. For one thing, it would be demeaning to the men.

"So you turned right instead of left," I said, "but guided by your nose."

"And now I'll be a junglejack forever." Kish grinned ruefully. He had a whimsical, expressive face, with twinkling blue eyes, and already a few smile-wrinkles to accompany them. I liked him, and rather wished that I myself had met him—the way that

62

I had first met Hasso in Verrino, before I found out why Hasso had been hoping to meet someone like me.

"Phooey!" said Lalo. "A junglejack? Why, that's nothing. I tell you, in the jungle you're usually better off *up* a tree. It's the creepy-crawlies down below that bug us. You'll need some good strong boots. And a stomach to go with them." She couldn't keep a straight face, though. She giggled. "Oh, I'm just kidding. Jangali's a decent, civilized place. Not like Port Barbra. That's where the really weird and queasy things happen, out in the interior. The fungus cult, for instance. Completely wrecks your sense of time and decency. Us, we just get smashed on junglejack like decent mortals."

"Tell me more," said Kish. "I like getting smashed, too. Preferably not by falling off a tree."

"You wouldn't, not with safety lines."

So we began to natter on about junglejack, the drink. Apparently this was distilled from the berries of some high vine. It went off quite quickly and didn't travel—alas for the export economy of Jangali, perhaps fortunately for the economy of everywhere else. And we nattered about junglejacks in general: the people who felled the hardwood trees and also harvested the tangled heights, picking fruit, tapping juice, scraping resin, collecting medicinal parasite plants.

I became quite enthused about the impending festival of acrobatics, vine-swinging and sky-walking, and also about getting smashed on junglejack, the drink.

As did Kish; which was of course why Lalo had timed her return for that particular week, to coincide. After a while she even had to remind him gently that not *everyone* in Jangali was a junglejack. There were also butchers and bakers and furniture makers, just like anywhere else.

And she went on more emotionally, now, about the beauties of the jungle, brushing aside the creepy-crawlies as of little consequence.

How I wish she had dampened my enthusiasm about Jangali rather than igniting it! Little did I know then that excesses of enthusiasm would result in my saving Marcialla's life—bringing me in turn a singularly horrible reward.

63

Saving Marcialla's life? Well, maybe I exaggerate. Let's change that to: rescuing her from an awkward and potentially lethal situation.

I was looking forward to arriving at Jangali—which was so decently distant from Verrino. I was looking forward to really enjoying the events. I even imagined that I was, in a sense, successfully running away. All the while in truth I was running—or sailing—*towards*.

"Sun's shining! Paint detail on deck!" came Credence's call from the top of the companion way. Why I had bothered cleaning my fingers, goodness knows. Except that if I hadn't, it would have been harder later on. Perhaps there's a moral in this: it's almost always harder later on. Everything is.

Jangali rejoiced in massive stone quays fronting the river, quarried and cut with steps and timber-slides. The town itself was founded upon that same great slab of rock, which ran back into the jungle before dipping under, submerging itself in humus and vegetation. In the original old town the architecture was of stone, with wooden upper storeys. The new town behind—which I was to see presently—was wholly of timber, and fused with the jungle itself. Some houses there incorporated living trees. Others were built on to them and around them. Some even slung from them cantilever-style. The entire effect of Jangali was of some strange metamorphosing creature which was living wood at one end and fossil rock at the other—or perhaps of dead rock coming gradually to life the further inland you went.

The locals reminded me of those of Verrino. Indeed, this might have been why Lalo had followed her nose to Verrino in the first place—though with no result. Jangali folk weren't as quicksilver-nimble and chattery, always scurrying every which where. Yet there was an elastic spring to their steps, a bounciness, as if they regarded the stone floor of the town more as a trampoline, ever about to toss them up into the treetops beyond. Its inert rigidity amused them and made them prance, just as a riverwoman sometimes feels about dry land after a long time afloat; they intended never to let themselves be bruised by it.

As I say, the locals weren't chattery. But they did address one

64

another in tones pitched to carry through tangles of vegetation in competition with the other chatterers of the beast variety; in voices intended to penetrate up to the very roof of the jungle. Conversations generally took place a few paces further apart than they did elsewhere, much more noisily, more publicly. Jangali would have been the ideal place for a deaf person to take up residence.

Thus the locals reinforced their sense of community. Otherwise, once you were in the jungle, the jungle could swallow you up, stifle you, isolate you, make you mute. I gathered from loud-voiced Lalo that people around Port Barbra behaved more furtively.

Before Lalo and Kish disembarked, they invited Jambi and me to visit them at their parents' home. Or more truthfully, Kish expressed this desire, so that Jambi (old family friend) could see him in his new abode; Lalo invited Jambi and included me in the invitation too. I suppose Kish was trying to keep a kind of psychological lifeline open to Spanglestream. No doubt he hoped that Jambi would continue to pay the occasional visit whenever she was in Jangali. Personally, I didn't think this was entirely wise—not at this early stage in their relationship. For "a man shall leave his mother and father, and sister and brother, and embrace the family of his wife". That's what it says in *The Book of the River*. In at the deep end, say I! Just so long as there aren't any stingers in the water (or at least in the hope that there aren't).

Yet maybe Kish was right. This established him from the start, in a strange town, as on an equal footing with his wife.

At any rate, it was their own business, and I soon abandoned any minor scruples I might have felt about us getting in the way when I learned that Lalo's parents lived in the new town, in a hanging home high up a tree. This I had to see.

And that's what we set out to do, the very next day. But before that, an odd thing happened.

We'd arrived in Jangali in mid-afternoon. There was the furling of the sails to see to, and the gangers to supervise as they unloaded our cargo: crans of fish from Spanglestream, barrels of salt trans-shipped all the way from Umdala, and pickles from Croakers' Bayou and such. By the time everything was boat-shape, we only had time to go ashore for a brisk walk round the monumental old town, culminating in a not so brief visit to Jambi's favourite bar—where I made my first acquaintance with the fiery junglejack.

The bar in question—the whole town, for that matter—was a-buzz in expectation of the festival. The normal population must have increased by half again, what with people trekking in from up-country and from smaller jungle settlements along the shore, not to mention outside visitors. Lalo pointed out women from Croakers' Bayou, and from Port Barbra. The former she identified by a more sallow look to them, and the latter by the hooded cloaks and scarves they wore—to cope, Jambi said, with occasional pesky clouds of insects in their area; besides Port Barbrans spoke much more softly. By contrast the Jangali locals seemed even noisier than I supposed they usually were. The Jingle-Jangle Bar lived up to its name; and I ended up later on with quite a headache—quite independent, of course, of the junglejack spirit.

The motif of the Jingle-Jangle wasn't trees, but carved stone. The bar was an artificial cavern of nooks and crannies and stalagmite-like columns, with fat chunky nude statues holding oil lamps. Around their squat necks hung strings of medallions, and around their loins brief girdles of the same. Presumably these medallions would jingle and jangle if you shook them. To my mind the whole mood of the bar was primitive and subterranean, with a hint of secrets and conspiracy, an odour of dark mystery.

The place was also very hot. There we were in the reeking petrified bowels of a jungle so dense that it had become a cave. I must say that the place had atmosphere: compounded of perfume and oil-fumes, sweat and mustiness, and partly of sheer hot air from all the babbling voices. I wouldn't have been surprised if savage drums had begun to beat; I noticed that there was a stone dais for entertainers, currently unoccupied.

And in the Jingle-Jangle I happened to notice Marcialla and Credence sitting over a drink. This wasn't in itself unusual.

What was odd was that they seemed to be arguing. Credence was insisting on something; Marcialla kept on shaking her head.

Every so often Credence glanced in the direction of a small, hooded group of women from Port Barbra; and Marcialla particularly shook her head then.

I should explain that Marcialla was quite a short woman, though in no way squat even if she must have been in her early fifties. She was wiry, and carried no spare flesh. Credence was big and busty and blonde, and at least fifteen years her junior. Marcialla wore her greying hair swept back in short shingled waves; Credence had hers in chopped off pigtails. All in all Credence looked like an inflated, coarsened girl.

"I'm peckish. Let's have a bite to eat," I suggested. So we carried our drinks over to the buffet bar—this was supported by carved stone female dwarfs, pygmy caryatids holding up the food table. On Jambi's say-so we bought spiced snakemeat rolls.

On the way back I ducked into an empty nook just round the corner from our boatmistress and her boatswain. This was just on impulse. Besides, our previous seats had already been taken in our absence.

I admit that I was curious and a little tipsy, therefore bold. But with all the racket going on around us I didn't really expect to hear anything. However, there must have been something of a whispering gallery effect in that nook. Also, the din was so incoherent that paradoxically this made it easier rather than harder to pick out snatches of two familiar voices—the way that a mother can hear her own particular offspring cry out amidst fifty other bawling babies.

Snatches was all that I did hear, but they were interesting enough.

"But suppose you doped the black current with enough of the time-drug. . . ." That was Credence.

A mumble from Marcialla.

". . . slow down its response, wouldn't it?"

"That fungus is a poison of the mind. . . ."

". . . test it by mixing some in a phial of the black current. . . ."

". . . and who'll drink it? You?"

67

". . . might do."

". . . to prove what?"

". . . achieve more *rapport*, Marcialla! Somehow to be able to speak to it, and it to us. Maybe our time-scales are too different."

". . . contradicting yourself. Slow *it* down? Slow us down, you mean. Anyway, it reacts fast enough when it's rejecting someone."

"Reflexes and thoughts are two different things. If I stuck my hand in a fire. . . ."

"Your trouble is, you're a true believer. Like your Mother; and so she named you Credence. You believe in the godly spirit of the river . . ." A surge in the level of the din cut off the rest of this.

"Besides," was the next thing I heard, from Marcialla, "take this notion one stage further. It's all very well to talk blithely of doping one phial with this wretched fungus powder. But suppose somebody then thought of dumping a few barrels of the stuff into the midstream, eh? Slow down its, ah, reflexes long enough to take a boat through, perhaps? Over to the other side . . . Where does that lead to in the long run? I'll tell you where: it leads to poisoning the current. It leads to making the river safe for men. What price your goddess, then? The whole thing falls apart. A whole, good way of life goes with it. Always assuming that the black current didn't react horrendously to being poisoned! What you're saying is sheer madness."

"Sorry, *Guildmistress*," said Credence unctuously.

"You know those people, don't you?"

"Which people?"

"The Port Barbra ones over there. Do you think I'm blind? You've arranged something. Now you want a phial of the black current. Or is it a bucketful? They want it. In exchange. Do they appreciate the dangers? Any more of this, and we'll be having to flash word to every boatmistress on the river to keep the stuff under double lock. Don't you think that would be sad? Is there no trust? No sense any more?"

Then the noise really did get out of hand. Some musicians had arrived, to do terrible things to my head—although they played pipes and flutes and banjos rather than bashing on drums. Jambi was growing restive about my noncommittal grunts and yes-noes as I sat with my head cocked, intent on other things.

"You in a trance or something?" she shouted.

"Hmm . . . ? No. Sorry! Cheers."

After a long lie-in the next morning, I was up and leaning against the rail at the head of the gangplank waiting for Jambi to join me—when along came Marcialla.

"Yaleen," she said thoughtfully, "saw you in the Jingle-Jangle last night." She waited for me to volunteer something.

"Quite a place," I said. "Oof. My head." I rubbed my tender skull.

"You meet all sorts in a place like that."

"All sorts are in town for the festival, I suppose."

"Even women from Port Barbra."

"Oh yes, Jambi pointed some out to me. They wear hoods and scarves."

And so we continued to fence for a while (or at least that's what I thought), and I was feeling fairly pleased with myself, though also praying that Jambi would hurry along and break it up.

"Weird place, Port Barbra," said Marcialla. "Odd people there, some of them."

"So I've heard. Strange jungly rites."

"People sometimes get attracted by strange things." When I said nothing, Marcialla went on, "Of course, you can't judge a place by its oddballs. Its extremists. After all, look at Verrino."

Did she know? Had word got out of what I had done, and passed along the river? I was talking—I remembered—to a guildmistress, no less. I'd heard that much last night.

"And equally," she mused, "people can get mixed up in queer things quite innocently, even the best of them." My heart was thumping. But then, so was my head. That was when Marcialla glanced up at the rigging and furled sails, her boatswain's special province, and sighed; and I realized that she had been thinking all along in a sad and lonely way of Credence, and simply associating me with her because I too had been in the Jingle-Jangle.

"Maybe," I said—I was trying to be helpful, without at the

same time betraying myself as an eavesdropper—"maybe people who believe deeply in things are all innocents, but it's a dangerous kind of innocence. . . ." And maybe I only said this to impress, in the hope that Marcialla would be amazed at my youthful perspicacity. What I'd said certainly wasn't true of the Observers at Verrino. Hasso hadn't been an innocent. On the contrary! Nor Yosef, either. Nor Capsi. Dedicated men, but by no means naive. If I had overheard that conversation aright the previous night, though, Credence was both dedicated *and* naive, deep down.

Marcialla obviously regarded me as the innocent, here. She smiled in a kindly way.

"You've done good painting work. Quite commendable. And if I hadn't kept you at it back then, there wouldn't have been time for a holiday now, would there? Don't let me keep you from enjoying yourself."

"I'm just waiting for Jambi." (Where was she, damn it?)

"Take care ashore," Marcialla added softly. More to herself than to me.

"Care, Boatmistress?" And I realized that I was echoing Credence's suave tone, of not so many hours earlier.

Marcialla stared at me, puzzled. "The booze, I mean, girl. Watch the booze; it's lethal." And she patted me on the arm.

"Don't I know it!"

Which was when Jambi turned up at long last.

So we sought out Lalo's home in the new town. We followed her directions scrupulously; but, as directions have a way of being, these ones were perfect so long as you had already been there once.

As we walked, the stone of the old town transmuted itself into the timber of the new. Homes were nuzzling against living trees, or were arranged around them in conical skirts so that the tree itself seemed like a huge, out-of-proportion chimney. Other houses climbed the largest giants in cantilevered or buttressed tiers—stepping around the great trunks like flights of steps by which some wood spirit could descend at night from the leafy crowns. Sometimes a walkway ran from one tree to the next, along a branch.

70

As yet, this was all jungle which had been thinned out and tamed. In the old town the sun was aggressively hot and glary; further inland the unbroken umbrella of foliage would surely blank it off except for vagrant shafts like spears of molten metal. Here then, in the new town, was the ideal compromise: the sunlight dappled down. Unfamiliar flower bushes hugged the roadways and paths, but there was no riot of undergrowth as such. Vegetable gardens were planted here and there, plump with tomatoes, courgettes, cucumbers, sweetgourds, meat-melons, pumpkins. Familiar fruits mostly, though their size was something else.

And of course we got lost. Or more exactly, we arrived just where we wanted to be not that day, but a couple of days later: at the festival site. I suppose this was because quite a number of people involved in the preparations were heading that way too. Like two stray fish caught up in a school of busier fish, unconsciously we went with them.

We came to a very large clearing, on one side of which workers were hammering, fixing and strengthening the terraces of a grandstand.

And at once I felt at home, for the area before the grandstand was like the deck of an enormous boat. Sparred masts soared up to the sky from the flat, stripped ground. Rope ladders ran up some of these; single knotted ropes up others. I spied trapezes, aerial platforms and crow's nests—with more ropes stretched taut from each to the other; while behind this array stood a dead, though still mighty tree. All the minor and lower branches had been lopped, but the surviving high arms were hung with more acrobatic gear. A few junglejacks dressed in tough baggy trousers, scarlet jerkins and flexible fork-toed boots hung from harnesses, checking belays and loops, wood-pitons and snaplinks; one man was abseiling down a rope.

After watching all this activity for a while, we made enquiries and were on our way again—this time in the right direction. My hangover had died away nicely by now.

As promised, the Lalo family home was a tree-house—one of those which "stepped up" around a jungle giant. We reached it

71

by way of a covered stairway bolted to the trunk which mounted the roofs of the houses below.

Yet scarcely had we arrived at the door, let alone met any parents, than Lalo declared that a picnic was in order "out in the *real* jungle". Kish popped out in her wake, bearing a hamper, and within what seemed like seconds we were descending the stairs again.

Perhaps Lalo's parents had hinted strongly that it wasn't good form to invite a friend from Spanglestream so very soon after Kish had left the place. Next thing, all his female relatives and friends might be descending on Jangali, to snap the house right off its moorings!

Or maybe it was Lalo, restored to her home and habits after her long wander-weeks, who had decided of her own accord that she had committed a *faux pas* by casually inviting two boating acquaintances. Kish himself seemed perfectly happy and at ease.

Whatever the reason, off we went into the jungle along a trail of perhaps half a league, which grew increasingly wild and noisy with hidden wildlife.

A jungle seen from afar, from the deck of a boat, can be utterly monotonous. At close quarters the same jungle becomes magical. There seemed to be a hundred shades of green: a whole spectrum composed entirely of that colour, as though the sun shed green light, not a bluish white. And in competition with this first, green spectrum was a second one consisting of flowers and flutterbyes radiating reds and oranges and azures, shocking pink and sapphire, like coloured lamps, the better to be noticed. Wings and petals seemed crystalline, glassy, iridescent, with an inner light of their own.

"Why, the flowers are shining!" I exclaimed. "Aren't they? And that flutterbye there!"

"They are—and you should see them after dusk," said Lalo.

Apparently when all the green leaves grew dim there lingered for an hour or two a parade of floral and insect firelight.

Lalo pointed out the occasional dangerous spine-tree, and a squat "boiler" out of which a burning liquid could gush, and oozing gum-sponges. She flushed out a whistle-snake which would shriek to scare you if you trod on it; but it wasn't dangerous except perhaps to your ear-drums. She sent a couple of land-crabs scuttling. These could take your finger off, though only if you stuck it in the wrong place.

She named for us the mammoths of the jungle: the jacktrees, hogannies and teakwoods. She showed us where honeygourds and blue-pears hung up high almost out of sight. We passed a miniature forest of white antlered fungi crowding on a fallen, rotten trunk. These, she said, were edible; whereas the tiny crimson buttons sprouting beneath were instant poison. They looked it. I'm glad I paid attention. I little knew it at the time, but this guided tour was a lesson in survival which I would be very glad of during the early weeks of the next year . . .

Vines dangled down as if to loop and strangle you. Indeed there was one variety known as stranglevine; but you had to allow it a good half-hour to tie itself round you. Moss-mats hung in greenly dripping masses, as though secreting some slime-venom—yet these could staunch blood and disinfect wounds. And webvines wove what looked suspiciously like enormous webs where surely something fat and hairy with lots of legs and eyes lurked; but didn't.

We finally came to Lalo's chosen picnic spot. Deep rock erupted upwards here in the form of a ziggurat rising a hundred spans above the jungle floor. As we neared this stone mass, it took on the appearance of an abandoned, overgrown temple. Briefly I imagined that Lalo was about to reveal an ancient secret to us: the work of some long-dead race, dating from before human beings ever came to this world, from somewhere else.

But no; it was a natural formation. Crude steps, now mossed over, had ben cut up one side of it; though perhaps the steps were natural too, due to fracturing and crumbling. We climbed up these to the top, which was flat and almost bald of vegetation except for a cushion of moss. Lalo uprooted a few plants and a shrub which had established themselves, and tossed them over the side—just as hill climbers elsewhere add an extra stone to a cairn. So, high above the jungle floor in this gap squeezed open by the ziggurat, we sat down. Kish unpacked a bottle of wine wrapped in wet leaves to keep it cool; and blue-pears, spiced rolls, smoked snake and a jar of pickled purple fungi.

We chatted idly, and ate and drank and admired the view, mainly of aerial webs and mats of moss—the brighter aspects of the jungle were below these middle levels, mostly. After a while I picked up the half-empty pickle jar and peered at the remaining contents.

"I was meaning to ask you, Lalo. You were saying that people at Port Barbra use some fungus or other as a drug to mix their minds up."

Lalo laughed. "And here in Jangali we always poison visitors with purple mushrooms. To keep them in our thrall for a hundred years."

"No, seriously."

"Why?"

"No special reason. It just seems weird. Interesting, you know?"

"And poor Jangali has nothing half as interesting on offer, alas."

"Oh, I didn't mean to imply . . . ! Why, this is fabulous." I swept my hand around. "I feel like a real junglejack perched up here."

Kish grinned. "I don't think junglejacks enjoy quite as much support as this."

"Anyhow," I persisted, "what *is* the story?"

Lalo considered, while she bit into a blue-pear.

"I don't know all that much about it. We hear bits of gossip now and then. About orgies in the interior. They use this fungus powder to make sex last a long time. To spin out the, um, sensations, so that they seem to last for hours and hours."

"So it's a drug which slows time down?"

"The trouble is, time gets its own back. So I've heard. You speed up afterwards. You run all over the place like a loony. You talk too fast for anyone to understand you. You gobble down heaps of food because you're burning it all up. If you go on using the stuff, you age before your time. You're old at thirty. Worn out, I suppose."

74

This business about rushing around and chattering nineteen to the dozen didn't quite seem to square with what I'd heard of the "furtive" conduct of people in Port Barbra and environs. But maybe the members of the drug cult kept themselves apart in secret places while they were liable to race about and gabble on. In any case this might just be a tall tale which the drug users fostered, to frighten people off.

"So it's mainly a sex thing with them? It's all just to make sex more thrilling?"

"I don't know that it makes it any more thrilling," said Lalo. "It certainly makes it last longer."

In her emphatic voice, this sounded like some ultimate statement. Kish blinked several times and shook his head as though he hadn't heard correctly. Jambi convulsed with silent laughter.

Lalo pulled a doleful face. "Oh dear! I think I said the wrong thing." And we all began to laugh; after which I couldn't reasonably get back to the topic without seeming obsessed. As if I wanted some of the fungus drug for myself.

Two days later Jambi and I were part of a huge crowd out at the festival ground. Lalo and Kish had promised to see us there, but of course we didn't meet up. There must have been ten thousand people. The grandstand was packed to bursting and the sides of the clearing were thronged. Certainly there were more people than I had ever seen in one place before. It struck me immediately that anything could happen in such a crowd while the acrobatic displays were in progress, and nobody would be any the wiser. Alas, despite the presence of at least a score of jungle-guild marshals patrolling and supposedly keeping an eye on things, I was right.

The clearing had been transformed with banners and bunting, with bright little tents and stalls beneath awnings selling snacks and drinks. There were side shows for the children; giant flutterbyes in twig cages to be won; wrestlers, clowns, conjurors, even a fortune teller.

A fortune teller. I had never had my fortune told. The tent was decorated with golden stars and comets; and when we came upon it there was no one waiting outside.

"Shall we?"

"No thanks," said Jambi. A conjuror was tossing a stream of shiny silver balls nearby. By some sleight of hand he seemed to be making them travel in figure-eights. "I'll watch him. You go ahead."

A fortune teller. Would the person read my palm? Or slit open a fish and examine its guts for auspices? How ancient, how quaint.

Inside, the tent was dim. So until I was already inside and committed, I didn't realize that the fortune teller was a Port Barbra woman. Her hood was pulled well over her head, and her scarf covered her nose and mouth so that of her face there were only two eyes staring out intently—observing the whole of me, while I saw precious little of her.

She spoke softly. "Please sit." On a stool, before a little table.

Which I did. By now I was wishing to flee from the tent, instead. But I was determined to be polite. Or was I too cowardly to rush out? Sometimes rudeness is the better part of courage . . . .

However, I placed upon the table a coin of the value stipulated on the notice outside, 50 scales, or half a fin. Not much, though not entirely negligible.

Cards: it was cards. She was a cartomancer—though maybe she could also turn a trick with fish-guts or palm-lines. Cards were probably faster and took fewer powers of invention.

She handed me a pack, face down. "Don't look. Cut and shuffle three times. Each time you cut, turn half the pack around." I did so, and gave it back.

She fanned the pack on the table, still face-down. There must have been a hundred well-thumbed cards in all.

"Choose nine."

I did so, quite at random. I had no special instinct for this one rather than that. She stacked the rest of the pack to one side then began to turn up the cards I had selected.

The first showed waves on water, with a schooner riding in the distance. The picture was in sepia tones, and pink and dirty white—as were they all to be.

"This is the River. This is you." Her voice was a dull monotone. I nodded, though I shouldn't have done.

The second showed a spyglass. "This lies behind you. You are

76

observant. You watch, though you don't always understand. But since this is behind you, you will understand more in future."

The third was of a babe in arms, but it was facing away from me. "This is your family. Reversed, it suggests negative feelings. You sail on the river to escape this." ("Oh no I don't," I said to myself.) "Or perhaps," she added, "by sailing the river you create these negative feelings." Obviously I had given her some facial cue. I decided to keep my features frozen.

Next was a signal-mirror, hand-held against a backdrop of rolling clouds with the sun just breaking through. Again the card faced away from me.

"These are your hopes or fears. The light of illumination. If reversed, you fear a message. Or a message has filled you with fear. The clouds are your anxieties, which cloud insight."

She turned up the fifth card; and I saw a handsome, laughing man, smartly attired. He reminded me of Hasso (of the dandyish flared trousers and striped shirts), though he was differently attired; but he was just as jaunty. Once again the card lay turned away.

"This is the influence at work: a husband to be sought, a lover. Yet he isn't really for you. Or else he is far away in time or space."

Number six was a cockerel crowing on a dunghill.

"Pride," she interpreted. "Indiscretion."

Indeed? Perhaps it made sense, at that!

Seven was a bonfire, with another cockerel rising in flames from it, flapping fiery wings. An arrow pierced the bird's chest. I had begun to sweat coldly, because this bonfire stirred hideous memories; but she said:

"This is the soul. Also, striving—which is betrayed or disappointed. Or else transfiguration which pierces the heart. The meaning is ambiguous." The bonfire certainly wasn't! "That card shows the *potential* outcome."

Number eight: three men with staffs sprouting green leaves were fighting with three women similarly armed. A fourth man strode away from the fight, his staff over his shoulder supporting a bundle. A house blazed, behind.

"Conflict. A husband walking home. Warfare. Alternatively:

77

resolute bravery, success. This is the *probable* outcome. Again, it's ambiguous."

She turned the last card over, placing it in the centre of the cross-shape she had made with the others. I beheld a river with a black band snaking along it midway. Several fishes gaped out of the water as though to gulp flies.

"The Black Current, what else? This crosses you, obstructs you. Or maybe . . . *you* will cross *it*." Abruptly the fortune-teller reached out and grasped my wrist. "What do you know of any of this?" she whispered fiercely. Her grip was tight. Outside, drums were beating, and I thought that they were beating in my heart.

"Nothing! Let go of me!" With my free hand I quickly forced her fingers open. After months of working boats this wasn't difficult. And this time I did flee, out through the flap of the tent.

"Hey!" cried Jambi, who was hovering impatiently. "You're missing the show! It's started. Come on."

Those drums beat louder now, unmuffled by the canvas; and pipes were skirling. Jambi had no time to ask me how I had got on in the tent; neither then—nor later.

If you want to commit a crime, the best place to do so is in public: in a place so public that dozens of other distractions are on hand.

How Marcialla actually got into the predicament she did get into, I never saw. Nor did Jambi. If anyone else noticed they must have taken it entirely for granted, as nothing unusual on festival day. When Jambi did spot what was going on, even she didn't at first register anything amiss. But she wasn't privy to the conversation I'd overheard in the Jingle-Jangle—nor had she heard Marcialla's veiled warning as we two chatted at the head of the gangplank.

It was a good three hours later. The main display was already over: the acrobatics, the climbing and abseiling, the rope-walking and trapezing by professional junglejacks male and female who had been practising for a week and more. That evening would see a fireworks display upon the great masts—the fireworks imported, naturally, from smelly Guineamoy. But the period from now until dusk provided full opportunity for those who weren't part of the official performance to show off their own antics. So when the last professional team had swung down sweating to the ground, a whistle blew. Teenagers, and men and women too, swarmed across the field to the tall masts and began to scramble aloft. Some went high up, some not so high.

"Accidents? Of course there are accidents," Jambi was saying to me as we watched these novices displaying their skill, or lack of it. "Lalo says that someone broke his neck a couple of years back. There are always sprains and fractures."

"It seems silly."

"Isn't it better if it happens here than out in the deep jungle?"

"I don't follow you."

She gestured. "There's a first aid tent. Bandages, bone-setters."

"Why should amateurs do it at all?"

"Oh, Yaleen! If somebody takes a tumble here, obviously they aren't ever going to make it as a real junglejack. The guild won't accept them."

"Oh, I *see*. *We* don't need competitions in mast-climbing, to become riverwomen. We just do it."

"The river's softer than the ground."

"Decks aren't. And don't forget the stingers!"

"Well, that's how they do things here. See: the jungle-guild marshals are watching what goes on, but they won't interfere."

"It seems a bit barbaric." Was it any more of a peculiar ordeal than having to drink a slug of the black current? A slug which might drive you mad? Less, perhaps. Less.

We were debating the pros and cons over cups of cool blue perry which we'd bought from a nearby stall, when Jambi broke off. She squinted and shaded her eyes.

"Isn't that Marcialla up the tree?"

I stared across the clearing. Marcialla, indeed. High high up, swinging freely to and fro on a trapeze. No safety nets of web-vine were hung beneath.

"Why does she want to show off? Surely she isn't thinking of quitting the water for the woods at her age?"

Marcialla's posture was . . . peculiar. The tiny distant figure sat immobile, with her fists clenched round the ropes. Her legs and her head weren't moving in proper time with the motion of the trapeze.

And when the trapeze finally swung to a standstill, Marcialla would be marooned high over a gulf of nothing.

At that moment I noticed three figures hastening through the crowd over to our left. They were heading away in the direction of the old town. One was blonde and big and very familiar. The other two were hooded. I couldn't distinguish their Port Barbra features, but something about the way one of them moved and clutched briefly at Credence to say something convinced me that she was the fortune-teller. For all I knew she might have been in the Jingle-Jangle too, a few nights earlier! Then the crowd hid the trio.

In a flash I knew exactly what was going on. (Yes indeed, the signal-mirror had just flashed an urgent message in my mind!)

"Jambi, don't ask questions—it's too urgent. You must do this for me: run back to the docks as fast as you can. Round up any crew you see—and secure Marcialla's cabin! Whatever you do, don't let Credence into it. Particularly if she has any strangers with her. Women in hoods."

"Eh? But I can't forbid—"

"Trust me. Do it!" And I set off at a sprint across the clearing.

I climbed that dead tree by rope ladder, as far as a notch where the main trunk forked. Here was the platform from which Marcialla must have been launched, but this was no use to me at all; Marcialla was way out of reach by now. The trapeze came less close to its starting point on each return swing. At least Marcialla hadn't fallen yet: she still sat propped on her seat like a life-sized doll.

A single knotted rope led higher up—thirty or forty spans higher—to where a lateral branch of considerable girth left the trunk. It was pointing in the right direction, but so many spans above. Craning my neck, I could see more rope lying on the branch, the coils bulging over like a nesting snake. One end appeared to be fastened by snap-link to a wood-piton driven deep into the trunk itself.

Quite how I managed the rest of the ascent I'll never know. It

80

wasn't like climbing up a mast at all. For me there has always been a certain feeling of elasticity about climbing a mast. Because a mast is rooted in a floating boat. There's a sense that your activities up a mast produce a certain slight reaction in the mast itself. No doubt this is perfectly illusory! Otherwise boats would tip over as soon as a few women swarmed into the rigging. But this tree felt like rock, rooted in rock.

At last I reached the branch which I was aiming for, and scrambled on to it, legs astride, beside the waiting rope. I was relieved to see other pitons set at intervals along the branch; otherwise I don't know how I could have tied the rope to it, given its girth. Unclipping the snap-link, I hoisted the coils over my head on to my shoulders. All coiled up, that rope was quite some weight.

Shuffling my thighs forward as fast as I dared, I soon arrived at a piton positioned above the mid-point of Marcialla's swing, and attached the snap-link again.

She was only swaying to and fro quite gently by now. The wooden bar of her seat was hardly a very substantial one; and I feared that she was in even more danger. While she had still been swinging fairly vigorously, sheer force of momentum may have adjusted her balance and even lessened her apparent weight. Soon there would only be gravity pulling at her. Pulling down.

Down. Much too far below the hard ground waited. . . .

How *did* one abseil down through mid-air? I'd watched enough junglejacks doing it that very afternoon! One of them had gripped the rope with his feet and had slid down while standing upright. Another had wound it around one thigh; and a third fellow around both thighs, with the free end tossed over his shoulder. Those two had descended as if they were sitting in a chair. The fastest junglejack of all, a woman, had simply slipped the rope through her crotch, under one buttock and up over her neck.

I settled on the double thigh rappel. It had looked reasonably safe, and within my ability. Laying the coil across the branch before me, I let out spare rope and looped this around my thighs and over my shoulder.

I realized that I couldn't just toss the rest of the coil overboard. I might knock Marcialla off her perch, and so undo everything. So I paid the rope down; and it was just as well that I did. By the time I had let it all down I knew that the weight of it, tumbling all at once, could easily have yanked me off my branch.

The end of the rope was fairly near the ground; though from as high up as this it was hard to gauge "fairly near". Ten spans short? Fifteen, even?

Then I went over the side.

Almost, I tipped backwards out of the rope; but I recovered myself. And now the rope squeezed me like a tourniquet. It gripped my breeches so tightly that far from tending to slide down like greased lightning, to my surprise I could hardly move at all. But then I recalled how the junglejack using this particular rappel had seemed to hump himself up "in the saddle" when letting out slack, so that he lowered himself jerk by jerk. I did so too. Down I went, bit by bit: dropping, jerked to a halt, dropping again.

It wasn't too far to the trapeze seat. I caught hold as gently as I could, steadied it, transferred my hold to Marcialla.

I was face to face with her, staring right into her eyes. She hardly blinked at all. Her pupils were dilated. Her lips moved slightly but she said no words—she only uttered a long moan. Perhaps this *was* a word, after all. But she was taking too much time over it.

I said slowly, "I'm taking you down. Let go of the ropes. *Let go.*"

For a while she seemed to be holding on as tightly as before.

"They gave you the fungus drug," I said. "The drug that stops time. I know they did. Let go. You'll be safe." No doubt this was a wildly optimistic promise. But there was no alternative.

Not at the time. It did occur to me later on that a better and less adventurous bet might have been to persuade some of the jungle-guild marshals that what was going on up the tree was far from ordinary; and so have them send experienced climbers aloft. But at the time I was remembering what Jambi had said about marshals not interfering. Besides, *I* knew what had been said in the Jingle-Jangle; they didn't. And then again, this seemed to me to be a riverguild matter.

Slowly Marcialla's grip did slacken. Maybe she had been sending signals to tell her fingers to unlock ever since I reached her. At last she came away—and thank the River that she wasn't any heavyweight! I hauled her awkwardly across my lap. The rope kept her pressed to my chest and tummy.

Now I had to heave our combined weight up while paying spare rope over my shoulder. When I slid, my right hand had to act as brake and anchor overhead.

It took a long time to descend. And it was a descent into worse and worse pain.

By the time we reached the bottom of the rope I could have screamed. My right arm was almost out of joint. My hand was rubbed raw and bloody; it hurt as if I'd held it in a fire. If Capsi had felt one half of this pain throughout his body . . . I put the thought away.

Even at the bottom of the rope I was still too high. Not too high to stop me from jumping and landing springily—if I'd been on my own. I wasn't. First I would have had to drop Marcialla like a sack of potatoes.

Luckily by now someone had realized that this wasn't just a spectacular display of amateur treetop-rescue. Marshals appeared beneath, stretching out a web-vine net.

"Let go of her! We'll catch!"

I did. And they did too; then they hurried the sagging net aside. I hung slumped in the rappel, letting my agonized right hand relax at last. Quickly they bundled Marcialla out of the net and stretched it again, for me.

"You, now! Drop!"

So I paid the last few spans over my shoulder, and fell. They caught me, lowered me quickly.

They had laid Marcialla on the ground. A marshal was kneeling by her, feeling her pulse. He looked puzzled that she was so obviously wide awake, but didn't move. A whole crowd had gathered round—foremost among whom I now spotted Lalo and Kish.

"Your friend over there," began one of the marshals, nodding in Lalo's direction, "she—"

Lalo ran forward.

"Thanks, Lalo!" I cried. I would have embraced her, except that my palm was running with blood.

"It's one way of making contact in a crowd, I'll say that! Your poor hand, Yaleen. What's it all about?"

"No time to tell! I must take Marcialla back to her boat, right now."

"It's the first aid tent for *you*," insisted the marshal.

"No!" Then I really looked at my hand. "Yes. I suppose so. Will you two come with me?" I asked Lalo. "Will you help me get her back to the riverfront?"

Naturally enough, there were questions from the officials. But I bluffed my way through these as best I could while they were busy cleaning and anointing and bandaging me. Someone mentioned drug trances, but I pointed out that Marcialla obviously wasn't from Port Barbra. She was given to crippling attacks of vertigo, I said—which explained nothing: neither how she could possibly be a riverwoman, nor how she had got up the tree in the first place. However, they let me get away with my blatant lies. I think they had plenty of other business to attend to.

Briefly Lalo, Kish and I debated the best way to shift Marcialla: borrow a stretcher, carry her between us, or what? I couldn't help much with my bandaged aching hand. Finally Kish hoisted Marcialla and slung her over his shoulder in a fireman's lift.

So, though not as swiftly as I would have liked, we returned to the old town. On the way there I swore Kish and Lalo to secrecy, and satisfied as much of their curiosity as I dared.

When we did at last get back to the *Spry Goose*, about an hour later, we found a strange situation indeed. Jambi had had the wit to pull up the gangplank—something which I hadn't thought of in the heat of the moment. She and two other crew members were guarding the gunwales with belaying pins clutched in their fists; though it did look as though their confidence was waning rapidly, as the prospect loomed of an ignominious beaching for life. For boatswain Credence was berating them from the dockside, as were three other crew-women who had turned up in

84

the meantime. These were innocent of what was really going on; to them it looked like a mutiny. And meanwhile the two Port Barbra women slunk in the background shadows, scarved and hooded. It was growing dark rapidly. Lamps had already been lit along the waterfront.

The situation clarified itself almost as soon as we hove in sight. Kish set Marcialla down, though he still had to balance her. The Port Barbrans whispered to one another, then took to their heels. After some hesitation—teetering between the chance of brazening it out further, and the prospect of what would realistically happen once Marcialla had regained her faculties—Credence shrugged and strode away; though with a show of dignity, I'll give her that.

The gangplank rattled down again on to the stone quay. Jambi and her two stalwarts looked mightily relieved.

We helped Marcialla slowly back on board her command. Shortly after that, the first rocket exploded high above the jungle, showering red and silver stars.

By midnight the distant pyrotechnics were all over, but ours were just commencing. Marcialla had speeded up. She rushed around her cabin, chattering, peering out of the porthole, pulling things out of drawers and stuffing them back in again, unlocking and relocking cupboards, scribbling illegibly on sheet after sheet of paper. We had to take the log-book off her to stop her from defacing it.

She sat down, she leapt up. She demanded hot snacks and more hot snacks, which a groaning cook provided, bleary-eyed, and which Marcialla wolfed down.

At one moment she wanted to run ashore to wake the quaymistress. At another she insisted on setting sail for Port Barbra at once even though it was pitch dark.

We used our initiative. Despite all her strident threats, appeals and protests we kept her confined to her cabin. Finally, around dawn, she flaked out at last. And Jambi and I could at last crawl to our own bunks.

When I woke up hours later I could feel that the *Spry Goose* was out on the river. The light was dying fast, so I must have slept throughout the day. Jambi still lay stretched out, snoring. She only groaned when I shook her. My arms and shoulders ached like hell, and my right hand felt as if it was bandaged in concrete, not linen. I climbed back into the sheets again, and didn't wake until the following dawn. Since the *Spry Goose* had already been under way by evening, Marcialla was evidently made of sterner stuff than me—unless the aftermath of the drug delirium was kinder to the flesh than the after-effect of abseiling from the heights.

It's only in stories that a snip of a deckhand suddenly gets promoted to boatswain; and Marcialla wasn't as foolishly grateful as that, merely because I had saved her life (perhaps), and because Credence had deserted.

By the time I came on deck again, Marcialla had already promoted Sula, from Gate of the South, to the post of boatswain. I couldn't help musing that slim, short Sula wasn't at all the sort of woman who could hoist a paralysed boatmistress all the way up a tree and sit her on a trapeze! ("Let me have those about me that are slight", to parody the ancient fragment *Julius Czar*.)

Of course Marcialla did thank me, and granted me sick leave till my hand healed. No more painting or hauling on ropes for a while for Yaleen! Actually this was a mixed blessing, since it meant that I had nothing to do but bum about the boat like a passenger, and watch the jungle pass by, and get in the hair of the cook by offering to help her one-handed. And all the while bottle up what had happened, like a dose of the black current.

I also had time to think about my fortune, as told by the Port Barbra woman. I had asked a few of the other women what they thought about cartomancy. (I hadn't asked Jambi, perhaps because I didn't want her to ask me in return what the cards had showed.) Only one woman thought anything at all about the matter, and what she thought was rather contradictory. On the one hand, the cards would always tell a story that seemed plausible to the person concerned. But on the other hand this story would be set out quite at random.

I puzzled about this and decided that the pictures on the cards were really so general that somebody other than me could have

86

extracted an entirely different personal saga from the sequence of spyglass, bonfire and such. And I myself could very likely have picked nine other cards, and seen the very same story mirrored in them too.

And yet. . . .

Even in their thumb-marked, washed-out dowdiness there had seemed to be something powerful about the cards, as though they and all their predecessors had been handled for so many centuries that, if there had been no truth in them to begin with, nevertheless by now the images they contained were fraught with generations of uneasy emotion. With each use—here and there, now and then—people put a tiny portion of their own lives and will power into the images on the cards; and this mounted up eventually, so that the cards became, well, genuine.

We weren't sailing under very much canvas, as though now that we had left Jangali safely behind, Marcialla wished to prolong the time till we next made port. Realistically, of course, this allowed Marcialla to keep a leisurely eye on how well Sula was coping with the sudden change in her duties.

Just a couple of hours before we were due to reach Port Barbra, Marcialla called me to her cabin.

She poured us both a small glass of junglejack from an almost empty bottle.

"Oh dear," I said, regarding it.

"It'll only go off. It doesn't travel." Marcialla smiled. "But you do, Yaleen. You get around. First of all you were in the Jingle-Jangle that night—"

Hastily I raised my glass and gulped half of the stinging spirit down to prompt my cheeks to flush of their own accord.

"—then up you popped at the top of that wretched tree, knowing just what was wrong with me."

"Well you see, Lalo had mentioned the fungus drug, saying how it made time stand still—you remember Lalo and Kish? They were—"

"I remember. They *did* help me back to the boat."

"So when I saw you sitting as still as that in such a dangerous spot—"

"You put ten and ten together and made a hundred. And a hundred was the right answer. I've already thanked you for your prompt and loyal act of bravery, Yaleen. At the time it would have been ungracious to ask you . . . why you eavesdropped on Credence and me." She waved a dismissive hand. "Oh, don't worry about that. I'm not offended. What I'm really interested in, being a guildmistress. . . ." And again she paused but I only stared at her, waiting it out, till she chuckled. "I think you ought to have expressed a degree of surprise there. You should have exclaimed, all wide-eyed innocence, 'Oh, are you?'"

"Word gets round," I mumbled; and I swallowed half of the remaining junglejack.

"As a guildmistress I have a duty to see that, how shall we put it . . . ?"

"The applecart isn't upset?" I oughtn't to have said this. Marcialla had practically forced me to complete her sentence for her, so long did she put off doing so herself.

"I was going to say: the order of things. Maybe you've heard people talking about the balance of our little applecart before. . . ."

This time I certainly did keep my lip buttoned.

"Well, whatever. I won't press you, since I'm grateful. Now I want you to swear that you'll say nothing at all about this particular insanity—this mad idea of doping the current—which is only really just a gleam in someone's eye, as yet." She reached for *The Book of the River* and the guild chapbook, both. "Otherwise people begin to gossip. Other people overhear. Sooner or later some man starts to wonder, '*Shall* we try it?' Before we know where we are, we're deep in the manure."

"I already said something—to Jambi. And Lalo, too."

"Oh, I don't suppose you told *everything*, did you?"

I swallowed. Not junglejack this time. I swallowed saliva—and my heart.

What was "everything"? The drug? The Observers at Verrino? The fact that Capsi had crossed the river without benefit of any crazy fungus drug, but by using a diving suit? The fact that over on the other side they burned women who loved the river, alive?

All these things together made up "everything". Surely even Guildmistress Marcialla had no way of knowing everything!

She peered at me quizzically. "You don't seem like a person who tells . . . all they know."

I took the two books and laid my bandaged palm upon them, wondering vaguely whether this meant there was a cushion between me and my oath. "I swear I won't say anything about what Credence was up to. What she had in mind. May I spew if I do."

"As you have spewed before, I suppose . . . Of course we must remember charitably that Credence was simply acting out of, shall we say, *devotion*: devotion to this river of women, and to the current which is its nervous system. Other people—men in particular—mightn't feel quite so devoted." Apparently satisfied, she took the books back and placed them on a shelf. "You've done well, Yaleen."

"Um, how did it feel when time stopped?" I asked.

Marcialla burst out laughing. "You're *impossible*, dear girl! But since you ask, it was . . . interesting. Though not all *that* interesting, in the circumstances. Imagine wading through molasses for ten days . . . No, I can't really describe it. I suppose you're fascinated by the current too? Yes, I see you are. Most people take it for granted. You can never ignore it, if you're going to be a guildmistress." Her eyes twinkled. "That, incidentally, is *not* a promise."

And she went on to enquire in kindly tones about my hand.

And so to Port Barbra. After all the excitement and the omens in Jangali I approached this town with some misgivings, as if I might at any moment be kidnapped by hooded women, and smuggled off into the depths of the jungle dazed by drugs.

Not so, however. Neither on this first visit, nor on the several return visits which the *Spry Goose* was to pay to Port Barbra during the next ten to twelve weeks. (For we started in on a local run: Jangali to Port Barbra to Ajelobo, and back again.)

Compared with massively stone-hewn and timber-soaring Jangali, Port Barbra seemed something of a foetid shanty town. The main streets were as muddy as the side lanes, though at least the major thoroughfares had wooden walkways along both sides, supported on stilts. Insects were a nuisance, not so much because they bit you, as that every now and then they liked to fly into your nostrils, making you snort like a sick pig on a foggy morning. I took to wearing a scarf, too, when I was in port; and a head scarf as well to keep them out of my hair.

Port Barbra exported precious timbers: the gildenwood, ruby-vein, and ivorybone—all of which trees were small and required no heroic junglejack antics. However, the inhabitants only used cheap woods for their own buildings and furnishings. They built as though they intended to abandon the town as soon as they had all made their fortunes. Except that there were no fortunes in evidence. Frankly I wasn't surprised if in such a place a few people took drugs. And perhaps a town which is one large slum either gives up trying—or else it cultivates a certain mysticism and inwardness. Certainly, in their quiet murmurings and hoodedness, and in their apparent contempt for comfort or luxury, the Port Barbrans appeared to have adopted the latter course. Though of mystical extremes I saw nothing. Nor on any visit did I run into that fortune teller—should I have recognized her, if I had!—nor Credence, either, supposing that she had made her way to Port Barbra with the help of her allies.

Naturally, I wondered what *had* happened to Credence. On our first visit to Port Barbra Marcialla spent a long while ashore closeted with the quaymistress. Subsequently I noticed many heliograph signals being flashed up and down stream: signals which I couldn't work out at all. Days later, when we were on the river again, more coded signals reached us, passed on by the boat behind. Later on, I noticed Marcialla observing me with pursed lips when she thought I wasn't looking.

And so to steamy, bloom-bright, aromatic Ajelobo, a paradise compared with Port Barbra.

I could have settled happily in Ajelobo. Jumped boat, like Credence. Signed off. Ajelobo was so neat and . . . yes, so innocent, at least on the surface.

The houses were all of light wood and waxed paper. There were hot springs just outside the town, where the population seemed to migrate *en masse* every weekend. Children, who were all dressed like flowers, flew kites and fought harmless little battles with them in the sky. Old men with little white beards played complicated board games employing hundreds of polished pebbles. There was a puppet theatre, a wrestling stadium—for wrestling was a local passion—and dozens of little cafés where people talked for hours on end over tiny cups of sweet black coffee, one of Ajelobo's prime exports. There were even three daily newspapers turned out on hand presses, filled with fantastic anecdotes, puzzles, serial stories, poetry, recipes and elegant long-standing arguments by letter (about costume, manners, turns of phrase, antiquarian fragments) which no one plunging into midway could hope to follow, but which regular readers savoured with all the avidity of someone reading an adventure story. Of which, in fact, many of the most exotic were written and published in Ajelobo, and exported.

And maybe Ajelobo was all surface, and no depths.

But equally, who needed to settle anywhere—when every town along the river was their home, if they wished it to be?

It was during our fourth call at Ajelobo, as the year was drawing to a close, that Marcialla made her announcement to the boat's company. The *Spry Goose* was going to sail all the way to the source of the river, to the end of the world under the Far Precipices: to Tambimatu, in good time for New Year's Eve. And one of our own boat's company was to be honoured—for good boatwomanship, and for initiative beyond the call of duty. She would be invited to volunteer to sail out to the black current at midnight, between the old year and the new.

Myself. I could have shrunk into my socks.

Not out of modesty, exactly. Let me be clear about that. Everyone loves an honour.

But because of the way it was phrased: "invited to volunteer". Could it be that the best way of keeping the applecart trim, when someone young and irresponsible knew something that they shouldn't know, was to . . . ?

No, it couldn't be that. More likely it was a neat way of making me feel extremely loyal—by putting me through an initiation ceremony, of the second degree.

Everybody on deck was staring at me.

I'd wondered before what a voice sounds like when it's quavering. If I was quavering when I replied, though, I wouldn't have known since I couldn't hear myself. "I volunteer," I said.

Hands slapped me on the back. Jambi kissed me on both cheeks. Sula pumped my hand; while Marcialla looked genuinely delighted and proud.

I still couldn't forget all those coded signals and wondered whether any searching enquiries had been conducted not only about Credence and her affiliations but also about myself, for instance in Verrino . . . turning up, perhaps, the fact that my brother appeared to have gone missing earlier in the year.

At this point I realized to my amazement that I had been chastely celibate for quite a long while. Whether this was somehow out of respect for my dead brother, or due to horror at the male fraternity across the water, or even from some perverse annoyance at my parents for breeding a new offspring, I had no idea. Maybe I had even been punishing myself by self-denial; and having effectively tortured my right hand on the abseiling rope at Jangali I had had enough of it.

I determined to repair this omission before we set sail again. I must confess, too, that in one little part of me I was wondering whether I really would see the next year in at all. Just in case not, I ought to enjoy some pleasures of the flesh.

So I drank Safe—not with Jambi, who ought to hunt down a languishing shore-husband, a married man, if she felt this way inclined—but with Klare, a jolly brunette from Guineamoy. It was she whom I had asked about the cards; and we went ashore together that night, the last night. As she put it, to celebrate.

I think I can say that we managed very well indeed. But one doesn't wish to boast of one's conquests. One shouldn't degrade men in their absence merely because we have liberty to roam, and they don't. So, like a proper lady of Port Barbra, I shall draw a discreet scarf and hood over a few very pleasant hours.

I was quite unprepared for my first sight of the Far Precipices. Fluffy white clouds with grey sodden hulls had been sailing along

all day, occasionally emptying their bilges on us. For hours I'd
been scanning the river and jungle horizon ahead for what I
presumed would look like an enormous wall. It was sticky and
far too hot, even on the river; the heat was soaking wet, unlike
the dry heat of my native Pecawar.

Klare happened by, on some errand.

"Where, where, where?" I complained petulantly.

"Lost something, Yaleen?"

"Just the Precipices. Surely we ought to be able to see them by
now!"

And she looked up into the sky—almost directly at the zenith,
it seemed. The clouds had parted there; into that high rift she
pointed.

"How about there?"

"Oh . . . goodness me." For that's where the bare peaks of the
Precipices were, all right. Up, up, and up above me, scraping
against space. I got such a shock. I simply hadn't realized. Of
course if it hadn't been cloudy I should have known sooner. As it
was, a god suddenly peered down at me from overhead. The tops
of the Precipices seemed to be floating free with no possible
connexion to the ground.

Though these connexions became evident enough by the time
we reached Tambimatu . . .

Not so much a wall across the world—as the end of the world,
period! A stone curtain, drawn across the rest of creation: one
which hung from the stars themselves at night!

It seemed to be toppling forever upon Tambimatu as though
about to squash the town flat. Yet the locals didn't see things
quite that way. On the contrary, they hardly seemed to perceive
the Precipices at all; any more than I had, when I looked for
them in the wrong place. The town of Tambimatu was a tight
maze of lanes and yellow brick houses leaning in towards each
other with overhanging upper storeys and machiolated attics.
The idea seemed to be nudge together and make tunnels of all
the routes. It was hardly possible to see those looming Precipices
from anywhere in the town itself. Domestically this interruption
in the smooth flow of the world did not exist.

By this style of architecture the Tambimatans also excluded the reeking jungle which clung around their town. The dank, festering mass of vegetation was quite unlike the bloom-bright tangles I'd seen elsewhere, quite unlike the noble halls of jungle giants. Spinach purée: that was how I thought of it. A tide of green pulp a hundred spans high.

Naturally, for those who knew, there were ways through it. And there was wealth to find—or there wouldn't have been a town. The wealth consisted of powder-gold and gems and other exotic minerals which turned up in the slime-ponds and mud-pools; as if, every now and then, the Precipices nodded and a scurf of riches fell into the purée. Actually this wealth was thought to leach and cascade down through the innards of the Precipices, into the water table, whence it oozed up into the jungle. Bright jewels for mythical magpies—to make them build their nests here! In Tambimatu town were gemsmiths and goldsmiths, cutters and polishers, artificers of sparkling ornaments. Unlike the dowdy shrouded denizens of Port Barbra these locals wore ear-rings and bangles and bijoux to match.

Slime and sharp facets; sparklers and gloomy mud!

Only from the quayside could the diligent eye follow the sweeping planes of stone upwards into the clouds which so often clung to them—picking out precarious trees, at first like green chaff, then like threads. Then dust, then nothing.

Two leagues south of the town, the river emerged. . . .

As a volunteer for the New Year's Eve voyage, first there was an obligatory call to pay on the quaymistress in company with my sponsor, Marcialla. This was soon over. More a matter of checking in, really.

Next there was a civic banquet in honour of all the volunteers.

Besides myself, there were six others. The boat which we would sail to the black current was only, in truth, a little ketch. Perhaps this was to present a smaller profile. The ketch was rigged with a lot of little sails, the better to manoeuvre it when we got in close, and keep us from fouling it in the current. At present it rode at anchor a little way out, conveniently separating it from any male influence along the waterfront. The hull of the ketch was painted black. Its sails also were black. It looked like a fabled boat of death, for freighting corpses, perhaps to be set on fire and scuttled. An extensible boom jutted from one side, to carry the collection bucket.

But I'm digressing from the banquet.

It was there that I met my six new boatsisters for the first time—and took an instant dislike to three of them; which is a very high antipathy score for new acquaintances in my experience! Maybe these particular women were over-proud, or pious, or otherwise screwed up by the honour bestowed on them. Maybe I was too. Screwed up, that is. In any case I was younger than all the others; and thus may have seemed presumptious. Bumptious, even. Consequently I put them on edge, just as they discomfited me.

Two of the others were all right, I suppose, and fairly relaxed. And the last one, I actually liked—and felt an instant sense of rapport with. She was called Peli, and hailed from Aladalia, which brought back happy memories. Peli was a burly woman in her thirties with a mop of straw hair and a red weatherbeaten face; or perhaps her blood pressure was unusually high. She was urgent, eager, informative, and talked very fast. However, she hastened to add, she was *not* artistic. Even so, she was the only one of us volunteers who had gone shopping in Tambimatu. Now she wore a coiled bangle which had cost her all of ten fish fifty (after bargaining). It must have been the only genuinely hideous gewgaw available in town. I loved her for it.

The banquet was held in the jewellers' guild hall, which doubled as a gem market at other times; however on this occasion there were no men in sight, since this was woman's business.

We mumbled words of introduction to one another; we drank each other's health; we ate grilled fish. Then the quaymistress rose and read out all our citations to the assembled throng. Mine sounded distinctly icky, as though I had won my place simply by swarming around masts like a jackanapes. (No mention, of course, being made of *all* the circumstances.) And won it too for being a dab hand with the paint brush. Since my hand was still visibly scarred, that seemed unlikely. "Someone's little favourite," I heard a voice mutter.

Afterwards we drank more toasts, and generally failed to get to know each other (Peli excepted); or at least that was my impression.

No matter! The quaymistress of Tambimatu, organizer of the New Year's Eve events, announced a leisurely trip to the source of the river the next day so that we could frame up into a working team.

Leisurely, did I say? Well, yes, that's true. It was leisurely. The Quaymistress accompanied us aboard the black ketch—which uniquely had no name whatever painted on side or stern, as though whatever was nameless could not be summoned, and compelled to come—and I have rarely sailed more gently before, except perhaps when we were idling away from Jangali after the fateful festival.

But otherwise! Maybe the quaymistress, as a local, could afford to be blasé about our journey. For me it was awesome, almost an ordeal of courage; though fascinating too in a nightmare way. Closer and closer we sailed to that seemingly infinite barrier, to the point where the river which otherwise flowed through our lives unceasingly, was suddenly no more. Where the river ended, vanished. Or rather, where it all *began*—but began as if created out of nothing.

The waters slid forth like tongues out of a thick-lipped mouth. Stanchions of rocky support, like teeth, stood hundreds of spans apart. Surely the action of the water would wear these supports away eventually—and then the whole Precipice would fall on top of us! Perhaps today.

Away to the west the black current emerged through a narrower supporting arch. Yet terms such as arches or stanchions convey the wrong impression. This suggests that the river was flowing from under a kind of bridge. In fact the cliffs extended right down to the surface of the water, and a little below, blocking any possible access or insight into what lay within this long hole in the Precipices. The supports were only visible because of bulges and ripples and what we could see through the dull glass of the water itself. So the river appeared to be oozing out of something solid—like the trail of slime behind a snail (only in reverse). Enormous snail, mighty trail!

I was glad that Peli was on board with me: so bluffly assertive—like the elder sister that I had never had. I was even more glad when we tacked about, almost within touching distance of the Precipice, to drift back towards the town.

The next day a kind of sacred conclave of the river guild was held on board the schooner *Santamaria*, which was also riding at anchor. We lucky seven were invited.

Several guildmistresses were present, besides the quaymistress and Marcialla. (She and I rowed over together from the *Spry Goose*, with myself at the oars.) There followed solemn readings from the private chapbook of the guild; then practical tips, and cautions. I left feeling more chastened than when I had arrived, at the prospect of our holy and dangerous duty. I can't say that I also felt inspired, exactly.

The day after that was New Year's Eve.

So the seven of us set sail in that nameless boat an hour before midnight. It was a clear night. Stars stood gem-bright in one half of the sky. In the other half, nothing: nothing but a wall of darkness. It seemed to me as I hoisted a sail that the black wall was an image of the coming year, containing only the darkness of death. No phosphorescent little beasties silvered the water here. Half-starlight was our only guide; though we did have lanterns, if we chose to light them. We chose not to.

As we sailed out ever so slowly, I brooded much upon the current. Too much, perhaps. The others likewise. Our little ketch was eerily silent, as though we were all holding our breath. Silent, that is, until Peli called out, "How about a song?"

"Be quiet!" hissed someone.

"The current doesn't have ears, dear!" And Peli began to warble one of our river songs out over the lonely deaf waters:

"The river
Is the giver

Of life,
Water-wife—!"

No, Peli definitely was *not* artistic. Tone-deaf, in fact. Though doubtless the tune she was singing sounded fine in her own head.

"Silence!" called the thin woman from Spanglestream who was nominally in command. "The current senses vibrations."

Does it? Did it? I brooded some more.

We finally hove-to within fifty spans of that deeper darkness which clove the dark waters. We dropped a drift-anchor. A lookout watched anxiously lest we glide closer, trailing drogue or not.

"Yaleen," came the thin woman's order, "extend the boom as far as it'll go. Peli, on the winch. Andra, prepare to receive the first bucketful. Salandra. . . ." Something else.

So I guided the first bucket, with its self-sealing lid, out above the edge of the current on the long boom, and waited for the word to dunk the pail in and haul out a portion of the black substance.

"All ready?"

"Aye." "Aye." "Aye."

"Lower away."

And the bucket smacked into the current. . . .

Madness seized me then.

Insanity rushed over me like flames. I still knew what I was doing. But why I was doing it, I had no idea. Nor had I any choice in the matter. It was as though that pack of fortune cards had sucked me into them, and imprisoned me in a picture! I still remember perfectly well how I scrambled up on the gunwale where the base of the boom was secured. I even heard Peli cry out to me, though I couldn't heed her. I even felt the brush of her fingertips as she tried to snatch me back to safety. I even heard the thin woman shout, "No! If it wants one of us, let it!" It made no difference.

Heedless I ran along that slim boom outstretched across the water—like an acrobat. But no acrobat was I. No way could I pause in my rush. No way could I pivot and return, had I wished to. As it was, I had no wishes of my own. Only my mad forward momentum kept me from toppling into the river before I even reached the current. But keep me it did; and I raced all the way to the end of the boom—and beyond. For a moment it even seemed that I was running onward through mid-air. But I fell, of course. And was engulfed.

Questing shapes swam around me, flashes of light dazzled me, soft tentacles slid up my nostrils, down my throat, and elsewhere too—they entered every opening in me. But I did not feel that I was suffocating; or drowning.

Yet my life flashed by me willy-nilly. Scenes of girlhood in dusty Pecawar. My initiation when I drank of the black current. My deflowering by Hasso in his attic bower. Verrino and its Observers. Bonfires on the further bank . . . All my secrets, all.

It was as if I fell asleep. And dreams had come to me. Yet not for my entertainment. They came to examine me, to walk around inside my skull and see what was there.

"*Yaleen*," sang the dreams. "*Ya-leeeen!*" they wailed.

I was aware of something immense and old and . . . I could not say whether it was wise as well.

It had been watching us, though not with eyes. Rather, with little cells of itself which migrated through us, flavouring us and savouring us before returning whence they came.

It had been feeling us, though not with fingers. Yes, with *vibrations*. But I didn't understand what kind of vibrations these were.

Or was this simply what I had already been told about the current? What I had mused about it? And now it was reading my musings back to me?

How could I separate myself from this strange state I was in— so as to know which was *me*, and which was *it*? I focused, like a dreamer trying to waken in a dream and be aware: not of the ordinary waking world outside, but of the world of the dream itself. I thought fiercely:

What are you?

And stars burned bright, and a world turned round underneath me, seen from so high in the sky that the world was only a ball, a plaything, a toy; and the sky was not blue but black.

What are you? I thought again, twice as fiercely—having no way to cry aloud.

And far away I heard a slurred voice:

"*The Worm of the World I am. There is no worm greater. The worm moves not; it flows within itself. On the day when it shall move, the whole world will turn upon its hinges . . .*

"*Till then, the worm shall watch . . . the flow of things.*

"*Of Woman and Man. . . .*"

Silence.

But why? How? Who—?

Something hidden reared and coiled around me. And within me too it coiled: it coiled around my mind. Crushing, suffocating, erasing. As I sank into oblivion I thought that I felt some other different creature, huge, slippery and scaly, rise beneath me.

To my surprise I woke to light and life.

I was soaking wet. Lying on a shelf of mud.

Raising my head, I saw spinach purée all before me, tangled up with tropic trees. One of my cheeks blazed as if I had been punched. The back of my right hand pulsed from the red weal of a stinger. But that was all there was, in the way of pain.

Pushing my palms into the mud, I doubled up, knelt—and looked behind me. The river flowed, almost lapping the toecaps of my boots.

I rose, to stare out over the waters. Far away—so far that they just had to be beyond the black current—I made out the sails and masts of a boat. A boat which could only be on the eastern side of the waterway.

And shivering in spite of the sticky heat, I knew: I was on the western bank. The sun was halfway up the sky. It was New Year's Day, and I was still alive. And I was all alone.

The black current had taken me and squeezed me through its substance—and its substance likewise through me—and then discarded me. I had been washed up on the far shore. Borne here by some giant fish of the depths, perhaps; a fish commissioned to carry me. . . .

*   *   *

My first irrational thought was to try to swim back to the eastern bank. Ignoring all stingers, since there didn't seem to be many hereabouts. Ignoring the black current. Crashing through it regardless. I would wave and shout, and be picked up by some passing vessel. Alternatively I would swim all the way.

I even went so far as to wade into the water, up to my ankles.

This frantic nonsense soon gave way to reality. I contented myself with quickly washing my hands clean of mud, retreated, and thought about my predicament.

Eventually, I decided that my only hope was to walk to the area opposite Verrino, where Capsi had first signalled to the watchers up the Spire.

I could search for his diving suit and anti-stinger mask. He must have cached them thereabouts. Maybe I could use them. Maybe the suit and mask were still where he had hidden them. No westerners ever willingly strayed near the water. Except for the river-witches.

And maybe the Sons of Adam had tortured the whereabouts out of him, and burned his equipment too. . . .

If I signalled with a mirror or a piece of broken glass, surely the Observers would see me from Verrino Spire! Only they, along the whole length of the river, would be looking for a signal from this side. Or if not actually expecting one, patient enough and obsessive enough to look out in any case.

Verrino! My only hope lay there: the only hope that I could tease out of this horror.

And here was I, opposite Tambimatu in the spinach jungle. Verrino was four hundred and forty leagues away—a distance rather more than half the length of the river.

Nevertheless, I set out.

Part Three

A WALK TO MANHOME,
AND AWAY

I had no idea how far I'd travelled. Or how many days it had taken. Seventy? A hundred? I'd lost count. There was no way to measure the leagues. On this sort of a hell-walk a league seemed an impossibly ambitious unit of measurement. I might have accounted for thirty, or five score. I was hungry, filthy, and fairly crazy.

Inventory for a hell-walk: stout river boots (good for a long journey), a pair of breeches, and a blouse, now tattered. Plus pocket knife and comb and a piece of string. Plus, of course, my wits.

I didn't eat well but at least I did consume enough to fuel me to tramp and thrash my way onward. I ate land-crabs and snakes and grubs, all raw. I ate tubers and fungi and fruit. I suffered stomach aches, and spent one whole day curled up in misery. However, I did remember Lalo's lore of the jungle. This jungle wasn't the same as the Jangali type, at least not at first. Even so, I managed to avoid fatal poisoning. I reminded myself that other creatures happily thrive on a diet of grubs and beetles and live frogs—down on gut level I was an animal too.

The first haul through the spinach purée was the worst; but I still had reserves of fat on me then.

I mentioned my wits as an asset.

In one respect my wits were quite disordered. For wit means knowledge, but what did I know? I knew the east bank from Tambimatu to Umdala. Of the west bank I knew nothing.

Yet the word "nothing" hardly sums up the quality of my ignorance. I hadn't exactly known Jangali or Port Barbra, before I sailed to them. Yet I knew where they were! I knew what *The Book of the River* said about them.

Here on the west bank *The Book of the River* meant nothing at all. It was as if the world had changed into another one entirely. And my map of it was blank.

This sheer blankness was the first shock I had to cope with.

For the first time in all my life no reference points existed. My only signpost was the river itself; when I could see it, which wasn't all that often. Once or twice when I was able to "camp" near the water at dusk, I spotted a tiny masthead lantern far away: that was all I ever spied by way of distant nightlights. My only real clue to my whereabouts came from the changing nature of the jungle itself: the decline of purée, the rise of occasional rubyvein and gildenwood, then at last halls of jacktrees and hogannies.

Yet the jungle seemed endless and chaotic. When I thought I had passed beyond one type of vegetation, it would reappear. I would be forced to seek the river to reassure myself that I wasn't simply stumbling back the way I had already come.

While in another respect: I had no *human* reference points. I was utterly alone with myself: more so than any prisoner shut up in a room with no windows, because that at least would imply the existence of people outside. I, on the other hand, could go anywhere I wished; and it seemed there would still be no one to speak to or to hear my voice, ever again.

When you're shoving your way through jungle all day long you don't spend a whole lot of time meditating or soul-searching in any very lucid or logical way. Yet your brain does churn over obsessively for hours on end. And what I was thinking to myself (if you can thus dignify the process whereby the milk of thought gets churned into stiff sticky butter which clogs your head up!), was that in all the time since I'd joined the *Spry Goose* in Pecawar I hadn't really been communicating with people.

Oh, I'd been talking: to Jambi, Klare, Lalo, you name it. I hadn't related, though. I'd been detached. I'd been viewing myself as a character in a tableau.

Here's Yaleen at Spanglestream, admiring the phosphorescent water! Here she is at Croakers' Bayou: behold the swamps and stilt-trees! And here she is shinning up a tree in Jangali. . . .

Even when I rescued Marcialla from that trapeze, I'd been a sort of actor or emblem of a person, like someone pictured on a fortune card.

So it seemed to my churning brain.

I tried to count the number of conversations I could remember

106

in any detail from the previous few months, compared with gabbier days of yore. This might be a more rewarding pursuit than trying to reckon leagues.

It wasn't. There weren't all that many.

If I can put it this way, borrowing from those critics writing in the Ajelobo newspapers, what I'd been living all that time had been narrative rather than dialogue. I'd made myself into something of a third person, so that what happened to *her* didn't fully affect *me*. I hadn't realized this, any more than I'd noticed until Ajelobo that I'd been doing without sex for months.

People! How I yearned for them, now that there were none!

"Oh Hasso, where are you? You who were gentle and witty!" I cried out, silencing the idiot jungle noise; then I stifled my cries in panic lest some savage Son of Adam heard me.

Many were the times I raved and rambled on to myself, and started imaginary dialogues—abortive ones which rarely got far beyond the opening gambits; whilst I ploughed through the purée, and subsequent jungle. Surviving. Surviving!

I guess in such a situation you either go mad, or else you grow up. You become yourself at last, your true self. Because there's no one else available—and "yourself" had better be big enough to bail you out of this scrape!

I grew up—I thought. At other times I wasn't so sure; and regarding this whole period I can't really guarantee the validity of my feelings or supposed discoveries about myself.

Sometimes when I stopped to camp—in the crook of a tree or under a bush—and when I'd been lucky enough to grab a bellyful of crab, worm meat and tubers, I loosened my breeches belt. I masturbated. And I thought hectically: not of insouciant Hasso or of my happy dalliance with sweet Tam in Aladalia in the days of what seemed my youth. But of the wearing of black robes. Of the private lives of humiliated women. Of a great grim Son of Adam who owned me, and was noble, but a brute. Black hateful fantasies, these!

Was this adult behaviour? Perhaps in a perverse way it strengthened my spirit. With my playful, clever fingers I embraced a hateful future. Coming to terms: you could call it that. I think I was sick with loneliness, and this was the only way I could discharge the accumulating poison. I think that to survive such an ordeal—one which just goes on and on remorselessly—you need something to hone you, to enflame you, to make you into a weapon, a mad thing. I could hardly revenge myself on the trees. I could hardly promise myself vengeance against any known individual. So instead I imagined humiliators and enslavers; and thus I advanced to meet them, day by day. I embraced what I most feared, to screw up the courage to continue.

By now I had somewhat discarded the bright idea that I was going to stand opposite Verrino Spire waving my torn blouse till some miraculous rescue party wafted across to me. . . .

My first menstruation of the journey I coped with, using wads of moss. My second flow was thinner; hunger and exhaustion were drying me up.

An heroic slog through wild jungles for weeks on end . . . Do you expect battles against giant reptiles with crystalline eyes (me armed with my pocket knife)—instead of a tale of what I did in my pants?

Well, there *were* incidents. Not many, but some.

There was the day when I stepped on what seemed to be a bed of moss. It was thick green scum, instead. I plunged through into a shaft of water. My flailing left arm was seized by teeth like needles. I never saw what was trying to eat me. Terrified, choking on the scummy water, I battered my free fist against the source of pain. Which let go. I wallowed and thrashed my way back on to dry land.

Blood welled from inflamed stab marks. But I spotted one of those dripping moss-mats which Lalo had assured me would staunch and disinfect. Leaping, I tore handfuls loose, to bind round the wound with my piece of string.

The remedy must have worked. My arm ached, but it didn't swell up or turn purple or throb with pus and poison.

Then there was the day I met a monster. It must have been the great-grandma of all croakers. It squatted in my path like a huge leathery boulder, high as my chest. Its eyes bulged at me unblinkingly. Its throat membrane pulsed.

"*Arrk! Arrk!*" I heard from directly behind. Naturally I turned

108

to look. At the last moment I recalled the ventriloquist trickery of croakers and hastily converted my turn into a leap aside, and a roll and scramble through undergrowth.

Crash! Where I'd been a few seconds earlier, now the great-grandma croaker sat slumped, a-quiver. Its eyes rotated. It shuffled about.

"*Urrk! Urrk!*"—again from behind. Scrambling up, I fled.

Nor must I forget the day of the piranha-mice.

A sudden hush came over the jungle, stilling the usual modest anarchic racket. In place of this, a moment later, I heard a rustling as of wind-blown autumn leaves down north in Aladalia or Firelight. A surging.

Ahead, undergrowth rippled. A grey living mass was advancing at speed, replacing the green. A million tiny creatures were gobbling everything in their path. Leaping, scuttling, climbing, dropping back—and chewing, always chewing. Leaves, flowers and moss became raggy in a trice, and vanished. Some thrashings and brief squeals marked where more mobile items of dinner took exception to being eaten. Something the size of a cat scrabbled for a tree. I couldn't identify it—it wore a second coat of squirming grey. The unlucky victim clawed bark, then fell back into the mass beneath. It seemed to deflate in an instant as if it had only been filled with air.

This happened very rapidly. In another few seconds I would have become hapless prey myself. The wavefront of hunger was nearly at my feet. I too scrambled up a tree, with a few grey scouts already hanging on to my boots. I crushed the ravenous little bodies against the trunk. I clawed and climbed higher. Obviously the things would eat anything. Even in my half-starved state I was a great prize of meat and guts.

I was terrified. How high would they climb? The grey mass heaped up around the base of my refuge. Parts of it made tentative leaps and forays. Tiny teeth darted. Hanging on precariously, I stamped and punched as best I could, bruising one fist then the other. A thin eager whistling rose from below.

But then—as though clouds had obscured some inner sun which lit up all their vicious little lives—the scouts stopped climbing. The mass subsided. The whole grey carpet ceased its flexing and writhing. It settled. It lay still.

Quickly comatose. Asleep.

The food-run was over. I was of no further interest. Nothing was, but slumberous digestion.

If I slid down the trunk right away, crushing little bodies by the score as I broke out of the cordon, mightn't they rouse again as one creature?

And if I waited . . . Tiny bodies, huge appetites! Mightn't they wake up just as hungry in another hour or so?

I brooded a bit then worked my way up even higher, to where a neighbouring tree tangled with my own sanctuary. I transferred. From there I moved with difficulty to a third tree. After about half an hour of awkward manoeuvres I descended on the far side of the sleeping pack.

For the next league or so I found a convenient roadway through the jungle waiting for me, stripped bare by the beasts. Marking their last few dozen food-sprints and mass snoozes. Presumably the total slumber that overcame the mice fooled other creatures into forgetting their peril. The impromptu road swung this way and that, and latterly vegetation had begun to reassert itself. I had to leave my tunnel when suddenly it veered off at a right angle.

Lalo had said nothing to me about these hungry hordes. Maybe they only lived in western jungles. In which case, what else lurked hereabouts? After quitting the corridor I was nervous and wary for a while, but no further animal prodigies crossed my path. The jungle cackled at me as if planning dirty deeds. Yet I never saw the owners of these voices; they did not follow me.

On the umpteenth day at last I came upon a trail—one which hadn't been made by piranha-mice. This was much narrower and had been hacked, not nibbled. Nor did it run nearly as straight as the rodents' single-minded tunnel spasmodically did. It took the line of least resistance amidst tree-trunks and tangles. Generally it ran east to west. I followed this trail inland, hoping that it would connect with some north-south route.

I could never see very far ahead because of the constant twists and turns. After marching along for a league or so I suddenly heard voices, coming from around the next corner or the one after.

Hastily thrusting aside, I concealed myself behind a mass of dinner-plate-leaves full of peepholes.

Only moments after, three men came along the path. Large boxes were strapped to their shoulders. All of the men sported untidy beards. They were dressed in baggy linen trousers tucked into boots, and coarse cloth shirts. Two wore floppy hats, one a white-spotted bandanna. All were armed, with knives and tarnished machetes. I didn't like the look of them one bit. These were wild men.

And I could have safely gone on not liking their looks—but for where I had chosen to hide.

A burning needle stabbed my hand as it rested on the soil; then another. I didn't cry out. I only gasped involuntarily and snatched my hand away—to tear two insects loose: red things the size of a fingernail. That was enough: the intake of breath, the rustle of leaves.

Boxes were shed. A knife came out. A machete was brandished. Boots crashed towards me; and I was hauled out upon the trail.

"What do we have here?" the hatless one said in wonder. "A girl?" His hair was a wild bush of bright ginger, as was his beard. He said "gairl".

"Obviously!" The black-bearded second man ruffled the tatters of my blouse. "In men's raiment. Mostly."

"Stop it," I squeaked.

"Runaway?" asked the third man, a rangy blond individual. "Witch?" He said "roonaway" and "weetch".

I was released, and Gingerbush put his knife away. "You a witch?"

"No, no." But of course in their eyes I supposed I was. I was a woman of the river.

"Do you think she'd tell?" snapped Rangy Blond. "What are you?" he shouted at me.

"If you don't think I'll tell, why ask me?"

"Ho, spirited!" from Gingerbush.

111

"Queer accent," remarked Blackbeard. "Audibly."

Rangy Blond gripped me by the shoulders, and I thought he was going to tear off the remains of my blouse. Maybe all my dark fantasies of the past few weeks had come home to roost. He shook me instead. "*What—are—you?*"

I stared into this wild man's eyes, suddenly inspired. "You're *upset*. Scared. *I* shouldn't be here. But neither should you!"

"Perceptive," said Blackbeard.

Rangy Blond seemed incensed. "Shouldn't be here? Why not? Who says? We're prospecting for jemralds." Presumably those were precious stones.

"Why shouldn't *she* be here?" mused Blackbeard. "A deaf man could tell you she ain't one of us. So where's she from? 'Tis obvious. She's from over the river. Ain't you?" He grinned— though not a cruel grin. "Shipwrecked, eh? You all use ships."

"Boats," I corrected him unthinkingly. And he chuckled in triumph. After all those weeks of isolation this was a game too fast for me. Blackbeard might look thuggish, but he was nimble-witted.

He turned to his companions. "Brothers, we've found us treasure."

"Okay," I admitted. "I'm from the other shore. I'm a river-woman. Do you want to know about it?"

Blackbeard laughed uproariously. "Do we, Brothers? Do we just!" He calmed. "So she came across the Satan-channel . . . Doesn't mean as how she was wrecked, though. . . ." Abruptly he caught hold of my hand and twisted it. "Sting bites, eh? You need ointment." Letting go, he unlatched his box and burrowed. Producing a glass jar, he salved my skin with something that stank. "Nasty buggers, those. So which is it? Boatwreck? Or sacrifice? Tossed overboard into Satan's black lips? Or a *spy*? Found a way over, set up a camp down south?"

Why had they hacked this trail towards the river? Simply to search for jewels? No . . . that was only their cover story—to hide what they were up to, from the eyes of other men. I felt sure of it.

* * *

After the comparative monotony of the past weeks, a lot happened in a litle while.

The three men cached their burdens beside the trail and escorted me back to their camp a league to the west, which a couple more men guarded. They gave me a new coarse shirt to replace my blouse, and fed me to bursting point on a stew of meat and veg poured over tapioca; then questioned me.

The camp consisted of a crude log cabin and a pair of tents, in a clearing with a stream nearby. Another narrow trail ran away north-west.

The "Brothers" didn't exactly introduce themselves, but it soon became evident that Blackbeard's name was Andri. Rangy Blond was Harld, and Gingerbush was Jothan. They weren't actual brothers, except perhaps in roguery. The two men who had been left to guard the camp were less savoury specimens: one with teeth missing, the other with a badly scarred left cheek. This pair eyed me but kept their distance, and weren't included in our discussions.

Andri paid intense attention to what I said, questioning me where he didn't understand and demanding the meaning of words he didn't know. I must have been interrogated for two hours. I even told about Capsi and Verrino. Yet Andri never went into unnecessary detail; he blocked in the general picture.

"Right," he said at last. "Yaleen of the River, I believe you. Mainly because no one could be such a thoroughgoing liar, except maybe Jothan here. Lucky you fell in with the likes of us. Saved your life, doubtless. Certainly saved you much pain. Wised up to our ways by those Watchers of yours you may have been. But not enough. Never enough."

"Was it entirely luck?" I asked. "That I fell in with *you*?"

He wagged a finger. "A story for a story, you won't get. Don't expect it."

"Because you're *danger*," said Harld.

"Potentially," agreed Andri. "S'posing she fell into the wrong hands. S'posing she blabbed her mouth, when those hands started twisting her."

"But I'm treasure to you, aren't I? More precious than

113

jemralds." I'd decided to stop being a lost waif, and to capitalize on my assets.

"Jemralds to one man: dung to most others, only fit for burning. After you'd shat yourself, in the cellars. S'posing you tried to hold back, like a costive. The Brotherhood would always think you was holding back."

"You don't have to try and frighten me."

"Spunky words, girl. But foolish. I simply touch on the truesoil."

"Do you. And which one man might I be jemralds to? The person you work for?"

Andri picked his teeth a bit. "Truesoil is," he said, "you won't be learning no names till you meet their owners. What you know not, you can't babble."

"What's all this 'truesoil' business?"

"Eh, don't know the word? Happen you wouldn't, either! Truesoil is the gritty, the down to earth. It's the permitted land. Near the river is all falsesoil. A lot I'll have to tell you. Evidently."

Which is what he proceeded to do, commencing as night was falling—until I found myself being borne in his arms into one of the tents, lantern-lit by Jothan. I'd flaked out.

Andri slid me into the luxury of a sleeping-bag. That night I dreamed I was in an honest bunk aboard a friendly boat.

My education continued the next morning, after I'd crammed down a huge breakfast. Harld seemed edgy and restless, but Andri insisted on wising me up adequately about life in the west before he would contemplate our setting off (for destination undisclosed).

"She has to know what not to say," he impressed on Harld. "What not to do. We'll get her a robe as soon as we can. Right now we have to robe her *mind*."

And learn I did: ten-thousandfold what anyone else in the east had ever guessed of the western world. . . .

Men had come to this world, said Andri, from another one called Eeden, a name unknown to me. And when people died here, their minds returned again to Eeden. The westerners were convinced that their physical bodies were artificial dummies or puppets; and these dummies were animated from a distance. This idea seemed a wholly lunatic one, but it did become more plausible—or at least self-consistent—the more Andri explained.

According to their "Deotheorists" real people couldn't live on any world except Eeden, for a hundred reasons which had to do with differences in air and water, foodstuffs, diseases, whatever. Consequently the "God-Mind" had sent forth to a hundred worlds artificial bodies capable of breeding and reproducing. A "psylink" existed between Eeden and our own world, such that babies were born back in Eeden yet they lived out their lives—their mental lives—in puppet flesh here. Meanwhile their original bodies lay entranced in cold caverns underneath Eeden, their growth halted at the infant stage, each to be "revived" when the corresponding puppet body died—as fully-experienced "cherubs" whose "afterlives" in Eeden would enrich the tapestry of that world gloriously, complexly, subtly. The cherubs would bring home to Eeden a hundred different histories, a hundred strange and varied ways of life, from all over the universe.

Yet here on this particular world of ours, Man had encountered the Snake of the River, an evil infiltrating creature intent on subverting the "psycolonists" and invading Eeden, only true Home of Humanity. The Snake worked its wiles especially through women, due to subtle differences in glands and blood and brain—which made all females potential agents of the Snake, Satan. Once infested, people could only be purged by pain and fire; which of course tended to kill them.

Naturally I was puzzled about the nature of this God-Mind, who had created human life here, and whose all-powerful will could cross the cosmos, only to be thwarted.

It appeared that "God" was a higher intelligence of "an ineffable nature". Inexpressible, beyond the comprehension of mere mortals. One day he would rule the whole universe, and create it. (Which meant that he both did rule, already, and didn't—the Deotheorists' ideas of time were really weird.) The arrival of dummy-people in the demesne of the Snake had awakened that other divine (or devilish) force to similar ambitions. Now there was a second contender for captaincy of the ship of stars.

What's more, the supreme God-Mind, the Lord of Creation, had himself somehow been produced out of the mind of Man; created, given birth to.

So.

This was both crazier, and more rational, than I'd expected. It wasn't simply that the Sons of Adam lorded it over women. They did—with a vengeance. But they actually had a reason. True, as far as I could make out, the average tenor of western life was cruelty, superstition and oppression pure and simple. Self-interest and rabid prejudice—coupled with distinctly backward circumstances. I noted how Jothan and Harld ogled greedily at some of the items I related of life in the east, ordinary items we took for granted. Still, there was a rationale behind their wretched system. The God-Mind, versus the Vile Snake.

I feared it might make me spew to play host to such a hostile concept of the black current; I who had drunk of it. To my surprise, it didn't. I was far from any eastern town or boat, far from the river, far from the community of women. I felt as if a persuasive influence had withdrawn from me; or perhaps it was just lying low, keeping watch.

That afternoon Andri, Jothan and I set off along the trail to the north-west. We left Harld and the other two men to get on with whatever business my arrival had interrupted—business which just had to be intimately connected with the forbidden river. Whose daughter had now fallen into their hands like a ripe peach.

Ripe? Ah well, perhaps "ripe" is an exaggeration! After my many weeks alone on sparse rations I was more like a shrivelled twig. Still, they loaded me up for the journey (I only realized later that they had burdened me lightly compared with the way a woman of the west would ordinarily have been weighed down). Andri and Jothan wore heavier back-packs.

Yet I stepped out relatively lightly. The trek wasn't so bad now that there was a definite path to follow, in the company of guides. That evening we made genuine camp, amidst jungle which seemed far less wild and chaotic.

Marching in single file allowed few opportunities for chattering. When we sat round a fire that evening Andri and I talked again, whilst Jothan busied himself boiling soup.

"Do you really think you're a puppet?" I pressed Andri. "Or a dummy-body, or whatever?"

He scratched his beard a while. "Look: our forebears weren't born here, for a fact. If you plunge into water, does that turn you into a fish? Likewise, if you plunge into a foreign world, why should you suddenly be at home?"

"We *live* here. We are at home."

He nodded at the cook-pot. "Why should we be able to eat what's here, and live on it?"

"Well, we do."

"That's no answer."

"We must have brought a lot of things with us to eat. Chickens, for instance! Some ancient writings mention chickens."

"Do they? How d'you know they're the same sort of chickens, eh? And why should chickens be able to peck around and live here? Unless, girl, unless we've all of us—chickens *and* people—been made into the sort of bodies as can live here. The Deotheorists say if you just dump a man of Eeden down on a strange world exactly as he is, he'll starve in a few days. He can't digest the local food. Or it poisons him. Same applies to the air and water."

"It couldn't have been *too* different here."

"Happen not. Otherwise maybe we'd have needed scales on our skin, or shells on our backs."

"That's silly."

"No, it ain't. We'd have been made differently. As would the chickens and cucumbers and everything else as came from Eeden. The Deotheorists say that all the kinds of life there are, are spelled out by different words. These aren't like our words, that we speak. They're very long magical words—so long, it would take you ten thousand pages to write but a single one of

117

'em. These words are written in our flesh. If you change the spelling, you change the shape of life.

"When we arrived here, whatever it was as brought us read all the words of *this* world back to the God-Mind. He thought about them, learned the language of life here, then he changed the spelling of our own words so as we would fit in.

"And on a hundred other worlds elsewhere, other words were read. And other shapes was born.

"Only the God-Mind can understand these words and change our spelling. It only takes Him minutes. Hours at the most. It would take us hundreds of years. I'll warrant He changed our stomachs and our blood quite a bit. Though not our outward looks. We look the same as we would back in Eeden."

If the God-Mind hadn't changed our appearance, why assume that he had changed us in secret, hidden ways? This seemed to be a completely unnecessary theory, in high need of the "razor of logic" to cut it out. I said so.

"Why is the idea handed down, if it's unnecessary?" demanded Andri.

"Because it gives the Brotherhood an excuse to rule the roost."

He grinned broadly. "Ah, you've solved it all in a twinkling! Simplicity itself!" He leaned closer. "Simple as a fellow shoving his squirter in a woman and making a baby pop out nine months later! Would you care to explain just how a baby is made, eh? Or how does a seed make a plant? Come on: tell me the recipe."

"A plant makes itself out of soil and water. A baby makes itself out of its mother and the food she eats."

"How? How does it make itself?"

I knew how to *stop* a baby, with a draught of Safe. But actually I was floundering. It occurred to me that maybe Andri's "long words" were what "genes" were; but "genes" was only a word itself, without much meaning. "It starts out tiny and gets bigger," I said.

"So this here fellow squirts a tiny baby into the woman, does he? Too tiny to see with the eye? How does *he* make it in the first place?"

118

"No, the woman has a tiny egg in her—"

"How does the egg become a person? What tells it?" Andri guffawed. "Look, girl: *words*—very long words written very small with a million million letters in each word—that's what makes a baby. The word of God. Made flesh." He gazed at me. "Don't have any such notions, do you? Never even give it a thought. Just get on living soft lives—"

"Hey, I resent that! Working a boat isn't any holiday."

"Like beasts, that don't question."

"We're beasts, are we? So now we come to the nub of it. What hatred you must feel for women! What a load of fear! Yes, I said *fear*. Let me tell you something, mister: you're no better than the rest of those Sons. Worse, probably. Whatever it is that *you're* after, you're screwing yourself up twice as bad."

"Maybe it is in Man's nature to torment himself, for truth. To strive."

I snorted. "And not in Woman's nature, I suppose."

"Yourself excluded. Naturally?"

This exchange seemed to be taking rather a vicious turn. Partly my own fault, I admit.

Just then Jothan cut in. "You've failed, girl. You wouldn't last ten minutes. You'd be in the ducking stool. Shrew. Scold. Argumentifier. Heretic. Disobeyer." Placidly he stirred the soup. "Why, you ain't even doing the cooking."

Andri actually winked at me. "'Tis true, what he says. You'll have to watch that tongue of yours. Or you'll end up pickled or cooked, yourself. The Brotherhood don't brook opinionated females. Us, of course, we're broad-minded. And we're still way out in no-man's-land."

"You'll have to act more appeasing," said Jothan. "Truesoil is, you'd better just stay shut up."

"Okay, point taken," I said. "No one's eavesdropping on us here. So, Andri, do you or don't you believe that you're an artificial person, a dummy? Tell me: I'm fascinated."

"Whatever you start out believing, Yaleen, you'll believe to the end of your days—even if you convince yourself you've changed your mind a dozen times, and turned all your thoughts inside-out. 'Tis true. You can't wash out the dye you're first dipped in. The best you can be is aware of this. Then at least you'll know what stains you always, even when you're going against the grain."

"Dipped in dye, is it?" And I had been dipped in the black current. . . .

How I rejoiced that I'd been born in the east, where people could be happy. Nobody could be happy on this other shore. They must be mad to give themselves up to such misery, when they could have used the river as the highroad to prosperity, variety, civilized lives. As I thought this, something deep in me and far below the surface seemed to agree and flood me with a wry euphoria.

"Soup's ready," Jothan announced.

We walked for the best part of another day till we reached a rough road running north and south. The trail stopped short of this road, leaving a mask of undergrowth. We must have veered quite a way inland, far from the river.

Andri jerked his thumb southerly. "Worlzend's that-a-way. We head north. We'll come to Pleasegod in a couple of hours. You'll stay out of sight with Jothan, till I find you decent raiment. If we meet someone beforehand—"

"I know. I'll dive into the nearest bush."

"That might look furtive. Just keep your trap shut. Glance demurely at the ground."

We did soon pass a curious contrivance: a cart loaded with packages, drawn by two huge hairy hounds, the like of which I'd never seen before. A skinny man trotted behind, clad in doublet and breeches, cocked hat and wooden clogs, flicking the air with a whip. He paid us scant heed, beyond a nod and a raking glance across me. Averting his gaze from my companions' machetes, he stepped up his pace and lashed the hounds.

"He didn't seem any too curious," I said when he'd passed.

Jothan grunted. "He couldn't be fool enough to fancy we'd rob him on the high road. I've no wish for a gibbet."

"What's that?"

"Gallows, girl, gallows! Hung up high to rot. God's Peace

120

guards the high road. Sons of Adam hunt you down, if you transgress it."

"The way they hunt witches down? How many women *do* disobey?"

"Not many. A few. Those as get seduced to the river, as if it sings 'em a song. Enough for entertainment once or twice a year, most places."

"You call the burning of women *entertainment*?"

"I don't, specially. Mobs do. We're all bloody ignorant savages compared with you, clever cocky superior Yaleen. 'Cept on certain matters such as Andri mentioned. Such as why we're here at all; and how."

An hour later we approached a laden barrow, pushed by a stout, black-cloaked woman. Her man strolled along with a single parcel tucked under his jerkined arm. Presumably it had bounced off the barrow and couldn't be fitted back on. The woman eyed me venomously, no doubt on account of my male attire.

"Ho," said the man, halting. He wore a bronze medal round his neck, with a circle and arrow design. In his belt was tucked a hollow tube of metal with a handle, which I assumed must be some sort of cudgel. "God's Peace, save you from Satan!"

"Save you," replied Andri with a smile.

"Who's she? Brotherhood business?"

"No, no. No problem, Brother." Andri made to move on.

"Wait a bit. I asked who."

"Oh, we're prospectors, Brother. We took her with us to cook, carry and comfort. Piranha-mice got her clothes. Had to lend her some." Andri had already told me that's what they called those ravenous little beasts.

"Piranha-mice? Close by?" The man looked dubious.

"Close enough. Better push on. Getting dark soon, isn't it?"

"I'm safe enough."

"Not from mice."

The man scrutinized me. Remembering advice, I glanced briefly at the ground. "What kind of cook is a skinny wretch without an ounce of fat? What comfort's she?"

Andri grinned wickedly. "Thieving cook. Had to teach her a lesson."

121

"Thieving cooks wax plump."

"Not if they're fasted."

"Doesn't figure. You cook the meals yourself, keep her tethered?"

"Oh, he's a born joker, this one." Jothan nudged Andri aside. Suddenly he looked alarmed, and cocked an ear. "Hark . . . Thought I heard a rustling."

"Mice, this far north?"

"First time for everything, Brother!" Jothan shoved me. "Get along, hussy, while there's still flesh on those bones. God speed," he called over his shoulder. And on we walked; though the man stood watching us till we rounded the next corner.

"Busybody," muttered Andri, once we were out of sight. "At least there ain't nothing like your mirror and lantern signals over here. Though one thing the Sons do have, is pistols."

I repeated, "Pistols?"

He stuck a finger in his belt, where the man had stowed his tube, pulled it out and said, "Bang. Kill you at a hundred paces. Hopefully. Cost a bit, take weeks to craft."

"Oh."

"I'd trust myself to throw a knife first. Pompous things, pistols. As soon explode your hand, as kill your enemy. In my opinion." His eyes narrowed. "Don't know about pistols, hmm? Mentioned none in your account of the east."

"You never asked," said I quickly. "Can't mention everything."

He caught and shook me. "Don't tell any lies, Yaleen! Lies catch you out!"

Soon, at dusk, we arrived on the outskirts of Pleasegod. I stayed in hiding with Jothan while Andri sallied into the town, returning after half an hour with a bundle for me: a ghastly ankle-length frock, with cowl, wrapped around a pair of rope sandals. It was pretty dark by now but I could still tell how hideous the costume was. Surrendering my own well-made serviceable boots and breeches from behind a bush, I watched them disappear into Andri's backpack. I never saw them again.

Being now in disguise as a penitent, slavish female, I attracted no attention in Pleasegod, where we spent that night at the

122

Gladfare Inn. The size of this institution puzzled me at first, till I realized that over here men must be on the hoof constantly. Our own eastern inns were simply places where you caroused. Most eastern travellers had their own floating homes along with them. Those women and girls who hadn't, rented private rooms chosen from the town register.

The Gladfare Inn was boisterous with boozers, in its long hall and out in its colonnaded courtyard. Above the hall rose two storeys of shabby bedchambers equipped with straw mattresses on trestles, ewers of water, soap like chunks of yellow rock. That evening I stayed in my room with the door barred, occasionally peeping down at the lantern-lit courtyard where Andri and Jothan had repaired to amuse themselves. Down below was a jollity in which I could not join. Apparently "a certain type" of woman drank in taverns. Subsequently I heard thumping and crashing on the stairways and corridors, shrieks, and giggles.

In the morning Jothan confessed that there was a more salubrious inn located behind the Donjon, where respectable men with respectable wives would stay. But we weren't seeking the company of pillars of society, were we?

Pleasegod in the morning was a sprawling, tatty, smelly place, with rubbish lying around in the streets, disconcerting nobody but me. Yet from early on it was bustling with barrows, porters, carts, costermongers—all the more bustling, I suppose, because of the low level of technical aids. In other circumstances I might have accounted the enormous marketplace as picturesque, but for me it was overshadowed by two of the buildings flanking it: the great brick prayerhall, and yes, the stern stone Brotherhood Donjon, before which lay a patch of ashes where no one trod.

The heart had quite gone out of travelling, for me. I, who had wanted to see the whole world! Never would I desire to add Pleasegod to the roll-call of other towns I'd visited—blessed names like Aladalia and Ajelobo. Even dirty Guineamoy and neglected Port Barbra seemed paradises by comparison.

I felt the same about the succeeding towns along our route: Dominy, and Adamopolis, each of them spaced apart by half a dozen intervening hovel villages. Life went on there, true; but it wasn't my idea of living.

North of Pleasegod we met an increasing volume of traffic on the high road; and travellers tended to gang up in bands of six to ten folk to while away the trudge convivially with songs and tales. But company was the last thing we wanted. We shrugged off invitations to join a party and attempts to tag along with us.

It had been ages since I had caught sight of the river even distantly. Once we left Adamopolis behind, though, the high road climbed up through hills verging on mountains. The jungle dwindled; and I thought I knew where we were now, for when I'd been sailing north of Spanglestream I had spied peaks inland to the west.

The highest point of our climb afforded a grand view east across leagues of land.

How could anyone enjoy the view? A grisly monument marked it. Boulders were piled together. From their midst rose a pole which supported a rusty cage in the shape of a human body: an iron suit, with a padlock fastening it. Within, a skeleton. This death-cage creaked and grated in the wind. But had the condemned person been dead before their body was locked in—or not? I didn't ask. A group of travellers had stopped to mumble and make signs, and glance furtively at the vast perspective. . . .

Far away, sunlight glinted from a long strip of water, thin and insignificant at such a distance. Even further to the north-east I noted a vague grey fuzz, like a blur in my eye. Could it be the smoke of Guineamoy?

"So here's Lookout Gibbet," Andri muttered sourly. "Don't stare at the river, Yaleen."

We hastened by.

Soon we were descending, somewhat riverwards, into forested terrain where I could see our destination nestling in the foothills.

Manhome South was a substantial town lying in the cup of a valley, fronting a thin crescent-shaped lake. From above, it almost looked civilized. Broad streets of two- and three-storey timber houses were set out in a grid pattern. These residences petered out into a mass of humbler dwellings built with mud-bricks and roofed with reeds—though the grid persisted

124

throughout. By the lakeside rose several large edifices of stone and proper brick.

Jothan pointed. "There's the Tithe Exchequer . . . That's the Brotherhood Donjon, and the Theodral nearby. . . ."

"Theodral?"

"The Deotheorist HQ. And over there's the Academy of Techniques."

Quite a centre of administration and learning! On such matters as how to build death-cages, or bore metal tubes which could kill people from afar. . . .

Once down in the outskirts of Manhome South, we loitered in a scrofulous public park till nightfall. Then we made our way through the blacked-out streets—lit only by whatever glow escaped from houses, plus starlight—till we arrived at a three-storey dwelling surrounded by bushes and a fence.

Jothan and I stayed outside while Andri slipped in through the gate. He was immediately greeted by the savage raving of a hound—which he must have known well, since it shut up quickly. Presently he reappeared, to conduct us round in the darkness to the back stoop where a door stood ajar, spilling dirty amber light. We entered a kitchen. A tall, freckle-faced man awaited us, dressed in a loose grey linen robe. Bunches of gingery hair like thin rusty wire sprouted from the sides and back of an otherwise balding, spotted cranium. On his upper lip grew an incongruously neat little ginger brush of a moustache. Standing there with his big hairy knuckles loosely clenched, he looked as tough as a plank. But he wore spectacles, too, glassy windows behind which his watery eyes were thoughtful.

"Upstairs," he ordered. "Bolt the door, Andri." Picking up an oil lamp, he preceded us.

And so I first made the acquaintance of Doctor Edrick.

I was to spend three weeks in his house, being questioned every afternoon and evening while Doctor Edrick made notes in spidery handwriting in a black ledger. At first Andri assisted in the interrogation; and where he had established general outlines, now Edrick filled in the minutest particulars.

I must have spilled out the whole of my life, and of all our eastern lives. And why not? Why should I have held back? Was I betraying our way of life, our river-way? Hardly! I felt more like an ambassador of sanity, showing these westerners how life could be conducted more satisfactorily than they obviously conducted it. Was I in any way their enemy? How could I be, when these two had helped and sheltered me? Had there been no Andri and Edrick doubtless I would have spilled out all the same details under much less comfortable circumstances, with a bonfire awaiting what was left of me at the end of it.

Besides, Edrick in particular had a nose for any pussyfooting on my part.

So I told; and told. Trying to put to the back of my mind the fact that I was trading my treasure of information, all for a hope and a song.

It transpired that Edrick was a Doctor of Deotheory: an influential man. He must be leading a double life, it seemed to me, if he was also mucking about with the river and was willing to protect me. Each Firstday that I was there he dressed in white robes, to proclaim in the prayerhouse by the Theodral. Though when I begged to go there, out of curiosity, he flatly refused; I knew none of the responses. Every weekday morning, wearing a less formal version of these same robes, he departed for the Theodral itself. While he was out of the house I browsed through a number of treatises from his small library. That was when I had finished cleaning the house, scrubbing clothes and platters, cooking, and feeding the hound. . . .

For those were my duties. Doctor Edrick had a "housekeeper" apparently devoted to him and thoroughly loyal. But he had sent her away on the morning after my arrival to visit her family in Adamopolis, something which she had been hinting at for many weeks. I was to be her temporary replacement. My presence was more explicable this way.

All in all, this was rather like being aboard the *Spry Goose* again—as an impoverished passenger, who had been set to work cleaning the bilges for my keep!

Edrick's library: it was small mainly because paper was scarce—a fact I had noticed in the night-soil shack out back, where a bundle of rags was spitted on a nail. What books there were, were crudely printed in very small editions—each with the permit of the worthy Brotherhood stamped in them. Maybe that was why paper was scarce, too. The censors restricted the supply.

From Edrick's books I didn't learn much beyond what Andri had already told me on the journey. Or rather, I learned *more*, but I wasn't much more enlightened by all the casuistical hypotheses and dogmas about the motives of the God-Mind, or the nature of the Snake, a topic with which I felt better acquainted than any westerner could possibly be. Nor did I gain an inkling of what Doctor Edrick's private river project was about.

He came back home one day to find me—with some cleaning chore suspended midway—perusing a yellowing old tract entitled *The Truesoil of Manhood*. Taking this from me, he tossed it carelessly on a table.

"You'll wear your eyes out, girl."

I was about to mention that his own peepers could well benefit by replacing those crude spectacles of his with some decent lenses ground in Verrino; however, he frowned as if anticipating some such impertinence. Though actually other matters were on his mind.

"Things are boiling up," he said. "Few know it yet, but it's so. That fine brother of yours set the cat among the chicks a year ago."

"Did he? He was more like a chick among the cats."

"I know, and I'm sorry. That was the decision of the local Sons in Minestead. Understandably."

"Did I hear you—?"

"My dear girl, those folk have to live close to the river, on account of the ore deposits. So they're specially sensitive to river-witchery. When the Theodral at Manhome North heard about the incident, they would far rather have talked to Mr Capsi in a lot more detail."

"Maybe Capsi was lucky they didn't get the chance!"

"At least they had his gear to study, at the Academy. The underwater garment wasn't destroyed. Of course, there's still the problem of men only being able to use the river once. . . ."

So that was where Capsi's diving suit had ended up!

"Manhome North: where's that?"

He looked amused. "Four week's walk and more. It's the other great centre. Anyway, since the Capsi episode there have been two schools of thought . . . I'll rephrase that: two schools have existed for a while. Now events are honing the intellectual conflict between Conservers and Crusaders. The latter being in the minority as yet."

"These Conservers want to keep things as they are?"

"They intend to keep our Truesoil secure and pure."

"Whereas Crusaders want to make contact with the East?"

"Contact?" He smiled grimly. "In a manner of speaking."

"And where do *you* stand, Doctor?"

"What a busybody you are, girl! Still, your family appear to have a history of poking their noses in." He hesitated. "I view myself as a sort of mediator between the two schools. The Crusaders, should they prevail, have it in them to provide us with much more exact knowledge of our enemy, the Satan-current, and its minions. All the better to safeguard our human way of life—not by crude fire and torment but by refined skills, by techniques."

"Hence your secret river project in the south?"

"*My* project? Not so! A project on behalf of the Crusaders! One from which I had high hopes of squeezing juicy knowledge. . . ."

"To feed back to the Conservers!" I was guessing, but this seemed likely.

"You make me sound . . . cynical. I would rather describe myself as a pragmatic idealist." He debated with himself. "That project was only in its first stages. Maybe now it's stillborn."

"Because I turned up?"

"And maybe it only needs twisting askew of its original aim. One item of great interest stands out from your narrative, Yaleen." Doctor Edrick adjusted his spectacles. "To wit, the existence of a certain fungus drug in the southern jungles."

"Oh no," said I.

"Ah yes," said he. "What a shame you never saw the plant itself!"

128

"It may not grow on this side of the river."

"You already told me that you survived our southern jungles because of your knowledge of similar jungles on the other bank. Therefore by and large the vegetation corresponds. Most likely that fungus grows in our jungles, too—further south than explorers have ventured recently. Though you have."

"I'm not going back there!"

"Could it be that you're going to Minestead? Opposite Verrino?" Edrick chuckled. "There to stand on the shore and wave a kerchief? In Minestead, where they burn people so impulsively."

"You could tramp around those jungles for ages collecting hordes of different fungi, and none of them the right one!"

"That, Yaleen, rather depends on the effort put into an expedition. The investment, the number of personnel. We'll need rabbits to screen out what's poisonous; and human volunteers to test what isn't."

"I'm not volunteering."

"Goes without saying. You're too valuable as a source of different information. Oh, we'll need lots of other women to cater for such a party, who can act as volunteers."

"So you see women as a superior form of rabbit?"

He wagged his finger astutely. "Point one: you've said that the drug is used in erotic orgies. Presumably involving men and women, though not provenly so. I can imagine many perversions of natural behaviour on your east bank.

"Point two: it's the *women* of your Port Barbra who orchestrate these lecherous rites; and the only time you saw the drug in action was in the case of a woman, your boatmistress.

"Point three: the female brain must have different gland-juices in it than a man's. Hence the woman's vulnerability to the Snake. The effect of the drug on women may be more noticeable than the effect on men. And the effect on the Snake. . . ." He looked pleased at his lucid grasp of the situation.

I could only feel an abject horror. I'd thought I had reached a sort of sanctuary. I'd imagined that somehow this might lead me back to my homeland. I'd fancied that I understood Doctor Edrick—the mediator who stood between me and the cruel Brotherhood.

129

I hadn't understood a thing. Instead, I was simply a traitor.

"Black current," I whispered silently within me, "*help me. Help us all.*" I prayed in the prayerhouse of my skull as a witch might pray to the Satan-snake.

No response. Alas.

Doctor Edrick fiddled pedantically with his glasses. "One adjusts to new circumstances, Yaleen. One adjusts. Have I not adjusted to your arrival here from the land of Satan? I trust I've conveyed *my* position well enough to help you adjust your own—to what must be."

One thing was obvious. I would have to escape from Edrick's house. I would have to get away from Manhome South. To flee, alone, to somewhere else. Probably with Sons and Crusaders hunting for me.

Where could I go?

I believe the black current may have heard my plea for help, across all those leagues of male land. . . .

That night I dreamed. I dreamed I was at Spanglestream with Jambi. We were standing together on the esplanade. Her husband was loitering some way off. Fishing smacks rode on the water, their emblazoned eyes lit by the shimmer of phosphorescence. Streamers snaked across the river like slow lightning flashes—silver arrows pointing the way from west to east. Pointing towards Spanglestream.

And Jambi said to me, in an offhand way, "Whatever the little beauties are, they seem to keep stingers away."

I woke with a start. Her words echoed in me. I repeated them aloud, over and over.

Had she really said that when we were on the waterfront together? Had I forgotten, or not noticed at the time, because I'd been tipsy? Had I not heard consciously—yet some part of my mind heard and recorded what she uttered?

I rose and paced the room in the darkness, thinking hard.

Was this wishful thinking? Dream fantasy? Or was it a sign? A response from the black current? *Which?* Why didn't *The Book of the River* mention that the waters of Spanglestream were free of stingers? If it were true.

130

Maybe the fisherwomen of Spanglestream—Jambi's old school chums—knew this but didn't make a big deal out of it, except that they felt less leery of sorting their nets by hand without using gauntlets. . . .

Maybe the waters *as such* weren't free of stingers? Maybe it was only the streamers that were safe? These streamers waxed and waned; so the water would indeed be infested sometimes. But not on the most splendid occasions. When the streamers seemed to stretch clear across the river in great swathes, only interrupted by the midway current, would there be a clear path all the way?

If I were to dive into such a silver swathe from *this* shore, and swim with it until I reached the current. . . .

Ah, the current. Problem.

It had let me pass once. Why not twice?

Thence onward to the east bank, safe in another luminous swathe. . . .

A long swim, even so!

Yet if I wasn't threatened with being stung to death, I could take my time. Vary my strokes. Even float a while to recoup my strength.

I tried to taste and savour my dream again. It had been so vivid, so lucid. But was it *true*?

Maybe Jambi herself hadn't spoken that sentence. Maybe I'd overheard one of her fisherfolk friends say it at the party. And maybe the current itself had spoken to me, through Jambi's dream-lips.

Maybe. Maybe. I could go round like this in circles forever. I decided to treat the dream as true.

I considered. Guineamoy must lie roughly north-east of Manhome South, if that tiny pall of smoke-polluted air I'd spotted from the heights of Lookout Gibbet had indeed been our grimy factory town. So Spanglestream lay to the south-east.

How many leagues away from Manhome South was it? Ten? Twelve? Perhaps no more. I could assume with some confidence that the Sons must shun *that* part of the shore even more fiercely: there where those bright emanations from the Snake coursed across to touch the very bank. All the country opposite

131

Spanglestream ought to be deserted for a long way inland. Once again my dream pointed in the right direction.

I made a mental note to avoid asking Edrick's opinion of the streamers, or show any special interest should he raise the subject. Then I climbed back into bed.

The next morning I began to steal food and store it in my room. Discreetly but busily.

As it turned out, it was lucky that I'd had to feed Edrick's hound. By now the beast thought of me as a friend. Or as something familiar, at any rate.

Otherwise, when I slipped out at midnight a few days later, the wretched creature would have barked everyone awake, in between tearing me to shreds. . . .

In the interim Doctor Edrick had said no more to me about his grand new project. But he had been absent longer than usual each day. On returning he had twice closeted himself in his study for ages with Andri and Jothan. Jothan departed the house a few hours after the second occasion, equipped for the high road. I had no idea whether he was heading back to the south—or northwards, as a courier to the Ka-Theodral in Manhome North. (*Ka*-Theodral was the formal name for the building, "ka" being some old word for the essence of a person, which rode the psylink back to Eeden when he died.) Whichever direction Gingerbush had taken, he was well out of the way. That same night I crept downstairs and unbolted the kitchen door.

I tossed meat to the dog, which appeared as if by magic. Before I had gone half a dozen steps it had bolted all the raw chunks down, and bounded after me. All the way to the gate, I had to soothe it and thump it in the manner which dogs seem to find friendly. When I shut the gate on it, pushing it back, the hound began to whine noisily. I tore a stick off a bush and hurled it far into the dark garden. Away I sprinted on tiptoe, hoping that when the animal came back, slavering on the piece of wood and thrashing its tail, and did not find me, amnesia would overtake it.

It must have forgotten. No barking rent the night.

Onwards through Manhome South I slipped. I'd gathered that

a woman out alone at night could only be a "whore" or a witch. But I was conveniently dressed in the colour of darkness, and there was nothing in the way of civic illuminations.

Three hours later, with the town well behind me, I was toiling up a forest trail leading out of the valley.

Getting across town and out through the shanties hadn't been too difficult. The grid layout proved invaluable. Even the fouler, rougher areas were arranged north by south and east by west.

I only had to hide once; and run another time, when I set a dog a-raving—but it must have been chained. I hope it choked. I tripped and filthied myself twice, out in the vegetable fields beyond the shanties.

On the far side of the fields was tangle. Finding a trail through all the bushes and trees took a long time. I had to backtrack. I had to circle to the north. Eventually I found a rutted road heading in the right direction—that direction being eastwards, riverwards.

Just as the sky was starting to grey with imminent light the road reached its destination: a timber camp. Ahead were long huts, felled trees, carts—with yokes and very long traces laid out for teams of men to haul. (Or teams of huge hounds. Or women.)

I debated my chance of racing through the camp, but it was too near dawn to run the risk of being spotted by early risers. And there might be dogs about. Instead I worked my way all around the slope, which had been thinned by felling. By the time the sun did rise, I was beyond.

And a clanging alarm sounded from the camp. My heart stopped for a moment—till I realized that this was just the signal to rise and shine; and toil.

I journeyed on for perhaps half a league more till I finally had to stop, exhausted. The undergrowth was thick but not impenetrable. No paths were evident other than minor runs trodden by small creatures unknown. I burrowed into a dense brake, squirmed round several times like a dog to make my bed, and slept.

When I woke in the afternoon, insects were zizzing about me, settling on my scratches and my sweat to feed. I fairly itched with their attentions, but I didn't immediately slap these pests away. Holding quite still, I listened: for any distant shouts, the baying of hounds, whatever. Nothing. I only heard the noises of the forest: a babbling murmur, occasional cackles. So I fed, then I emptied my bowels, burying the evidence with the aid of a stone. I forged onwards. Downhill, now. Away from the heights that lay inland. I navigated by the brightness of the sun.

It took eight days to reach the waters of Spanglestream. I didn't hurry unduly—often I *couldn't*. I avoided easy, exposed routes, though after the first day or so I didn't expect to be overtaken by pursuing Sons. Doctor Edrick must surely decide that I had struck off north in the direction of Verrino. Or perhaps less likely, that I might have fled due east straight towards the enchanted river to lave my witch's limbs in it as soon as possible.

Instead I slipped south-east diagonally across the land.

This was no mean journey. Yet with ample food on hand, and compared with those weeks of travel up in the far south, at times it almost seemed a stroll.

At last one evening as the world was darkening I pushed through brush and creepers for the last time, to stand upon the river bank once more. I beheld silver streamers snaking upon the waters, and my heart rejoiced. As night fell, the phosphorescence glowed ever more brightly.

Dream and reality seemed to merge. Once again the myriads of beasties were putting on a show for me, and this was such a show as seemed more allied to my dream than to my memory. As far as I could see in both directions liquid silver floated, hardly broken at all by straits of black water. Even if I drifted downstream I should still be safe.

One tongue of white fire lay particularly close to the shore. It was as wide as could be: three hundred spans, or four. It angled down from the south-east. Faint twinklings of light visible far off in the north-east were perhaps the harbour lanterns of Spanglestream itself.

I slipped off my women's black weeds—they were certainly the worse for wear. I discarded my undershorts. I kicked off my frayed rope sandals. I cleansed myself of the West. I was determined to plunge into the stream quite nude. If any Son of Adam could have seen me, he would have known that a witch was going home, and would have covered his eyes. Or else he would have stared, and lusted for fire.

I plodged out to where the mud fell sharply away—and launched myself upon the luminous highway.

When a light wind stirs even the gentlest of waves, on so wide a river after a while you lose sight of the bank entirely. Stars spread above me in a second river; mainly of silver, with several sapphires and rubies scattered through that setting. I took the constellation of the Axe for my guide, remembering how it would turn about the Pole as time went by.

No stingers attacked. If great shoals of pollfish, ajil and hoke were grazing upon the streamer, I felt no mouths bump or nibble at me. My arms were haloed in a warm white fire. My head, too, I suppose—though I never dunked my face as I swam.

I don't know how many times I varied my stroke—breast, butterfly, crawl—or whether an hour had gone by or longer, when blackness loomed immediately ahead. The ever-splashing silver had begun to blind me to the stars of the Axe; that blackness gave me back my sight.

I didn't tread water or hesitate.

But I did think fiercely in my head: *Worm of the World, it's me: Yaleen! Let me pass!*

If I'd expected it to drink me deep, then spew me out again with a giant fish to bear me senseless to the eastern shore, I was wrong.

I swam through the current sluggishly, breasting what felt like soft butter or congealing lard. And while I swam, it explored me. Dreams strolled around inside my skull, examining the contents once again, laying out the wares. I never sank into the depths, of the current or of unconsciousness. In the midst of my "hallucinations" I remained aware of where I was. Thus I was swimming briefly through the southern jungles—then along the high road in company of Andri and Jothan. Next I was floating in Doctor

135

Edrick's house. Here, the current seemed to shudder, to wobble. . . .

As before, it drained me. It didn't speak, though. Maybe it was too busy with what it was learning from me of the western land to spare time for my immediate problems. For little me, lost in the middle of the river. Maybe it had already communicated enough by sending me that dream. Perhaps I had to be truly unconscious, before it could connect on the personal level.

Or did it communicate? Not in words as such?

Somehow I sensed that it was satisfied with me. Somehow I suspected that I might be able to pass through it in future whenever I wished, or needed to. This was nothing vouchsafed to me directly; no more than an intuition.

Certainly this second passage was far more smoother than my first brain-crunching, suffocating inadvertent one.

Then I was through.

And flailing about in ordinary river water. Phosphorescence dazzled me once more. The invisible shore lay another three-quarters of a league away. I was as far from land as could be. And quite wrung out.

I felt dreadfully, absurdly let down and abandoned. All of a sudden my relief at passing through was replaced by rage. In retrospect I think this was a necessary rage—like my screwed-up emotions on the jungle trek weeks earlier—which gave me the strength to carry on.

"Help me, damn you!" I cried. The current ignored my appeal. I was of no further interest.

"You heap of shit!" I howled.

Then I gathered myself, and struck out again along the quicksilver road, not so quick for me.

Eventually—on the hundredth or thousandth occasion when I craned my neck—I saw lanterns distinctly, tiny pools of light, irregular dark humps of buildings lightly rimed by starlight.

Suddenly: masts spoking the stars, a fishing smack lolling on my left by a moored buoy, another on my right.

Quite unexpectedly I was there.

I stroked along that last lapping shining tongue. I sidled along

136

the base of the wharf. I touched a stone step. I hauled myself out.

Dripping silver, I crawled painfully up the flight. I weighed a ton. Each separate step was unbelievably solid and unmoving.

At the top I slid forward and spread out like a boneless jelly. But before I passed out I decided maybe I was wrong about the imperviousness of stone. Spanglestream quayside suddenly felt more comforting, more tenderly cradling, than any other place where I had lain my head to rest for a very long while.

I'm hazy about the exact sequence of events thereafter—I was discovered presently, still lying there—however the night certainly ended with me wrapped in a blanket on a spare bunk aboard a brig, the *Cornucopia*.

Next day was confession day.

After I'd been lent new togs, and had devoured a huge plateful of good fried river fish, I confessed to the boatmistress of the *Cornucopia*. That afternoon I repeated my story to an emergency mini-meeting of the river guild—consisting of the quaymistress, Halassa, and two guildmistresses who happened to be in port. One of these had been present at the conclave held on board the *Santamaria* at Tambimatu, prior to my New Year's Eve departure. She was able to vouch that I was the person I said I was.

To these three women I told my whole story, Verrino included. And how I had informed Doctor Edrick about the fungus drug. And how men of the west believed that all of us on this world were made of artificial flesh; and when people died, their minds returned to Eeden—home of the God-Mind which originally sent us forth to populate strange planets, and multiply. All of it, all.

Many were the urgent coded signals flashing up- and downstream during the next few days; you can be sure of it!

And me?

I was quartered at the quaymistress's own home in town till a full guild meeting could be convened. Halassa wavered between regarding me as a miracle, and a miscreant. Or perhaps as

137

somebody who had contracted a lethal disease and survived it uniquely, to carry its seeds around henceforth in my veins. I was a prodigy—and a bit of a pariah. Heroine, and renegade.

The mini-conclave had sworn me to keep mum about the bulk of my tale. (Though what exactly my oaths were worth when the black current itself had twice allowed me passage, was another matter. . . .) The bulk of it; but not all. That was impossible. Word had spread around the *Cornucopia*; and had leaked ashore, as well as to other boats. Nor did Halassa try to keep me penned in her house. If she had tried, she wouldn't have succeeded. Halassa's home wasn't—*couldn't* be—another Edrick's. After my months of exile, I had to rub shoulders with real life again: streets, taverns, cafés, waterfront. I was on a leash, but not too short a one.

As I wandered about, I attracted a certain amount of attention. To those in the know, I was a bit of a wonder, to point the finger at. Look: there's the first riverwoman ever to cross the current—and cross it twice! She's the first of us who knows all about the west! Does she not have horns on her head now, or a jet-black tongue, or some other mark of strangeness? Maybe she can read the current's mind and foretell the future! That sort of thing. Some women would try to pump me for information, either back-slappingly or unctuously.

I enjoyed this for a while; then it began to oppress me. Presently—and none too soon—life settled down again. People stopped staring and asking silly questions—or not-so-silly questions, which I dared not answer. Six weeks after I'd swum ashore, a full conclave of eight guildmistresses was held aboard a schooner out of Gate of the South; and I confessed in full all over again.

This conclave spanned four full days. The guildmistresses were not so much sitting in judgement, but more as a tribunal of enquiry: to delve into all available facts about the other half of our world, facts which might cast a new light on what we thought of as the certainties of our existence.

They always conducted their deliberations with me present, and free to contribute. Until near the very end I was never sent

138

out of the elegant cabin, with its silver wall-sconces, gildenwood furniture, and its tapestry of the Obelisk at Port Firsthome. Still, I fancied there was a certain whiff of trial about the proceedings.

On the last day the youngest mistress present—a handsome blonde woman of Sarjoy named Tamath—raised the matter of that obelisk.

The monument rose from a rocky butte overlooking the town. A popular picnic spot, that, commanding a fine view down meadows towards Port Firsthome and the river. Whoever had woven the tapestry had included several family parties. Scarlet and orange rugs were spread, to contrast with the rumpling background grass that rose (in the tapestry at least) to meet the grey conical roofs of Sarjoy, and the blue of river and sky—the heavens wearing a few fluffy clouds for contrast. Some naked children skipped in the foreground, a young couple kissed, and an old man capered curiously, brandishing a flask of wine. The seated mothers and fathers were mostly squat, as though their threads had sagged or the weaver couldn't manage figures at rest. An open hamper spilled fruit and fishes and strings of sausages on to the rug. It looked as though the antic patriarch had kicked the hamper over, in pique at their having forgotten to cook most of the food.

The Obelisk of the Ship was a basalt shaft a hundred spans high, shaped like a sleek fish with tail fins to support it. Really, it ought to have dwarfed the picnickers more than it did. An attempt at perspective had been made—unsuccessfully. The column was leaning, about to topple and crush the people below.

I suppose the tapestry was charming.

Inscribed on one of the black base fins in tiny letters was a simple legend:

HERE PEOPLE FIRST CAME
INTO THIS WORLD

Into it they came, with rugs and a hamper, arses like barrels, no clothes on the kids, and a drunken grandad. . . . That was, I recalled from my own visit, the actual inscription carved in time-worn letters on the obelisk. Verbatim.

Tamath rose, crossed to the tapestry, touched the legend.

"Isn't that an odd way of phrasing it?" she asked. "Not 'landed upon' or 'arrived at'—but 'came into'. Almost as though people first *came into* existence on that spot . . ." She eyed Nelliam, a senior guildmistress of Gangee, an ancient wrinkled woman with the face of a prune. She eyed her hopefully. "Doesn't our guild agree?"

"Language changes with time," suggested Nelliam. "The sense of words."

Tamath pressed on. "How do we really imagine we got here? Were thousands of human beings crammed into a ship of space? What would they eat? Consider the cargo problems! Consider, too, what Yaleen has said: a foreign world may not be immediately hospitable."

I looked attentively at Tamath, careful not to grin in gratitude or stupid pride that she valued my report.

"To be sure, it must have air and water and life on it already, or else it's no use whatever. But why should the life be life that people can live with? Why should the air be air they can breathe? Why should the plants and fish be edible at all?"

The more I looked, though, the more I began to suspect that Tamath was, well, speaking out of fright. As people will babble pointlessly when they don't know the answer; yet they're compelled to speak for the sake of it, to keep up their presence. That sort of fright.

She had raised the matter because she had to raise something—vigorously. The tapestry was on hand to suggest the very thing; as well as providing the pretext for her to parade elegantly across the cabin.

She was only repeating what I had said. She continued repeating it forcefully, as though it was her own idea.

Nelliam shrugged. "Life's life. Air's air."

"Is it? Are they? Maybe we did have to be 'made'—or 'remade' —for this world of ours?" And now Tamath had to conjure something new out of the hat. I could almost see her reaching, straining herself. "If so, then the only place to make us was *right here*."

Oh well. I supposed some people had to psych themselves up to excel.

140

But now Sharla, a senior guildmistress, spoke up. She was of late middle age, and if any ultimate secrets were in possession of the guild, surely she should know them. Obviously she didn't; obviously there weren't any. . . .

"You know," drawled Sharla, "that obelisk has always puzzled me on another score. It's a symbol of a ship of space, right? So where's the hulk of the ship itself? Something tough enough to travel between the stars ought to last for lifetimes after it lands—even with rain and rust attacking. Yet there's nothing at all."

Tamath crossed quietly back and resumed her seat. During the next several minutes while Sharla expounded, Tamath nodded sagely, to convince everyone (except perhaps Nelliam) that she had made a valuable contribution by midwifing a truly original idea. . . .

"I wonder about the nature of this ship," mused Sharla. "Need it have been built of metal or anything similar? Imagine for a moment that we could harness a giant fish. Suppose we built a deckhouse on its back and planted masts and dug holes in its body. Imagine that boats were like that—not of wood, with a bit of metal.

"Could this ship of space somehow have been built from living tissue? Could it have manufactured our bodies out of itself, and so consumed itself?"

"You have an over-active imagination," remarked Nelliam.

"Yet the black current is a great living being—of a nature we can't understand. Subtle and immense! Why not the Ship? Imagine that a ship could be a living being, which carried *no* crew or passengers—because it was *its own* crew and passengers. Something godlike, beyond our comprehension." Sharla had whipped up her own enthusiasm now; her voice was awed, ringing with sincerity.

"Yet it was manufactured by people?"

"Maybe people made something greater than themselves— which then produced something even greater: something alive, superbly wise; and it was *this* which built the ship. Or gave birth to it, even. The people who started the process wouldn't be equal to the end result."

141

"And how could this be, Sharla?"

"A baby grows into a girl—who grows into a woman. The woman is entirely changed from the baby she once was."

Nelliam sniffed. "Whereupon the woman gives birth to another baby. Back we are where we began."

"It's just a comparison."

"Perhaps it's a good one," said Tamath. "Or perhaps: like a leaf-worm changing into a flutterbye?"

"*I* vote we should concentrate on what is sure," Nelliam said. "Such as the likely capers of the Observer-men at Verrino, when Yaleen decides to favour them with an account of her recent travels."

"I wouldn't!" I protested. "Honestly! Why should I? My brother isn't there any longer."

"No, but your lover is. And other acquaintances." Nelliam tutted impatiently. "That's beside the point. I think we should consider enlisting the support of those Observers. If the westerners are so sure that we're the Devil's daughters, maybe they'll try to build bigger pistols to shoot right across the river. Or they may try to take to the air. I suggest an approach in confidence to the Observers, so that they'll report any unusual sightings across the water. I'll go further. We should build observation towers ourselves. Convert the present signal stations. Erect more, and taller. It'll help communications. I can name several blind spots where a message can get held up for hours, if a boat isn't in the right position to relay. A year ago I'd have said no message could be that urgent. . . ." She brooded.

"Yes, but what about the *women* in the west?" I wanted to know. "The vile lives they lead. The burnings."

"Nothing we can do, Yaleen. Not without wrecking our own world."

"But—"

"What would you suggest?"

"*We* could take to the air!"

"We don't wish to. For reasons which I'm sure even you must appreciate."

"Besides," drawled Sharla, now on the "Conserving" side, "supposing we crossed the river on a wind, how could we be sure

142

of getting back? If we did cross over, what then? Do we land, and make speeches about freedom and happiness? Till they put us on a bonfire. . . ." Sharla, I realized, was one of those who would argue both sides of a case with enough flair to convince you that she was deeply committed . . . to deciding nothing.

Nelliam tapped her finger lightly on the table. "I see a more basic objection against intervening. Something Yaleen appears not to have realized, despite her experiences over there. A vital difference between us and them. One which the Sons should surely work out, given all that Yaleen fed them—if they aren't utterly pigheaded." She looked around the conclave. "Well?"

"The forms of social organization?" It was Marti, the dusky veteran quaymistress of Guineamoy, who answered, Judging by her tone and her raised eyebrows she was telling us, not asking. An ally of Nelliam's, then.

"Exactly," said Nelliam.

"How do you mean?" I asked. "What did I miss?"

It was Marti who told me, briskly. "It's like this, Yaleen. Technically those Sons are more primitive than us. But they possess centralized authority: this 'secular arm', the Brotherhood. That isn't in the least like our own guild system. Their two Manhomes, North and South, are obviously twin capitals, *ruling* towns. Here, no town rules any other. Over there they have what might be called a 'government'."

"Two, surely? If there are two . . . capitals."

"They will need twin capitals because of the slower communications. That doesn't imply two separate countries. On the contrary—judging by the names."

"Oh."

"Our way of ordering society is invisible and unobtrusive. Theirs is visible and brutal. Harsh circumstances lead to harsh solutions. The circumstances of those Sons are tough because they've denied themselves the river—"

"Which itself orders affairs invisibly and unobtrusively?" I hazarded.

"*You* have more knowledge of that than us, girl!"

Nelliam raised her hand, though rather limply. "Whatever mumbo-jumbo's in the Chapbook, our guild isn't founded on

143

mystic wisdom. We're rooted in tradition: *practical* tradition. That Brotherhood is dogmatic. It *is* rooted in mumbo-jumbo — with practicalities playing second fiddle."

"The Chapbook is mumbo-jumbo?" I echoed incredulously. Two or three of the other women, notably Tamath, looked quite shocked.

"Obviously I'm exaggerating. I do so to make my point. We pay lip-service to what's in the Chapbook, because it *works*. If you're to ply the river for your livelihood, the river must accept you. We drink of the current. We obey certain codes. Then basically we forget about it. We don't grovel on our knees on deck every morning and pray to the river-spirit. We don't make a big deal of the black current, always and ever, remorselessly. But they do over there. They're obsessed—with denying it. The current is our background; that's where it belongs. It's *their* foreground, even though they cower away from it."

Silence in the cabin, for a while. If a Tamath had said such things, perhaps there would have been uproar. But then, she wouldn't have.

"Talking of practicalities," said I, "what about Doctor Edrick's scheme for poisoning the current?"

"May it fail," said Nelliam tightly. "May he thrash around for ten years, never finding what he seeks. May he fall between those two stools, of Conserving and Crusading, and get squashed. Really there's nothing we can do about it."

"We could tell everybody, from Umdala to Tambimatu. Put people on their guard. Tell them about the west."

"Why? So that everybody lives in a state of permanent anxiety? So that any malcontents have a lever against us?" Nelliam leaned towards me. "So that your fame spreads far and wide?" Yet her tone was whimsical rather than malicious.

Shortly afterwards the conclave began to wind up. I was left with the odd sense of being high in the councils of the land—yet these councils making little difference. The guild could trim our sails a bit; but could it ever actually alter course? On a long and rather straight river which leads forever from A to B is there even any concept of altering course? Any need to?

After I was dismissed, the 'mistresses must indeed have come

144

up with some last-minute practical conclusions: about the building of better signal stations which could double as spy towers (if equipped with Observer-style telescopes). Some sort of consensus must have gelled, since I was to see the results before too long. Yet basically I felt enormously let down. Once again. First by the current, now by my guild. . . .

When I came to think of it more coolly, what actually could be done? On any scale corresponding to the size of the problem? Reacting prematurely might make it a problem. Once you identify something as a problem, it tends suddenly to get worse.

One of the last things said before I was dismissed came from Tamath:

"Mumbo-jumbo or not," and here she glanced at Nelliam, "may the black current show us our true course." Her look was respectful—but there was a slight edge of, shall we say, ambition in her voice. She was a handsome, engaging woman, as I say. She must have worked hard, and pleased people. And all the while, perhaps, a little frightened of doing the wrong thing— while needing to speak out, proffer her opinion, make decisive choices. She would be admired for it, and she would never quite dare believe it herself.

"To be sure," conceded Nelliam. "Pardon my impieties. Blame them on the crotchets of an old lady. I was just trying to make a point."

'May the current show us our course. . . .' Tamath had no idea how soon and how drastically the current would show us something!

Oh yes. One other final thing was that I was assigned a berth and duties on board Tamath's own command, the *Blue Guitar*, now bound for southern waters.

As so I would continue my life as a riverwoman. Just as we would all continue our lives.

For a while.

And so I did. And so did we all—for the next half year, till New Year's Day came round again, anniversary of my awakening washed up on a strange shore.

This particular new year found me on no strange shore. The *Blue Guitar* was tied up at the stone docks of Jangali. . . .

On New Year's Eve I had walked out through the old town to visit Lalo and Kish, whom I hadn't seen for over a year. The young couple ought to have moved out of the parental home into a place of their own, though it was to that tree-house that I went first, to enquire.

Lalo's mum turned out to be a portly swarthy woman whose hair was a mass of wiry black wool and combs and strings of agate beads.

She directed me in the usual emphatic Jangali style, then added, "If you'll hang on a mo, I'll take you myself. I'm baby-sitting."

"Baby?" I suppose I gaped. "But how—?"

"Why, in the usual way, dear!" Her laugh boomed out. "How else?"

"I guess it's a while since I saw them."

"Best to get your brood hatched early, I always say! Then all that bother won't wear you out in your prime. They'll have three babies, I think. The first one's a darling little boy, so the next should rightly be a big strapping girl."

I wondered whether Kish would ever learn to raise his voice as loud as hers. . . .

"Has a woman called Jambi visited recently?" I asked on impulse.

"Who?"

So I described Jambi, reminding Mum that she was a friend of Kish's family and that we had both been on the boat which brought Kish and Lalo home.

"Oh, I remember! She did call once. Rootless, gadabout woman! Can't say as I took to her hugely. One shouldn't encourage that kind of thing. It's too unsettling, when a young man's trying to adjust to a new style of life."

Poor Kish. . . .

"I expect you're right," I said.

"Of course I'm right. Now if you'll just wait a mo! There's ever so nice a view from that balcony."

"It really doesn't matter! I was only intending to pop in." I

146

slapped my brow theatrically. "Oh dear, now I've remembered something else I had to do!"

Mum scrutinized me. "Have you really? So what name should I mention to my Lalo?"

"None. Don't bother." I retreated. "Obviously they're busy. Anyway, I'm quite a rootless gadabout myself!"

"What a peculiar whimsical way to behave! Well, *goodbye*," said Mum, and shut the door.

I left.

As I headed back towards the river, I thought of my own mother and father. I still hadn't been back to see them. Yet that was hardly my fault! Tamath's boat had kept me to southern waters since my return—far from Verrino, so that I wouldn't over-excite the Observers, I suppose. We were scheduled to sail downstream "sometime" but I could be fairly sure I wouldn't be permitted to hop boats to any old vessel I liked, for an earlier passage north. Tamath was keeping an eye on me.

I had written a couple of times to my parents—initially from Spanglestream—and had had two letters back. The second had been awaiting me at the quaymistress's *poste restante* when we docked in Jangali.

Mother's first letter had conveyed a certain air of reproach at my having absented myself for so long without sending word. (Naturally, I hadn't told her that I'd spent some of the time gadding footloose and fancy-free about the western world!)

I detected a degree of anxiety about Capsi, too. (*That* still required a personal explanation face to face. However, any adequate explanation was so intimately bound up with other events on which I shouldn't enlarge that the problem had only got worse with time.)

All in all, both letters from Pecawar were quite complacent. A child had been born, of course. A girl. Her name was Narya. By now she was a year and a quarter old. Things were fine at home. Narya was a joy. Her first word had been "wain". It had rained in dusty Pecawar, impressing her.

Maybe my parents were weeping in private, but I doubted it. The keynote was complacency.

And Lalo's mum was militantly complacent.

And guildmistresses were fairly complacent too. Because in their guts, they couldn't imagine anything ever being very different. For them, the extent of foreignness was somewhere distant like Umdala.

Not, I hasten to add, that I thought there was any inherent virtue in striking up acquaintance with the really foreign, the west. Still, the west existed. And it was pulsing with people, whose souls were sick; some of whom at least were hatching plans which had to do with us.

Such thoughts occupied me while I walked back to the *Blue Guitar*. Then I put them from my mind.

That night a gang of us were planning to hit the Jingle-Jangle for a fine old thrash to celebrate New Year.

Whilst down at Tambimatu a boat with no name would sail out slowly to the mid-stream. Without (thanks be!) any Yaleen on board. . . .

And a jolly night it was indeed. Music, talk and singsongs—as deafening as ever. A lot of joshing, some kissing (and resort to a certain upstairs room for a six-way tangle), even a bit of a brawl, though a half-hearted one. This time no Port Barbra women were skulking about the premises. I collected a hangover, which I nursed through most of the morning in my bunk; as did many of us.

At last I just had to empty my bowels. So I dragged myself up. I raided the galley for a bite of eel pie then crept on deck, to lean on the rail and recover.

I decided that I, too, felt complacent.

Partly this was a consequence of the hangover: I had no desire to exert myself. Mainly it was due to being there once again on deck at Jangali dock, just as I'd been once before. It seemed as if nothing essential had changed, after all.

So I lazed about. Had lunch with the other walking wounded. Played several hands of cards, winning a few fins and losing them again. There was desultory talk about mounting a return expedition ashore that night, though no one was overly enthusiastic. The air was a hot muggy blanket. The sun boomed down on the river.

148

At around two o'clock the tall new signal tower to the north of Jangali began to flash. (Oh yes, there *had* been little changes.)

Idly I spelled out the message, which was in plain language.

A moment later I was not so idle.

"Tamath!" I screamed. "Boatmistress! Someone tell her to come!"

Minor commotions occurred on other vessels, too, as more people began to notice the flashing and pay heed.

Tamath was by my side in record time, sprinting from her cabin. She too stared. She had missed the start of the signal, but that didn't matter. It was soon being repeated. Briefly Tamath hesitated between dashing to the lookout station where young Melesina—about the only person actually on duty—was copying the signal down. As the message sank in, she stayed by me . . .

The contents?

Urgent alert. Ex Umdala. Repeat onward. Black current withdraws upriver ex sea. Head of current passes Umdala midday. Speed 17 LH. Wake upsets small craft. Head of current size of small hill. Look of giant croaker. River clear where head has passed. No current remains. Umdala endit.

Two hours since that signal had set out! The black current was withdrawing upstream at a rate of seventeen leagues per hour. Soon the "head" would be passing Firelight. A little over an hour later, Melonby.

Maybe something wild and terrible in the ocean had driven it upstream . . . I doubted this. The current was winding itself back towards the Far Precipices, like some huge rope being winched in. And on the end of that black rope was the living head which had never been seen, or even guessed at, in all our history! A head the size of a hill!

Tamath called to boatswain Hali (no relation to the Hali of the *Sally Argent*) to send someone aloft with a spyglass to observe the midstream; Hali climbed the shrouds herself.

"Nothing can possibly have happened at Tambimatu," Tamath muttered to me. "Last night, I mean. Not to provoke this. Or we'd have heard by now. So has your precious Doctor Edrick doctored the current, after all?"

"How do I know? How can a current flow *up*-river, Tamath?"

149

"Ah, its substance is curious." She was quoting the Chapbook of the guild, not telling me anything new. Her voice was sing-song. Her eyes looked glazed with shock. "It seems a liquid. Yet it flows within itself, and is One. Like an oily sinew, like a tapeworm."

"A worm with a head, so it seems!"

"It doesn't really flow like water. Waves simply pass along it; it remains."

"Till now it did! Incantations aren't going to help us any, Boatmistress!" I spoke as sharply as a slap on the cheek.

She recoiled, then recovered herself. "No, of course not . . . You're right."

"So is there a brain in its head? And eyes that see? And a mouth that feeds? And speaks? Maybe speaks!"

"Speaks," she repeated dully. "What could it say? Now that anybody can cross the river? Now that anyone can sail? The world's turning upside-down. . . ."

"It told me the world would turn on its hinges, on the day when it moved. Now it's happening. Today. Maybe Edrick didn't start this. Maybe the current decided long ago."

"What's going to *happen*?"

From the topgallant Hali called, "I can see ripples rushing all along the midstream water. It's moving, all right!" Hali ordered Zernia aloft to take over the watch, and began to climb down.

"What's going to happen, Tamath, is that it'll pass us here in Jangali. Unless it decides to halt halfway."

"If the head displaces enough water to upset small craft . . . then we'd best slacken our moorings . . . Or even put out, a hundred spans or so. Hali!" she shouted to the descending boatswain.

"Hang on." I interrupted. "It's withdrawing at seventeen leagues per hour. If it keeps on coming, it won't pass here till. . . ." I calculated. "Um, tomorrow, around midnight. Maybe very early, the day after."

"Oh yes, of course . . . Quite right."

"And I want to see it pass," I added. "From close by."

Hali had joined us by now. "Do you just?" Her tone was sarcastic. "We hear and obey. Right, Boatmistress, let's all jump to it and sail the *Blue Guitar* right out so that Yaleen here can get an eyefull!"

Tamath pursed her lips. "Yaleen has a . . . special . . . reason for wanting to be close. It may well be that we all *need* her to see what happens . . . Hmm, yes, we'll probably sail."

Hali stared at us incredulously. She didn't know my past history. By the time the *Blue Guitar* had arrived in Spangle-stream for the conclave, six weeks had passed since I'd swum ashore. The waves of gossip had slackened into tiny ripples.

"The crew won't want to get anywhere near *that!*" Hali protested.

"I'll speak to them. Tomorrow. Or tonight. In a nutshell, Yaleen here has crossed the current twice already. It knows her. She spent many weeks on the west bank. And she got back."

"Oh," said Hali. She looked hurt. Because Tamath hadn't taken her into her confidence earlier. "Oh." If I'd been in Hali's boots, that was about all that I could have found to say.

Hali was deeply hurt; and because of this I could see she was very sore at me.

Tamath turned to me. "Isn't the current at its lowest ebb as the year changes? Surely it should have grown *more* sluggish with the drug—not less?"

"Yes, the drug would make it sluggish, at first. Then it would speed up." Just as Marcialla had speeded up, rushing frenetically about her cabin . . . "It would go berserk."

Excluded from this exchange by ignorance, Hali looked even more resentful.

As the afternoon wore on, more signals came our way.

Ex Firelight. Head passing. River clear downstream. . . .

Ex Melonby. . . .

We might have stayed up half the night watching for signals—latterly, lantern flashes—spelling the retreat of the head upstream. However, Tamath ordered us all below quite early. The next night would be a long and risky one. She explained why; and stunned the crew with her explanation.

* * *

151

Going on for ten the following night, we were readying the *Blue Guitar* to sail, working by the light of our own lanterns and those on the dockside.

Dispute had broken out (not least from Hali) as to whether to risk a fine schooner in this enterprise. A little tub would be less of a loss, if loss there was to be. Though equally, a little tub might more easily founder when that living hill rushed by.

Two of our crew had deserted, though Tamath was only willing to consider them as temporarily missing ashore.

And I was in the peculiar ambiguous position of suddenly not being very popular, since I was the reason for this nocturnal jaunt to danger—while at the same time I was something of a miracle. From the way some of my boatsisters spoke, you'd have thought I was personally responsible for the present misconduct of the current.

We cast off. Slowly we sailed out under light canvas, to take up station.

We were about halfway out when, in the darkness to the north, the powerful signal-lantern began to wink. Tamath was loitering near me on the fore-deck. I had been relieved of my ordinary duties; who could say what my extraordinary ones might be?

Urgent alert. Ex Verrino Spire, I spelled.

It was the first time I'd seen such a call-sign. So some accommodation had been reached between the river guild and the Observers. Unless this was a spontaneous message, breaking into the chain of light.

. . . *Repeat onward. Explosion in town. Fire. Screaming. Confusion. Quayside appears under attack. Large rafts landing ex river. From West. Alert all towns: arm with any weapons to defend shore.* . . .

Tamath clutched my arm savagely, hurting me. She seemed to imagine her fingertips were pressing words into me.

"It's the Sons," said I, wincing. "They've invaded Verrino. . . ."

Sick at heart, I visualized the Sons of Adam rampaging through that lovely town, where in their eyes every woman was a witch. "Arm with any weapons" indeed! With knives and needles? With pitchforks and mattocks?

Tamath finally found her voice. "The head can only have passed Verrino fifteen hours ago! How could the West have rafts ready? And men, and weapons? Unless Edrick's plan worked! Unless he did poison the current! Damn you, Yaleen, for this thing you've done. *Damn you*. You told them how. And you've destroyed our lives!"

And at Verrino quay were berthed real river-going vessels, for the Sons to seize and press into service. . . .

Of a sudden our world was cut in half.

It all seemed so abominably unfair. Only a while ago the whole river and my life had stretched before me, full of tantalizing distant towns, vistas, bright adventures, friends, lovers, boats, dreams. Anything whatever that was good, within the changelessly rich fabric.

It was all over now, forever, before it had really begun. I felt as though a giant hand had abruptly doused the sun and stars, and drained the river dry.

Because I felt so dry, I wept.

"Don't be such a baby!" sneered Tamath. "What way is this to greet your only friend, who's rushing to visit you? You'll need to see straight, to pat the worm's head."

"Damn it," I gasped. "This is *grief*! Don't you understand? How many of us have ever known such grief before?"

"Congratulations, Yaleen. You're the bringer of grief." How bitter Tamath sounded.

And so the *Blue Guitar* continued onwards towards my tryst with the head of the worm; while three hundred leagues distant, a war had begun.

Part Four

THE WORM'S HEAD

THE WORKSHOP

For a while I'd been hearing a twanging sound. At first it was like singing in my ears. As the hour of our rendezvous drew closer, the noise grew louder; though never so loud that it could have been heard from the shore, I don't suppose, unless you placed your ear directly on the water.

It was the sound of a single enormous chord being strummed; it was the hum of the current winding itself back elastically towards the Far Precipices.

The night sky was two-thirds full of stars; the rest was cloud. With our lanterns doused and our eyes adjusted to the darkness, visibility was about fifteen hundred spans.

Visibility? Ah, that's taking liberties with the word! We would hardly be able to spot details much beyond two hundred spans—and only really when the worm's head sped by at its closest.

I was about to add, "so long as you had the reflexes of a cat". But we used to have a cat back home in Pecawar. Opinion has it that cats can see things that are invisible to human eyes. Well, it isn't true. Half the time cats are simply looking in the wrong direction. . . .

When that head rushed past, we would have about fifteen seconds to see it, but only two or three seconds of clear observation. Unless, of course, the head intended to pause and chat with me. And this I rather doubted.

I was risking lives for a whim—and Tamath was clutching at straws. I already knew that I was going to disappoint her; and anger her more. I was on the point of swallowing my pride and begging her, "Let's call it off. Let's go back." But this would also be dishonest. What, opt out at the last moment? And thus shift the blame? I could tolerate Tamath's hatred (I thought), but not her contempt. Not hers; she didn't deserve to scorn me.

Ah, my famous self-esteem again! Why should I flay myself for it? But I did. It seemed I couldn't win.

"Here it comes!" cried Hali from the mizzen top. Hali wouldn't allow anyone but herself aloft. I hoped she was lashed securely. I clung to the rail, peering aft.

A huge bow-wave tossed the *Blue Guitar*. Our boat heeled to starboard. Never had a deck sloped so crazily. From a midships came the noise of skidding, crashing and cries.

And in the midst of this: a dark enormity, a minor hill raced by, as if shouldering our schooner from its slopes. A mound of inky jelly, stiff as muscle . . . For an instant in the starlight I saw its face, but an instant was enough.

I'd faced a giant croaker in the jungles: a leathery boulder with bulging eyes and a beaky gash of a mouth. I'd seen gargoyles jutting from the gutters of the Donjon in Pleasegod: twisted faces, perhaps modelled on people burnt alive.

This was worse. The gape of its mouth was a slash through the tissue of the hill, wide enough open to gulp a skiff and crew; a mouth which dripped thick strings of glue. A ledge of a chin scuffed the water below. And above: ridges of bulges and pustules—then two hooded eyes. These eyes were set far apart: long, triangular and white. In them was no expression, no life; as though the salt of the sea had caked them over.

A face sculpted by a lunatic! More awful that it should have such a face, than have no face at all. Surely the worst thing in the world would be to stray anywhere near that mouth, those eyes. The creature was a great grotesque tadpole: simply a head, with a tail hundreds of leagues long. . . .

Already it was gone again into the night.

No sooner had the *Blue Guitar* righted itself than we were heaving down into the gulf to port. The boat jarred shudderingly as it met a wall of water rushing back to fill the trough. Something smashed to the deck from aloft. I feared for Hali. (Or was it myself I feared for, if it was she who had tumbled down?)

In fact we had snapped our spanker gaff.

Presently our lanterns were re-lit. Just as well they'd been doused, or we might have caught fire. And presently Tamath counted the cost.

"So Zernia broke her ankle. And Challi cracked her skull—let's hope it's only concussion. Then there's the spanker gaff—"

"Maybe the wood was rotten inside." It probably was, but why didn't I keep my big mouth shut?

Tamath rounded on me. "Don't you *dare* speak of anything on my boat being rotten! Unless it's yourself!"

A whimper of pain mounted to a sudden shriek; Zernia's ankle was being set.

"I'm sorry they got hurt," I said. "Truly sorry."

"Are you indeed? That's very small beer when people are being hacked to pieces in Verrino! So what did you learn, Yaleen?"

What had I learned, indeed? Once again the image of a tadpole came to me. The huge head, the inordinately long tail.

"I think . . . maybe it's about to change. Like, yes, like a tadpole which has no further use for its tail."

"You think," she mocked. "And of course by sheer coincidence, just when it decides to 'change', those bloody Sons decide to attack us."

To this, I had no answer.

"Well, what wise thoughts did it communicate?"

"None," I had to admit.

"None," she sneered.

"Mind you, last time it spoke I was right inside its body."

"So maybe this time we ought to have tossed you overboard, with a line attached! As bait for the worm's brain." And away she stalked.

We spent the remainder of that night in midstream on deep anchor. This was the first time any boat had anchored quite so far out; but our hooks caught on the riverbed with a link of chain to spare. I lay in my bunk during those dark hours like an unhappy, chilly plank. I was sure that I didn't sleep a wink; though I somehow found myself waking later on to the light of dawn.

When we were hoisting sail that morning, a signal flashed that the worm's head had passed Tambimatu at seven o'clock. . . .

* * *

The *Blue Guitar* headed back to Jangali, where the two crew-women who had deserted slipped back on board again before the day was out. In time for supper, to be exact. Tamath said nothing to them about their absence, and pretended not to notice.

But neither did she broadcast her opinion that it was I who was responsible for the invasion—otherwise the mood might have turned really ugly. As it was, I only had Boatswain Hali's sullen enmity to contend with. And Tamath's controlled hatred. And some sour looks from other women, who took Zernia's injury personally. Challi had woken up with nothing worse than a headache; and she wasn't the sort to harbour a grudge.

Incidentally, the spanker gaff *had* been a bit rotten at the point where it snapped. It ought to have been replaced, not held together with paint.

Much happened during the next few days, though to begin with little of it happened in Jangali. We learned of events thanks to signals from Tambimatu, and from points north to the Spire at Verrino.

(What *did* occur in Jangali was: anxious crowds gathering on the quay, flurries of panic, rumour rampant, and a besieging of boats every time a signal tower flashed—since shorelubbers couldn't read the signals. The quaymistress soon appointed a herald to proclaim newly-logged messages; and then to pin up the texts on a board in the market place. I don't know that this did a great deal to restore daily business to normal.)

From Tambimatu we learned that the worm's head had ended up jammed in that rocky arch below the Precipices. The head now occupied that point of exit and entry like some ghastly gateway, some portal of black flesh—with its drooling mouth agape, its white eyes staring blindly. The guild had sent the ketch with no name to inspect; thus the crew reported.

Maybe the worm's head had grown in size during the millennia since it first emerged, and now it was too large to slip back inside the mountain. Maybe the bowels of the mountain were already packed solid with its body, leaving no more space within.

Whether it was still alive, or dead and slowly corrupting, who could tell?

160

From Verrino we learned that the Spire was still in friendly hands. What the Observers saw from their vantage point obviously disinclined them to throw in their lot with the invaders. They signalled that the Spire could withstand an eight-week siege; longer on starvation rations.

On the day after the invasion the signal towers north and south of Verrino had both been burnt to the ground; news which scared us all. Why burn something which could be seized and used? Unless the guild signallers had held out, and been burnt along with their towers. . . .

Yet in the confusion of that first violent night one yawl had somehow evaded capture and set sail. This yawl took up station upriver. After the towers went up in flames, the yawl could still relay signals from the Spire, southwards. No such facility existed to the north of Verrino, thus all contact was lost with the whole stretch of river from Sarjoy to Umdala. Three whole days passed before a brig set sail from Verrino to bear down upon that yawl. The brig was crewed by women, but ineptly so—at least until one of the women was thrown overboard by the men in charge, with her hands and ankles bound. Then the brig's performance improved dramatically. The yawl had to flee upstream; all contact with the Spire was broken.

During those three days the Observers reported rafts being rowed back to the west, then returning with more armed men. Had the Sons been able, obviously they would have pressed real boats into service at once; but it had taken them till the third day to round up a scratch crew for the yawl. So most of the boat crews must have deserted to hide in the town. It might have been even wiser to scatter far inland—though I don't know that this would have been *my* first instinct, or any riverwoman's; and soon, of course, the chance was gone.

From aloft the Observers spied murders, and rapes by the raggy soldiery.

But then men wearing robes arrived from the west; Edrick's colleagues, and maybe the man himself. Vicious incidents tailed off quickly, in full view at least. Corpses were piled and burnt. Looting ceased. Cordons and roadblocks were set up. Patrols prowled the streets, enforcing order. Perhaps the western war-

161

leaders deliberately let their soldiers storm around to begin with, to terrorize the town, so that the people of Verrino would feel grateful for the contrast later on. Or maybe the leaders hadn't risked crossing over till the terrain was secure. By the time we lost touch with Verrino, at any rate, an uneasy calm reigned. As yet, the Sons hadn't piled faggots to burn people alive individually. . . .

From Pecawar, dear Pecawar, word continued to flow that all was well. From Gangee and the other towns, likewise. In each a militia was now being hastily raised, though how effective these might prove I could hardly judge by the example of Jangali. Jangali had always boasted an athletic, spirited, tough guild in its junglejacks. Before long, teams of 'jacks were marching about Jangali armed with machetes, axes and bill-hooks. No doubt this was fine for morale—but good for what else? There was only wild jungle opposite, and for long leagues northward.

Meanwhile, leaders of the jungle guild and our own river guild conferred for days on end about what to do. Coded messages were flashed, as well as plain—shorelubbers noticed no difference. I began to worry that Marti had been all too right about the absence of authority.

But then, ten days after the invasion of Verrino, a tight-lipped Tamath instructed me to accompany her to a meeting at the hall of the jungle guild.

The Jay-Jay Hall, as it was known locally, was a massive wooden edifice on the edge of the new town: a real temple of tree-trunks roofed by great beams and naked rafters, with clerestory windows for light and air. Entering the Hall was like boarding a great landship, largely devoted to an empty hold. The principal chamber contained no furniture at all, as though it was an insult to giant trees to trim them into tiny chairs. Instead, everyone sat on tasselled cushions arrayed on the waxed plank floor—and you'd better be sure to leave your boots in the lobby.

I was seated cross-legged beside Tamath. Twenty 'jacks and riverwomen were present in all; and before very long a 'jack dressed in the typical baggy trousers and scarlet jerkin, and sporting braggartly black moustaches, was asking:

"And why should Jangali be invaded *soon*? Tell me that! If I was a westerner, sod his guts, first I'd secure Verrino. Wrap it up tight. Rule the place till the people knew nothing else. After a year or two I'd pick off Sarjoy, then Aladalia, as leisurely as can be. Sew them up too. Where's the hurry? It's us who are in the mess, with our trade routes cut in half. We're wasting our time marching round the town with axes on our shoulders, that should be lopping trees."

A boatmistress said, "Well, *I'd* hurry. Because the current might come back!"

"Come back? Why should your mascot come back? You're crying for the moon."

I'd sometimes wondered what a moon must look like. A ball of rock floating above the clouds? A kind of cold sun? The jibe was insulting.

"I hope you aren't suggesting that women have become like children suddenly. To operate our trade routes you need fully experienced—"

"Persons. Male or female. And s'pose those Sons send boats to raid, like pirates in some Ajelobo romance, who'll be best to fight them off? Those as knows sails and needles? Or those who know axes?"

"Mister, it takes time to learn the ropes."

"And maybe we've got time. Five or ten years."

Another junglejack spoke up. This man was older, with a birthmark—a squashed cherry—on his cheek.

"You riverwomen certainly need to buck your boat crews up with those of the axe, as my friend says. A woman's no match for a hefty man in most fights. But there's danger in hanging back from the fight too long. We might find ourselves stuck in mid-air with no momentum. We simply can't let those Sons pour thousands of soldiers over the river. And I'll tell you why. Judging from what that stupid snitch of a girl said, those westerners are a lot poorer than us materially. Now they'll have heaps of our own goods to use against us. No matter how much they mess up the places they capture, they'll only get richer and stronger."

So the river guild—or Tamath—had already told the jungle guild about my travels. . . .

163

I was incensed; I spoke without thinking. "That stupid snitch is sitting right here!" I said loudly. I only realized after I'd let this out of the bag that I must have been present for a reason: as a card for our guild to play. But what card could I be?

There were a few intakes of breath. Men's eyes bored holes in me. Women looked embarrassed. Tamath snarled softly, "Shut it!"

"Okay, okay," I muttered.

"Well, well!" declared Moustache. "I'd say the river guild owes us one for that. Why's *she* here? So that we can send her up a jungle giant without a safety line? Or spit her on a spine-tree? Or stick her on a bonfire? Then both guilds shake hands afterwards?" His loud voice sounded more threatening than perhaps he meant it to, I had to remind myself.

Surely this wasn't the card that Tamath hoped to play? To toss me up into the treetops as a way of repairing inter-guild relations?

"We don't *quite* go in for that kind of thing," Moustache went on acidly. "You misunderstand our little annual festival."

"Nothing of the sort was in our minds," protested Tamath. "We can discuss *her* later on." She addressed the man with the birthmark: "Sir, we agree with you that time isn't our friend. And when I say 'our', I include everyone living on the east bank—man or woman, from Jangali to Gangee. So therefore. . . ." And she glanced at the quaymistress of Jangali, a plump silver-haired woman named Poula.

"So therefore," continued Poula smoothly, "we must urge the recapture of Verrino as soon as possible. How may this be accomplished? First, we should restore communications with the towns of the north so that we can co-ordinate efforts. We should build balloons to carry couriers over the occupied zone—and spy on it. This can be done."

A 'jack whistled. "Can it, just?"

"We think so. There'll need to be tests."

"And lightweight couriers! Now I see where the girl fits in."

Poula ignored this. "Next, we need weapons which can match those pistols of the Sons. Guineamoy will have to manufacture these. Therefore Guineamoy must be strongly defended. The Sons might attack Guineamoy next."

164

"Knowing about its workshops, as they do." Moustache glared at me.

"Oh, a fool could tell from all the smoke!" said Poula.

"Really? Then why didn't the Sons attack Guineamoy to begin with? Why Verrino?"

Maybe the answer to that was that Doctor Edrick had wanted some decent spectacles . . . I suppressed this flippant thought.

"Three reasons. Guineamoy must have seemed our strongest town. They may not have known quite what they were up against."

"Now they do. And the answer is: not much!"

"Next, Verrino is close to Manhome South, where those 'Crusaders' might be more influential. Unless we strike back and win, they'll soon be influential everywhere in the west. Finally, the Sons had a convenient launching place at Minestead. So now Guineamoy must be defended." Poula looked round the meeting. "Defended by whom?" she asked rhetorically. "And who will recapture Verrino with the weapons made in Guineamoy? Success in this enterprise requires a stout team who can lay off their ordinary guild work for weeks without disrupting essential supplies such as foodstuffs. . . .

"In a word, the junglejacks. Women 'jacks can carry on jungle guild business in the meantime, on a trimmed-down basis."

Moustache stared at Poula. "So what you're proposing is that we prune our own guild down to the women members—and turn the other ninety-odd per cent of us into your army!"

"It'll be *everyone's* army: the army of the east. But an army, yes. Meanwhile, riverwomen will be busy ferrying fighters and weapons. Don't worry, we'll be doing our bit."

"Aye, by shipping us off to a foreign town. Men don't go gadding about like you lot, with a lover in every port. Some would say: what's Guineamoy to us that we should quit our homes, leaving Jangali unguarded? Some might say we could survive quite well on our own, from the Bayou down to Tambimatu."

Surely some Jangali men must have come from Verrino originally! Yet it was a truism that new allegiances thrust out old.

"Don't worry about your home town. The jungle protects Jangali adequately from attack."

165

"Exactly!"

Poula wagged a finger. "Until the day when the Sons come sailing upstream—picking off one town then the next!"

"She's right, you know," said Birthmark.

Moustache subsided somewhat. "So we're to pack our bags, and garrison Guineamoy?"

"Yes," she said.

"While the Guineamoy guild make lots of pistols and things, for us to go to war with?"

"We haven't time to mince words or be diplomatic, Sir. Yes, yes. It's the only way. Guineamoy are prepared to tool up to make swords and pistols. And explosive bombs which you can catapult from a boat deck, or drop from a balloon. And incidentally," she added, "please don't think too harshly of Yaleen. She did tell us about their guns and how the Sons govern the West; that's useful."

But I wondered whether she was defending me personally, or simply the honour of the guild. . . .

"Almost as useful," snapped a 'jack with a vein-smashed drinker's face, "was what she told them about *us*! And about the poison those Barbra weirdos use."

I winced. I did manage to stare back at him, though perhaps my face was as flushed as his.

"We'll need to discuss your proposal," said Moustache. "We'll give you an answer tomorrow."

"Guineamoy already agreed," said Poula.

"Maybe that's because they're closer to the action, and a bit more exposed? And maybe the almighty river guild promised to remit their cargo fees for the next couple of years?"

Poula snorted. "Next you'll be fretting in case we charge you for troop transport!"

She didn't actually answer his question, though. This, I thought, was foolish. If the 'jacks sailed to Guineamoy, sooner or later they would discover whether there was anything in this wild surmise. And who would fight with a stout heart if they even suspected that they were being diddled?

Yet who was I to criticize?

"Tomorrow," repeated Moustache. He stood up, in one smooth scissoring action. Other 'jacks followed suit.

"Wait. One thing more. We haven't discussed the motives of the Sons enough. Their beliefs."

"So? You can turn that one loose on the savants and nitpickers up Ajelobo way."

"We may indeed."

"Marvellous! That'll amuse us while we're on guard duty, and exploding ourselves and dying messily. I wonder how many cords of wood they'll need to print their fantasies?"

Poula remained patiently sitting. Reluctantly a few 'jacks sat down again. Not Moustache, though.

"You have to know what your enemy thinks," she said. "One key to this is, what the black current is."

"What it *was*, you mean."

"Is still! Coiled up as it is, within the Precipices."

"Who cares? Sod all effect it has on the river now."

"Yet it still reaches into all of us, who are of the river," Poula said patiently.

Moustache looked blank.

"I assure you of that, Mister 'Jack. May I vomit if I lie, or betray."

"What on earth are you talking about? What's wrong with you?"

Poula was shivering. Her face had blanched. She bit her lip. Moustache stared hard at her then nodded—as though persuaded, of something at least. Abruptly Poula fainted and keeled over. Her neighbour tended her, tucking a cushion under her head.

"Okay, so I'm impressed," said Moustache. "What conclusions am I meant to draw?"

Tamath took over again. A little too slickly for my taste, as though this incident—genuine though I knew it to be—had been rehearsed beforehand. "And the key to the current," she said, "must be in its head. Where else? Tambimatu tell us that its mouth gapes open." I mistrusted her tone mightily. "An open gateway is an invitation."

"To be swallowed?" Moustache laughed. "Maybe its mouth just stuck in that position. Maybe it's dead."

167

"In that case, Poula would not have felt so sick and fainted."

"Poo to that," said the florid-faced 'jack. "Some folk believe an idea strong enough, they can make their own hair fall out."

Yet Moustache looked impressed despite himself. "So the thing has a key stuck in its throat. What of it?"

"We will send someone through that open mouth to investigate. We will send the only person who claims to have talked to it. We'll send *her*."

Me.

I'm sure if Poula had been conscious she would have announced this with less vindictive relish.

Moustache guffawed. "Heh heh! That's one better than sending her up a jacktree without a line."

But the 'jack with broken veins looked troubled. "Hang on a bit! Is it in our interests to have that thing meddled with? I say leave well alone! After a bite to eat, it might revive."

The 'jack with his cherry stain broke in. "Let's face it: what's going on is an invasion. An invasion by barbarians—who'll probably like you and me just as much as they like the ladies here. If jumping into the thing's mouth helps us any, I say we should welcome it."

"Another reason for honouring Yaleen with this special mission," added Tamath, with a nasty smile, "is that she seems to have a certain talent for survival. For popping up again. For being regurgitated."

Which did nothing to diminish the very hollow feeling I had in my tummy. . . .

The next day the 'jacks did give their answer, though I wasn't present myself; and the answer was yes. Yes, they would transform their guild into an army to defend Guineamoy. Yes, they would liberate Verrino. Not try to. They *would* liberate it. When a 'jack decided to fell a tree, that tree fell.

So a day later the *Blue Guitar* set sail for Tambimatu with everyone on board in relatively cheerful mood. Now that Tamath had won a victory or two, she was more relaxed. And when she told the crew the purpose of our trip—that I had volunteered to enter the worm's head—they eased off in their attitude to me. ("Just so long as we don't have to pilot her personally," observed Zernia, who was up and about now and hobbling on a crutch. "No, no," Tamath hastened to assure her. "The black ketch will carry Yaleen.") Even Hali softened her heart towards me, and became less abrasive.

Ah, my chance to save the guild! To be a heroine, pure and simple. Or a dead one.

During that voyage I often found myself recalling my glimpses of the lunatic head: the blind eyes, the mouth dripping glue . . . I tried not to dwell on this, but I had time on my hands. I was forbidden to undertake any strenuous duties—just in case I broke a leg, accidentally on purpose.

So I spent my spare hours reading the *Blue Guitar*'s small library of Ajelobo romances, studying the antics of their heroines and heroes in disbelief. Nobody ever asked *them* to stuff themselves down a giant dripping gob. Now that some days had lapsed since the plan was mooted, it seemed the height of craziness to try to communicate with the worm by this means. What would *you* think if a bug tried to make friends with you by leaping into your mouth? The venture semed ever more like some primitive rite of human sacrifice; oh yes, I found a fine example of *that* in one romance—though naturally the heroine rescued her boyfriend in the nick of time.

We passed Port Barbra without putting into port. Soon we were approaching Ajelobo, source of those fantasies which had delighted me once; Ajelobo, whose wiser residents would soon be set the nut to crack, of whether we were free individuals or puppets. To gnaw at this nut, while 'jacks died for freedom's sake; I could appreciate Moustache's sarcasm. No doubt Ajelobo savants would still be debating when a tide of Sons rolled up the river to answer them with steel and fire. Long after *I'd* been digested as a worm's breakfast.

With Ajelobo half a league ahead, Tamath came to where I was lounging in a deck-chair; she was rubbing her hands contentedly.

"Signal just came. The first lot of 'jacks are sailing. Isn't that great?"

"Great," I agreed. "And what happens when they've won

169

Verrino? Will they go back to chopping wood? Will they disband of their own accord?"

"If the current doesn't return, I suppose we'll need a garrison in every town from the Bayou northwards. For a while, at least."

"For a while—or forever? We'll need a standing army, Guildmistress, and our river guild to serve it. That's quite a change."

"In that case we might have to *invade* the west, and depose those Sons."

"That's no answer, either. What price the rules of marriage afterwards? What of the wander-weeks for girls? What of men staying put? What of *The Book*? All down the drain."

"Yaleen, you're forgetting the economic power of our guild."

"And you're forgetting how that power depends on us having a monopoly! I don't see any way back to where we were before. Paradise is lost, because the worm has gone."

"In that case," said Tamath tightly, "it had damn well better come back. You'll see to that, won't you, dear? Then you'll be promoted to 'mistress, just like me.'"

"Oh sure, I'll see to it. Dead easy, really! I just pat it on its snout, gaze soulfully into its eyes and ask, 'Is oo sick, Wormy? What medicine makes oo well? Me? Am I oo's medicine, Wormy? Tell-ums, then!'"

Tamath slapped me briskly on the cheek, and strode away. Soon there was cheering on deck, and up aloft, as she shouted out the decoded signal.

With watering eyes I returned to my romance, *The Cabin Girl and the Cannibal*. One by one I tore out pages, folded them into darts and launched them over the rail. Soon we had a little paperchase behind us; though nothing much compared with the expanse of water.

Tambimatu again! The Precipices soaring up through the clouds; spinach purée humping up against a town which couldn't see beyond its own roofs nodding together . . . Jewels and muck.

I blew my accumulated cash, upwards of sixty fish, on a

splendid diamond ring. If I was doomed to plunge into foul saliva, I might as well be properly dressed for the occasion—if only on one finger.

The guild had other notions of how I should costume myself for the encounter. Somebody must have had a fine sense of irony: the guild had prepared a sort of diving suit.

"For your protection, Yaleen," explained Maranda the squat, bland quaymistress; she who had skippered us to the Precipices and back, the year before. On a table in her office rested a glass helmet, a tight pigskin bodice with a brass collar to clamp the helmet to, and lots of straps on the back; and a tough belt with a padlock of a snaplink.

"Why not naked, rubbed with costly oils and unguents?" I'd found the "unguent" in *The Cabin Girl and the Cannibal*. It sounded sexy.

"You might need air, Yaleen. We've considered the way your brother crossed the river. See this valve here, in the glass? You'll carry several compressed air bottles linked in series on your back—enough for two hours. The finest craftsmen in Tambimatu have made them. The bottles are going through final trials right now."

"Are they of gold and silver?"

"And there'll be a long rope fixed to this harness, so we can pull you out."

"Oh, won't I just be the fly on the angler's line! Shouldn't I have a hook in my ribs? So you can winch the whole worm out of its hidey-hole, when it bites? Then the good boat *Nameless* can tug it downstream all the way to Umdala."

"I'm glad to see you've braced your spirit for what may prove something of an ordeal."

"Ordeal? Gosh, I'm used to it! The only thing that mildly worries me is, how will it *hear* me through the helmet?"

"You can set your mind at rest on that score. If there's no result, we'll send you in again without a helmet. Now here's the lamp you'll use. . . ."

At least this time, unlike my first trip to the head of the river, we would be dispensing with any banquets or solemn hoo-hah. Who needed them? For some curious indefinable reason I felt

171

quite off my food—and as for solemnity, whatever flip badinage I might utter, you can believe I felt solemn enough inside. In the pit of my tummy.

I was to transfer to the black ketch immediately. Departure time was set for a day hence.

So out to the moored ketch I was rowed by an apprentice, the oars dabbling like ducks on a pond. As our rowboat neared the ketch, a face peered over the gunwale: a face as ruddy as the sun through morning mist, a red orb topped with straw—and the sun rose a little in my heart.

"Peli! Peli, it's you!" I cried.

A moment later I was scrambling up the ladder, boarding. Peli from Aladalia! The water-wife with the warbling voice!

For five seconds we simply stared at one another. Then Peli cried. "Why, let me take a look at you!" and did just the opposite, rushing to embrace me and thump me about the shoulders to check that I was solid. I laughed and laughed; so did she.

"Oh, it's so good to see you!" I gasped, when we untangled. "But what are you *doing* here? Surely you haven't been stuck in Tambimatu ever since—"

"What, faithfully dragging the river for your body? No fear! Mind, I gave that skinny bitch what-for. The one who wanted you overboard. Don't know if you heard me. . . ."

"I *was* a bit busy at the time . . . No, but I did hear you cry out. And I felt your fingers trying to save me."

"Bless you, when I saw you leap on this gunwale and scuttle along the boom!"

"Did you sail to the current again, this Eve past?"

"No, I was in Ajelobo. The guild summoned me here. I'd been with you last time, that's why. Thoughtful of them, eh? The crumb of comfort. Some of the other 'sisters who'll be with us, *they* sailed to the head this time. And I can tell you they're definitely a better bunch than that tight-nosed lot *we* had. The only fly in the ointment is old Nothing-Bothers-Me—she's the skipper."

"I know. I've just come from her office. She's been working

172

overtime, welding me a wedding costume. It sure looks tight. That old worm had better not put me in the way of a baby."

Peli laughed, and caught my hand to admire the diamond ring. "Is this the wedding band? Won't the worm have a job slipping it on? He's a bit on the fat side."

"Oh Peli! Same old Peli. I bought the ring to make me feel good. *Something* has to. Well, *you* do. Being here."

"Hmm, not completely the same old Peli. Bit bothered, in fact. About Aladalia. I was down there in the summer, and now what's going on?" She sighed—but then her sun shone brightly again. "Oh, the hell with that. You've got enough worries for six people. And six just happens to be the number of the crew. Come meet your 'sisters!"

They were indeed a much better bunch. Three of them—Delli, Marth and Sal—had just sailed to the head and the midstream. Laudia and Sparki were veterans from way back who had been in Tambimatu when events, also, came to a head.

Laudia was a boatmistress and Sparki her boatswain. These two had been together a long time. Laudia was as blonde and elegant as Tamath, though with none of Tamath's ambitious insecurity. Sparki was dusky, diminutive and peculiarly boy-like. Peculiar, in the sense that the current hadn't thought so when she drank her slug of it. Sparki looked just the sort of person I thought the current weeded out: like a boy who had run away to the river in girl's clothes—as in one daft romance I once read, written without any knowledge of the actual facts.

Plainly enough this bosom couple were the two individuals on board most trusted by the guild; on account of their love of the river and love of each other, which were intertwined. The way of the river was the bond of their relationship; I could tell that from a dozen touches and tones of voice. Lose one; loosen the other? Perhaps. So Laudia and Sparki could be relied on to do whatever the guild required. At least I felt sure they wouldn't behave like martinets.

Five. And Peli made six. Me, seven.

Only, *I* wasn't crew; I was something else. I was the bucket to dip in the current's jaws.

After our supper of pork stew and rice that evening, we drank delicious strong green tea: Tambi-maté. In its storage jar Tambi-maté looked like a dollop of the local purée, dried. Generous wads were infused in boiling water in individual glass tumblers with real silver caps. Then you sucked the liquid through a thin metal pipe; and quite hard you had to suck, too. Sal, herself from Tambimatu, did the honours. The drinks set was hers, presented by proud parents when she was chosen for the New Year's Eve trip.

We drank quite a few glasses, getting a queer untea-like buzz from the drink, a buzz quite different from tipsiness. This was a clear-headed bright elation, accompanied by a slight anaesthetizing of the body so that after a time I couldn't tell whether I'd had enough to eat, too much, too little, or nothing; and I didn't care which. If only I'd had a jar of Tambi-maté with me a year earlier! It was perfect for someone lost in a jungle, with only grubs and roots to eat, and keep down. Though I'm not sure quite how I would have heated the water. . . .

"Will you sign your glass?" asked Sal, after the fourth or fifth infusion.

"Eh?"

"Your glass. Sign it with that diamond. Delighted to see you supporting local crafts, by the way!"

"You want me to scratch my moniker on this glass because I bought a jewel in town?"

"No, of course not! I want you to do it because there'll be songs sung about you in future years, and tales told."

"If there are, let's hope *I* get the chance to write them, or else they'll be a pack of lies."

"You will. I know you will! In fact, start scribing now: your name, I mean." Sal giggled. "Please! For luck."

"Go on," urged Delli.

"Well, okay then." Feeling rather peculiar about this—and realizing that I hadn't escaped ceremonies after all—I tucked the glass into my lap and inscribed "Yaleen" as legibly as I could.

Sal held the glass up to the lantern to admire, tilting it about; she had to, to make any sense of the spidery scratches against the sodden leaves within.

"I've spoilt it, haven't I?"

"Oh no! Absolutely not! I'll treasure this."

I felt light and euphoric. "It's my glass gravestone," I joked. "Will you put flowers in it if I die?"

She grinned. "No, but I'll drink Tambi-maté from it. All my days."

A while later, Peli blinked repeatedly as if to bring a bright idea into focus. "Yaleen, I've been meaning to ask: why *did* the current call you, a year ago? It wasn't objecting to you, otherwise you'd be dead. So what was special about *you*? I don't mean that as a put-down—"

"No, no, you're right!" She was, too. It seems astonishing in retrospect, but I had never actually asked myself this. I took it for granted, because it had happened to *me*. Like everyone else I was the heroine of my own life, the centre of the universe *et cetera*. Why shouldn't something extraordinary steer itself my way?

"Maranda wondered about that," volunteered Laudia.

"What, old Nothing-Bothers-Me?"

"*That* would bother her. She's been presiding over the annual trip for years. So when she heard you'd come back from the West, and hadn't been driven mad and drowned, she started puzzling. And she came up with an answer. You were very young to be honoured, Yaleen. I don't know why! Not quite two years on boats, and there you were sailing to the current—"

"I could tell you why, but it's a long story, full of junglejack festivals and. . . ." (And fungus drugs. Better not tell it after all. . . .)

"Let's just ascribe it to your sterling qualities, eh?"

"Um. Right. Qualities now in demand again . . . But what's the answer?"

"That you'd drunk the current more recently than anyone else who ever made the New Year's Eve trip. So maybe that's why it called you. Because you were more in tune with it."

"More in tune? That doesn't figure. The current can call a girl who fails her initiation, from a whole league away! It can call a man who tries to travel twice—"

"It can't *talk* to them, only craze them and destroy them.

175

That's why Maranda is bringing a fresh slug of the current on board tomorrow: some of the new vintage for you to drink. Plus some left over from last year, in case this year's has something wrong with it."

"Oh, shit! Look, I got through the current again just a bit ago. I probably swallowed dribbles and dribbles of it."

"But did it talk to you? Maybe it couldn't quite reach you."

"Maybe it couldn't be bothered."

"So another slug or so should tune you up nicely."

"Tune me up, indeed!" I swung round. "Peli, dear Peli," I begged, "give us all a real tune."

"Okay." And Peli gave voice.

Now, this might have been unkind if we had just sat and listened, grinning within. But we didn't. We all joined in; and not simply to drown Peli out. For the song was that irresistible one:

> *Under the bright blue sun*
> *River-run, river-run!*
> *Under the stars on high*
> *Sails fly, sails fly!*
> *Under the masts so tall . . .*

Presently Sal held up the signed glass again, canting it to catch the light. "Our boat ought to have a naming, too!"

"Why not?" agreed Marth. "Fat lot of use Old Nameless'll be if the current never comes back."

"What name does the current need to heed?" Delli thumped the bulkhead. "Boat, I name thee *Yaleen!*"

"I'll go one better," promised Sal. "I'll paint *Yaleen* on the prow tomorrow."

We all laughed. I didn't think she would do it.

Next morning Quaymistress Maranda boarded, bringing with her the "diving suit", air-bottles and rope. And when she boarded, Sal was hanging over the side, just finishing daubing my name in yellow paint. Maranda grumbled and growsed at this defacing of her precious ketch, till Laudia exclaimed exasperatedly, "We can always black it out afterwards!" Sensing unified opposition, Maranda conceded.

I drank her slugs of the black current, to no very noticeable effect; and soon we set sail.

All too quickly for me we reached the head of the river—and the worm's head, protruding gargoyle-like from that submerged stone arch with its chin resting on the water.

Was the sight more appalling by daylight? I'd feared it would be. Yet I found I could control my rising hysteria by telling myself that this thing wasn't alive—it was simply a mound of crudely-sculpted mud, or maybe basalt covered with mould.

When I'd last seen the worm's head, it was moving. Now it wasn't. The only movement was of water lapping it. Just so long as it didn't move! Just so long as a white eye didn't blink—why, that eye could be a slash of chalk! Even the drool in the worm's jaws hung motionless, like slimy stalactites.

We manoeuvred the *Yaleen* through some down-beating air turbulence almost up to the lip itself, deep-anchoring in the very lee of the Precipice where there was a pocket of calm.

The Precipice! Ah, better that I hadn't looked upwards! I couldn't believe that what loomed above could be a vertical rockface. It just had to be the real surface of the world. In which case, how come we were floating vertical to it?

The whole world bent abruptly at right-angles here, causing an awesome sense of vertigo. For a moment I imagined this was the effect of the slugs I'd drunk. But no; it was a consequence of the planet being hinged in half. I didn't dare look up again or I would fall, fall upward.

We worked silently most of the time, and spoke in hushed tones if we had to say anything. I don't think this was for fear of alerting the worm. No, it was because any words would be as stray melting snowflakes in that place; they would vanish before they could make their mark.

Sparki and Sal helped me don the diving costume. They strapped the bodice skin-tight, then slotted in the air-bottles behind, which effectively blocked access to the straps them-selves. The helmet was clamped to the brass collar, a valve was turned and I breathed bottled air smelling faintly of burnt oil. Maranda locked one end of the thin tough rope to my belt at the base of my spine; the rest of the rope lay in loose coils, with the far end tied to the capstan. She lit my lamp and clipped this to the bracket on my helmet. Then Peli thrust out the gangplank, on to the lip of the worm.

We were ready. I was ready. (And a little voice was gibbering somewhere, "Ready? How can anyone ever be ready for *this*?" I ignored the voice inside my head, since it was my own and I didn't wish it to reach my lips.)

Peli squeezed me in her arms, provoking one of the few sounds: a loud "*tssk*" of disapproval from Maranda, in case any of my fine equipment, product of the best Tambimatu artificers, should get scratched or crumpled before the worm could have its way. . . .

Then I walked the plank, with the rope paying out lightly behind me. I stepped on to the lower lip cautiously in case it was slippery and I skidded off into the water. Which would be an uncomfortable and ignominious beginning. But in fact the surface of the lip felt tacky, like paint which hadn't quite dried; and it yielded to the pressure of my feet, giving lots of grip.

Turning, I saluted the *Yaleen* with my diamond ring upraised. I don't know that the crew recognized the gesture as a salute; maybe they thought I was giving them the finger. I elbowed a dangling rope of drool aside—it didn't snap, just bent. I elbowed another gooey streamer, and shoved my way between them.

The inside walls of the mouth were bulgy and bumpy, and so dark they seemed to drink my lamplight. To see, I had to swing my head from side to side. Shadows ducked and dodged, as if racing round to ambush me from behind. I couldn't flick the beam too fast without dizzying my brains. Above me I saw a dark dome, sprouting warts the size of cushions. . . .

Hard to look down, encumbered as I was with helmet, bodice and bottles . . . but a ridgy floor below. Slicker and firmer than the lip.

As I stepped on in, my legs started to shake. Scared? Of course I was scared.

And of course that wasn't why my legs were wobbling.

To say that the floor split open under me would be too precise by far. It would grossly flatter the chaos of the next few moments. Before I knew it, I was a toddler careering down her first carnival slide, shrieking aloud . . . Rope snaking behind . . . Black jelly curve above . . . Light swirling, head thumping and bumping . . . Then the lamp went out. I only realized I'd been swallowed when I was already halfway down the gullet.

The tube swooped upwards briefly. Impetus carried me over a brink. I sprawled in pitch darkness.

And now I *was* shaking like a leaf. I'd pissed myself too. Hot at first, then clammy-cold. The blackness was absolute. In fact, you couldn't even call it blackness. It was *nothing*. I might as well have gone blind.

I lay very still. Or tried to. Since nothing further happened, I rolled over after a bit and felt about. Soft clammy texture here . . . Slithery and harder over there, like muscle . . . My fingers closed on a tentacle, shied away. Ah, it was the rope! My safety line. Should I jerk it? Give three tugs for "Pull me back, quick"?

But beyond being gulped down, nothing dire had happened. At least I wasn't floundering in acid juice. I continued exploring, very gently. Each new span my fingers touched was so much extra safety, so much breathing space. And so much extra cause for jitters, because the very next grope might bring me up against . . . who knew what?

I thought my blind eyes were playing tricks: I saw a flash, a flicker.

I shuffled about, and focused on a spot of shimmery blue. This brightened to a glowing patch. I held very still, hardly breathing. Perhaps the light was only a few spans from my face. In which case, it was far too close! The glow continued to intensify, but since this had no effect on the darkness near at hand, it must be distant. Then all of a sudden everything adjusted mentally, and I *knew* that I was peering along a tunnel of some kind, which eventually debouched into somewhere far larger that was aglow with blue light. I stood up, stretched tall, and my fingertips brushed the roof above. Shuffling to left then to right, arms outstretched, I discovered curving walls; these were squashy, though interspersed with stiffer "muscle-ribs".

So I began to plod forward in the direction of the light, holding my hands ahead of me. After the first ten paces I stepped out more boldly. And the glow increased in apparent size.

A few minutes later I stood in the doorway to a cavern that was eerie and enchanting. Curving walls and vaulted roof were ribbed and buttressed with blue bone, or stiffened muscle. All across a misty floor fronds waved like underwater weed. Warts humped up through the low mist and hairy "vegetation" in a line of stepping stones. And all glowed softly in various tones of light or dark blue: the fronds were almost mauve, the warts a brighter turquoise as though to mark the way. The cavern was long, long. Far off, the ground mist seeped upward to become a general dense azure fog. Was this cavern part of the Worm—or was the Worm's substance coating cavern walls?

The stepping stones led straight to a kind of island: a large hump of milky, veiny powder-blue. "Opal Island", I thought, giving it a name.

And here was I, held back in the very doorway by that damned rope! Which Maranda had so thoughtfully locked on to me, in case any meddling little fingers inside the Worm unknotted it. By now the rope had reached its limit.

Retreating a few paces, I gathered slack—and set to work fraying the rope with my diamond. Obviously I had to go on into the womb-cavern—why else had it lit up for me? I sawed away till I thought the stone might part from its setting; but Tambimatu craftsmanship prevailed. As well it should; I'd paid a whole bag of coins for the ring! At last the strands parted.

Pry as I might, I couldn't budge the air bottles; though at least I could unclamp the helmet, which was steaming up. . . .

The cavern air smelled faintly of dead fish and humus; nothing very stomach-churning—no swamp-gas or intestinal stenches. Once the helmet was wrenched free, the bottled air blew an annoying draught against my neck; I would probably end up with a stiff neck or earache. . . .

Still and silent stretched the cavern, save for a slight bubbling or susurrus amidst the misty fronds.

Should I bellow out, "I'm here"? The worm must know that already. I kept quiet.

I trod across the stepping stones—without any bother—and reached Opal Island. Closer up, this took on the proportions of the glazed buttock of a giantess: with veins of milky blue flowing within, and a large vague shape like a huge bone, inside towards the top. A rim ran right round the base. As soon as I set foot on this rim, the whole island quaked. Hastily I hopped back on to the nearest stepping stone.

The trembling quickened; shivers ran up the slope, overtaking one another—then there was a sudden loud "plop". The whole top of the island split open.

Two seams flopped apart, and a human arm emerged. It wagged about as though waving to me. A bald head and bare shoulders followed. Unsteadily, a naked man stood up. His skin was the unhealthy white of someone newly unwrapped from a long spell in bandages. He looked like a big jungle-grub. His groin was as nude of hair as his skull.

The man regarded me out of watery blue eyes—then he took a step, and slipped, and skidded all the way down the side of the island on his buttocks, fetching up with a thump on the rim.

"I—" he croaked. Abruptly he retched up a volume of thin white liquid. Maybe I hadn't too much to worry about from this fellow! Wiping his chin, he tottered erect, and contrived a smile—he pushed at his cheeks with his fingers as though trying on a mask for size.

"Hullo, I'm to be your guide. The current took me . . . some time ago. I tried to stow away, see. The current kept my body intact, so now I'm representing it."

"A *man* is representing it?"

He examined himself in surprise. "Goodness, I haven't been a man for ages. . . ."

"You haven't been . . . Are you *crazy*?"

"Actually, I'm dead . . . It kept my body, see. I've been living other lives, in the *Ka*-store."

"In the *what*?" For "Ka" was the name the Westerners gave to the mind-part of a person. They said the *Ka* flew back to Eeden when the body died. Flew to another world . . . "Are you from the West Bank?" I demanded.

"No . . . Sarjoy, once. . . ."

"You did just say '*Ka*', though?"

He nodded.

"Are the Westerners telling the truth, then? About the God-Mind on Eeden? How can there be a *Ka*-store here? What *is* it? What does—?"

He flapped his hands in distress. "Please!" The dead man gestured at another line of stepping stones continuing along the cavern towards the azure fog. "Could we possibly . . . ? Sooner we go, sooner I get back to my dreams."

"Go where?"

"To the *Ka*-store."

"How can there be a *Ka*-store here? This isn't Eeden. The current isn't the God-Mind—or is it?"

He slumped down and clasped his hands around his knees. Maybe he had difficulty standing up, after being dead for so long. . . .

"I suppose we've time to spare," he conceded.

"Time? You do realize there's a war on? That good people are being butchered? And all because the current withdrew! Was it poisoned?"

"If only you'd stop bombarding me . . . Yes, I realize there's a war on. No, the current wasn't poisoned. Will you listen to me? The black current can store the *Ka*s of the dead, so long as people were close to it in life. As it links more *Ka*s in its store, so its mind grows in power."

"You mean to tell me that all riverwomen who ever lived are still alive here?"

"Well, they're dead, but yes. They dream each other's lives now. And as they interweave, so the creature who was here before us all seeks . . . seeks the mind-key to the universe."

"Oh." The mind-key to the universe. Tamath had speculated that there was a key stuck down the worm's throat . . . So it was the key to the universe, was it? But apparently the worm, too,

182

was still hunting for it. Just then I remembered what Andri had told me: that people couldn't simply arrive on a foreign world and merrily fit in from the word go. "Did the current *shape* this world for us?" I asked.

"I don't follow you."

I did my best to explain. "Did the current alter this world so we could eat and drink and breathe here?" I ended up.

"Quite the contrary! The world grew of its own accord. So did the current. I don't quite know how its body works, but I do know that it takes energy from water. It splits and burns and changes water . . . Well, aeons ago it floated off down the river. And it made a big mistake. On its own, you see, it has no more brain than a worm in the soil. But it can use *other* minds. It has a thirst for them, it can drink them. And after drinking them it can start to think."

"I sometimes feel that way myself."

The zombi looked irked. "Really? Well, the current sensed dawning minds on the land. So it exerted itself to use these minds. But they were only dawning, and it quenched them instead. They withered and died out. Then for aeons more it just lay inertly, sensing only the slow dim wits of fish and the like. It hoped other creatures might become aware, if it let them alone."

"How could it *hope* for anything, if it hadn't a mind of its own?"

"It sensed. It *felt*. The flow of its being is to *know*, through others. To absorb, to drink. . . ."

"So then I guess the Ship from Eeden arrived at Port Firsthome?"

It had indeed. Yet for aeons the creature had been sluggish. It had simply been existing at the bottom of the river like a vegetable.

Before it could grasp what was happening, the world had half changed. New plants and fish and animals were mingling with the native ones, in some cases pushing the old life aside, in other cases even cross-breeding.

Suddenly as if from nowhere, bright strong minds were present. Young minds, printed with mature purpose, newly dressed in knowledge. This was the first generation of settlers.

Amongst whom, the current dimly detected two varieties of

being: those of Flow, and those of Thrust. The one, compatible with it; the other, alien. Excited, confused, it rose from the depths, putting forth its senses—to be dazzled, blinded.

It still couldn't "think" about any of this—which in any case after all those dormant aeons seemed to happen instantaneously. And almost immediately, a vast intelligence from far away shone through these bright new minds as through a window; touched the current, tasted it, tried to extinguish it.

This distant intelligence was a being of Thrust, rejoicing in its grandeur and dominion. So, at any rate, it seemed to the current, when the current tried to analyse events long afterwards. However, this ambitious intelligence had already transformed almost the whole of its local substance to breed plants and animals which would be at home on the new world, and then to build human bodies, and to light their minds with *Ka*s from afar.

Instinctively the current lashed out to save itself. And there was madness on the land: a storm of forgetting, a whirlwind of disruption. The worm wasn't quite sure whose fault the mind-disaster was. It suspected that the far intelligence might have tried to extinguish its *own* experiment upon this world, to break the link with the creature it had woken.

Some settlers lost less of themselves, some more. All were deeply confused. Two groups survived: one on the west bank, where the far intelligence was remembered, though chaotically; another on the east bank, where its origin was quite forgotten.

Down succeeding centuries, as the current established a rapport with Those of the Flow, in the east, and drank the spirits of the river-dead, it began at last to *know*.

Thus spoke the zombi. His name, he added in an afterthought, was Raf; though he seemed to attach little significance to it, as if it had been centuries since he last used it.

And now events were on the move.

"Poisoned?" Raf chuckled. By now he behaved more naturally, though he wasn't exactly my notion of convivial. "Not on your sweet life! The current got just the ingredient it needed dumped into it. The rennet, to curdle the milk of its mind. To

184

thicken it, enrich it. It had been trying to influence those cult-women inland from Port Barbra, but they were hard to get hold of. . . ."

"What? Say that again!"

Credence, boatswain of the *Spry Goose*, hadn't been so hard to get hold of! Suddenly that whole episode of the Junglejack Festival took on a startling new perspective—and I found myself pitying Credence. She had been manipulated in her beliefs, used as a tool—to be discarded when she couldn't prise open Marcial-la's cabin door. Credence mustn't entirely have known why she was conspiring; otherwise she might have proved more effective. Hell, who was I kidding? With Marcialla unpersuaded and marooned up a tree, it was only by a hair's breadth of bad luck—known as Yaleen—that Credence failed.

Raf looked dreamy. "Ah, I have been one of those cult-women. She fled from her coven to sail the river . . . She could see how young they all died, and looking so old! Oh, I've known the Timestop, and the Timespeed . . . But never mind about it now."

Never mind? In one sense Credence hadn't failed at all. All unwittingly, she had set *me* up as her successor.

And this, Raf was only too happy to confirm. For the second time within a few seconds my perspective on events swam inside-out.

"You came along just at the right time," he said. "The current read you. *You* proved better. More economical! You solved another problem, besides: how to lure those Sons of the God-Mind closer, so that the current could drink enough dead *Ka*s to really get to know them—and taste and test the link to that far puissance. . . ."

"Hang on! Do you mean to say the current provoked this war? Just so that Westerners would get killed, and it could harvest some of them?"

"That is putting it a bit crudely."

"How can it harvest dead Sons now it has *quit* the battlefield?"

"Never fear! After a while it will return downstream. It can judge the progress of the war by the *Ka*s of newly dead riverwomen. Since they're in tune, they still die into it."

"And am I supposed to applaud this clever scheme? Which brings agony and death!" If I'd thought Doctor Edrick was unscrupulous, then surely here was his match!

"Well, it wants to become a God, you see."

"A . . . *God*?"

Raf glanced around. I did, too . . . and my blood chilled. Surely the cavern walls had crept closer while we were talking? Surely the roof was lower than it had been a while before?

"The Sons would have waged war in any case," Raf said reasonably. "Sooner or later they would have found a means. In fifty years or a hundred. The time isn't important."

"It is, to anybody who's alive!"

This part of the cavern definitely was shrinking. The fronds sprouting out of the ground-mist were getting agitated.

"No, it *isn't* important! Not when you can live a host of other lives hereafter. Nobody who is taken into the *Ka*-store regrets it. And remember, when the current becomes a God, all those *Ka*s will be part of that God too."

"According to you."

"You'll find out soon enough, Yaleen. The current is pregnant with itself—"

"Uh?"

"I'll rephrase that: soon the current will give birth—to something greater than itself. And it feels it should be fertilized—"

"For crying out, doesn't it *know*? Who ever heard of getting fertilized *after* getting pregnant?"

"I don't mean literally fertilized. It *senses* that it needs the intimate presence of a living person during the change. Here is the womb; you are the man-seed."

The womb. And right now the womb was undergoing a contraction. . . .

"I'm a woman, you dumb corpse!"

"Please! The current is the Flow; you are the stone that shapes the Flow. You are the agent who helps it change, without changing yourself. It'll keep you in dream-life while it broods around you."

"It brooded round me twice already! And crept and crawled inside me. This is getting to be a habit."

186

"Ah, but this time—"

"Third time lucky?"

"This time you will be a legend, Yaleen. When you finally walk out of its mouth, salvation will be at hand."

"What if I don't want to be a legend?"

Frankly I didn't think the current had a chicken's idea what it was doing. If it had, I didn't think much of the plan. Not when the worm was content to start a war to get its way. Even if it did immortalize assorted fallen victims.

Those walls!

That roof!

"Look, I don't want to sound abrupt, but the place is caving in. Goodbye!" I turned and quickfooted it over the stepping stones towards the tunnel mouth. Fronds writhed up over the warts ahead to block my way.

"Stop!" cried Raf. "The mouth's closed!"

I did stop. "What?"

"The mouth has shut."

Maybe I shouldn't have paused. Fronds were questing for my ankles now. I kicked at them. Maybe the zombi was lying?

"There are such rewards, Yaleen! Access to all the lives that women have lived!"

And maybe if I did fight my way out, with my mission unaccomplished, Maranda and Sparki and Laudia would toss me back inside . . . While I hesitated, the ceiling slumped a little closer. Obviously the cavern was a hole in the Worm's body, a big bubble it had blown in itself within some vaster subterranean space.

Kindly consider the absurd horror and lunacy of this moment. Outside, the world was in chaos. A giant tadpole wanted to make love to me, or something. And the roof was falling on my head. In such a moment, what could save a girl but a sense of humour? (Or a sense of *rage*—somehow rage didn't seem a useful reaction at this point.) I began to laugh. I doubled up. I creased myself.

"What's wrong?" cried Raf anxiously.

"Oh nothing . . . !" With an effort I controlled myself. "It's so bloody funny, this business of becoming a God! How lucky cats and dogs are, never having to try! Just look at it: this collapsing

187

Ka-theodral of a womb . . . a zombi for a guide . . . the spirits of the dead spun in a yarn . . . barrels of minced fungus gotten by devious guile . . . all in the guts of a worm . . . a war thrown in! And at the end of the tunnel, what: power and visions? Life is quite absurd!"

"But the universe itself is paradoxical," called Raf brightly. "Existence is. I mean, why should anything exist at all? So maybe true knowledge and absurdity are twins. Maybe the one is the key to the—"

"Oh, shut up!"

Already the wart-stones beyond had all vanished under writhing fronds; where I stood was similarly infested.

"I'm coming back, damn it!" Swiftly the fronds at my feet shrank away.

We set off promptly for the far end of the cavern. Now that I was on the move in the desired direction, the shrinkage back at the island end appeared to have stopped.

So off I trod to confront my destiny, and the Worm's destiny, and the world's; loaded down with useless bottles of fresh air; sporting a jewelled ring, with the power only of cutting rope; and guided by a hairless animated corpse . . . As I followed Raf's lead along those wart-stones, I decided that Doctor Edrick and his cronies would never get anywhere with *their* quest for knowledge. They were far too serious about it. The real and the true could only be seized in a laugh, a laugh which would rattle the stars.

And the trouble was, at the same time it all *mattered*; mattered intensely.

Still, I was determined not to be too tense. It's no good tensing up for love, eh? And our worm had decided to love me. Somehow.

I was in the midst of finding out how to be mad and sane simultaneously. I hoped the Worm could perform the same balancing trick. Then maybe it *would* graduate into a God. . . .

I hadn't known what to expect. A mound of jelly shot through with sparks? A pool, depth-full of flickering darting starlight: *Ka*s held in suspension?

What we arrived at finally, somewhere in the azure fog, was a fountain-basin: a phosphorescent powder-blue bowl some nine or ten spans across, bubbling with denser violet fog like foamy suds.

A coldly boiling cauldron. A chalice of flesh. A bathtub.

Of course all the "architecture" hereabouts had to be a purely temporary affair. This chalice, or bath of suds, had been laid on specially for me. I had no idea what the *Ka*-store might look like the rest of the time. Perhaps like nothing at all.

"You climb in," advised my friendly zombi. "You lie down."

The basin bore a certain resemblance, also, to an enormous sphincter muscle. "It won't close up on me, will it?"

"It won't *eat* you—never fear!"

Why did people say things like "never fear" when that's just what anyone in their right mind ought to be doing?

"Perhaps I could assist you with those things on your back?" Raf offered gallantly. "They look cumbrous to lie on."

"Ah, so comfort *does* come into this! That's nice to know."

With a certain amount of fumbling, Raf managed to detach the air bottles. He had no such luck with the locked belt and tail of rope.

So I climbed aboard that basin. As I did so, a sigh of satisfaction seemed to sough through the cavern. I lay down in the violet fog; at once I felt myself departing, into a different kind of place . . .

And I enter the *Ka*-store. . . .

I'm Lalia, a woman of Gangee, thirty years old, dark and tall and strong.

I'm borne along within her life. A stick floating downstream, I go where the water wills; unlike a fish, which can turn and oppose the stream. . . .

I'm a stowaway in her. I wear her like a glove. I see what she sees, feel what she feels, speak what she says, go where she walks. I regard Gangee not as a dingy hole but as home, a drumskin of familiar beats.

She, the Lalia who is experiencing her life unfolding, remains unaware of me. Yet a later, more complete Lalia seems to know me, and nod in recognition. My life as Lalia isn't continuous. I experience her in spurts, like a gashed artery from which her life-blood springs. Several days, then a skip forward.

Men of Gangee are planning an expedition to cross the desert. By investing in supplies the river guild has bought me a place on this expedition as their observer. Maybe another river flows somewhere beyond the sands?

Why, this must be hundreds of years ago! Yet equally it's *now*: the urgent present moment, the moment which matters above all others.

Which matters most . . . and least. The present moment, the moment you're living through, is often rushed away impatiently for the benefit of future moments. Or maybe you stand quite still and try to halt time, to savour the present moment to the full; but what you're really saying to yourself is: "Look! Concentrate! I'm here now at this point in space and time. I hereby fix this moment in memory forever—so that I'll understand and treasure the meaning of it . . . in another hour, another week, another year. Not now; but *then*." Only when a moment lapses and is gone, can it be really known. Thus the moment is everything, and nothing too.

Yet since I, Lalia, am living each present moment ordinarily, but also as part of my whole completed self, this treachery of time is healed now. Each instant becomes radiant and luminous. Every act and word is a dewdrop and a diamond.

This is the joy of the *Ka*-store; it could also be the horror, if the moment was evil and agonizing. But even horror is outshone, when the light emerging from each moment is so bright that pain is blinded.

We march inland from Gangee to the verge of the desert, accompanied by a gang of porters laden with supplies. We set up base camp in the dusty outback beside a tree-fringed pool, the last well. Beyond, there's only a plain of fine gravel horizoned by distant dunes.

We have planned well. Taking turns, we lead teams of porters far out into the Dry to lay down caches of food and waterskins filled from the pool. The first such sortie takes a couple of days, to go one day's march and return. The second sortie penetrates twice as far. And so on. In this way we scout a full week's

190

journey into those far dunes, preparing the way, always returning to base. These preparations occupy several weeks and limber us up marvellously.

Then we dismiss all our porters and set out alone to cross the Dry. Six of us: five men, and myself.

Thanks to our preliminary forays, the first week's journey is easy—even though the ridge-dunes we have to cross are soft underfoot and complexly interlinked. We find all our caches without any fuss. Dunes may creep, but not that quickly; and only gentle breezes blow. It's the calmest time of year, the Lull. The river, of course, is breezier even during the Lull, but we're far away from it. We have six weeks before the winds blow strong again.

A sea of star-dunes succeeds the ridge-dunes; we can thread our way through these at speed. On scattered rocky outcrops, landmarks in the arid ocean, we stash food and drink for our return, further lightening our loads.

And I fall in love with one of the explorers, Josep. Likewise, he with me. But this is wrong. He's a man of my own home town. We could only have fallen in love by being so far removed from the breath of the river. By being so isolated.

Isolated! Yet always we are in such close proximity to four other Gangee men (who mustn't guess; yet do) that we can do nothing at all about our love. This is both a torment and a blessing. We burn with frustration and yearning and dread, as surely as we burn in the heat by day. To me Josep seems uniquely brave and beautiful.

Three weeks inland; and still no change in the dearth and death of the landscape. Only minerals grow here.

Impasse: the other four want to return while there's time. But Josep cannot bear to fail—though this is one of those enterprises where even to have attempted it is a sort of success. Josep wants to journey at least a fraction as far as *I* have travelled, on the river; but in his own direction. Only such a one could I love, who mirrors me.

After a parched conference, it's decided that three will stay here, camped in a jumble of crystal-crusted rocks in a shattered region of shale. Three will scout onward: Josep, me, and Hark.

A day later Hark decides that we're marching to our deaths. And maybe we are. Maybe my bones will lie down locked with Josep's bones upon a bed of sand.

Hark and Josep quarrel; not violently but in a softly hateful way. Hark acts as though Josep is betraying the spirit of our expedition, by pressing on with it. Hark can't bear to be within the aura of our love, which grows fiercer the more it is prevented.

He leaves us early in the morning to retrace his steps to where we left the others. When he reaches them, they will stay two more days, then depart, taking all the food and water with them; that's the threat. The promise.

As soon as Hark has gone, Josep and I set out for the nowhere beyond nowhere. We have just one more day, one night.

How defiantly we spend that night! It seems as though the entire purpose of our expedition, all those weeks of preparation, all the porters and supplies, is simply for us to make love. Will we return and report, "Oh yes, we discovered *something*—we found each other"?

Yet at sunrise, when we stir again in one another's arms, the suspicion dawns on me that Josep is making love not to a woman, but to the desert itself—to this naked emptiness far from the river where no codes of river life apply. My breasts are as star-dunes, my flanks a dune-slope under his sliding fingers. Between my thighs is the well of liquid we have not found. I'm the desert made flesh. Only thus can he master it; he who must master something.

That day we return in silence to the place where we parted from Hark. That night, when we unroll our blankets on the sand, Josep is impotent—because he is withdrawing from the desert now. Although he clutches me cruelly and forcingly, in a way I have never known a man act before, he achieves nothing. At last he turns aside in an agony of shame, so that I have to comfort him; and this is worse, for he weeps like a child.

In the morning when I wake his tears are still falling on my face. It feels that way. Actually stray raindrops are spitting down on my skin from a solitary cloud.

Off to the west, an impossibly dark mass of clouds bunches

low, dispensing rain; dirty sheets of water drench down. Within an hour the clouds have fled, the sky is clear.

And when finally we reach the jumble and the shale, first we find one drowned corpse then another then a third. The freak flood has vanished; the desert is parched dry again. Waterskins have been washed away and ripped by shale, so that there's only a slop of liquid left in those we recover. We find a fourth corpse, Hark's, his skin already turning to leather.

"You brought the river here!" Josep screams at me insanely.

Thankfully my life as Lalia jerks forward at this point, lurching towards its close.

A few days later, somewhere further west amidst star-dunes, Josep falls down dying of thirst. As I am dying too. . . .

And for a moment I believe that a miracle has happened, and that actually I *have* commanded the river and it has come to pour down my swollen throat and slake my terrible thirst!

But I'm dead; and the black current has received its daughter into it from afar. As I soon discover. I've come home—to myself at last; and it's this which illuminates all other earlier moments of my life . . .

I'm Charna, a teenager of Melonby, eager to join the riverguild in another year or two.

Right now it's the cruellest winter in memory. The river has frozen over. Boats are locked at their moorings, with ropes and spars crusted by frost just like the decorations on iced name-day cakes. No river traffic moves.

With my best friend Pol I venture on to the ice, skating and skidding, and scuffing up the dust of snow in lines and arcs. (It's so cold, the snow is dusty not moist.) I carve my name upon the river for all to see.

Some of those who see are boys, who begin to dare each other, for it seems as if the river has become as safe and solid as a road. They admire me; resent me. They're scared, and proud. In the bitter calm cold they grow hot-headed, jeering and teasing, us and each other. Presently the boldest and most foolish of the boys steps on to the ice himself, and skids along beside us.

"You'll have to walk for a wife now!" warns Pol. "You've used up your one go."

"Nonsense! I'm not on the river, I'm on ice—on top of it! I bet you could cross all the way to the other side!"

"Oh no, you couldn't. The ice'll be thin in the middle. Maybe no ice at all."

"Wheee!" He runs, and crouches into a skid. He tumbles and pratfalls all along the ice. Scrambling up, he slides back to the bank and hops ashore. "Come on, you lot!"

"No fear!"

"Not likely!"

"Chickens," he sneers, and jumps back to his ice-sport. Leaps on the ice a second time.

"Oh, I'm a river-boy," he sings. (Of course, the real song is about a river-*girl*.) "My boat is quite a toy! She brings me heaps of joy—!" (He's just making up the words, mocking them.)

Suddenly he screams: "Destroy! De-ssss-troy—!"

He windmills his arms wildly. He begins to race. Out, out. . . .

We all watch, numbstruck. Soon he's hundreds, a thousand spans away. In his green coat he's a leaf blowing over the ice. Then he's no more than a sprig of grass. Finally, far away, he vanishes. The faintest twang sings through my feet. The ice has cracked, out there.

And a death has happened, because I wrote my name on the river.

I'll *not* feel guilty! Of his death I am innocent!

I'm a boatswain of Firelight, a happy and fiercely passionate woman. How can she be both at once? She is. I know; I'm her. She burns like the dancing jets of flaming gas in the caldera outside the town; yet inside she is sunned by her passions, not consumed or exploded. . . .

I'm a multitude of lives, all linked, reflecting into one another. All those vistas and ventures I ever dreamed of as a little girl— and was robbed of so abruptly—just as suddenly are mine; to overflowing. . . .

* * *

I am Nelliam, aged guildmistress. . . .

Nelliam? Guildmistress from Gangee? But *how*—?

I'm in Verrino, residing with the quaymistress. I've been here for weeks, engaged in negotiations with the Observers. Perhaps I'm not the best choice of intermediary, since I can't possibly climb that wretched Spire in person . . . But I meet a young man on neutral ground, usually one of the many wine-arbours. He has coppery skin, lustrous eyes and a pert little nose. If I were only forty years younger, and less sadly wise than I am now. . . .

(My own heart lurches—for of course, the young man is Hasso, my erstwhile one-night lover, he who plucked the first flower of my flesh.)

From another point of view, that of someone who can look back down many thousands of days of life, maybe I'm the best person for the job. But only maybe.

So I set my sails to the task, applying gentle persuasion, as though I'm out to seduce this young man; and only occasionally do I lose patience with him.

Much has been agreed in principle, and even put into practice; but now I want those panoramas of the west bank which the Observers have been collecting and hoarding for a hundred years. I want these sent to Ajelobo, there to be engraved by craftsmen—and printed in a gazetteer which our own signallers can emend by pen.

All of Yaleen's information will be printed in this gazetteer as well. It will be a second *Book of the River*, a ghost guide to a world hitherto unknown. Or maybe I should describe it as a second Chapbook, since its distribution will be strictly limited. No additional, unofficial copies will sneak out; of that I can be sure. Those Ajelobo publishers depend on us to freight their wares.

Tonight is the night before New Year's Eve, and the wine-arbour is lit by fairy candles. The arbour isn't heavily patronized this evening; most people are saving themselves up for the morrow. A couple of riverwomen natter together. A lone old man broods. Two lovers—husband and wife of a few week's vintage, by the look of them—whisper in a nook.

Apart from these, only Hasso and I. Age wooing youth—

195

except that Hasso is a little *too* experienced, suave and cautious. Personally I could do with an early night. No rest for the wicked, though.

"What guarantees can you offer?" he's asking.

"Our word of honour," I repeat. "Your panoramas will be perfectly safe. We just want to borrow them. We'll return them inside a year. It'll take as long as that."

Lights flicker softly around us. There should be music to serenade us. But no; music would lull me to sleep.

"Okay, *I* believe you. I'll consult. . . ."

We agree to meet again in this same arbour on the night after New Year's Day; it should again be quiet, in the aftermath of all the parties and revels.

But come that night in the New Year, the arbour isn't quiet at all. It's packed and noisy. Because the head of the black current has passed Verrino. Now everyone is telling everyone else about it, offering explanations, contradicting each other. Instead of peace and privacy there's pandemonium.

It's a clouded black night, as black as the current which has now abandoned us. All those fairy candles are just petty twinklings lighting up the tiniest part of our fearful darkness. Crowds have sought sanctuary in this and the other arbours, away from the now naked river.

And I know that I, Nelliam, am about to die . . . Soon, and bloodily. I try to make myself stand up, to flee while there's time. But that isn't how it was; Nelliam's legs don't heed Yaleen.

Unsurprisingly Hasso turns up late for our appointment. He chucks down two glasses of wine straight off before whispering to me what the Observers saw of the worm's head through their telescopes. I can hardly make out his mumbling, with all the surrounding din. "Speak up, will you!"

He recoils, brows knit, offended.

"I'm sorry, Hasso, we're all on edge. Pardon my tetchiness."

"That's all right. I understand. So *then*—"

A sudden scream from the direction of the waterfront cuts across the babble. Momentarily the hubbub dies—then it re-kindles, doubled. People leap up and crush into the alley.

"Wait here! I'll be back." And off goes Hasso, too.

196

Before long, bedlam is spreading this way. A murky red light leaps up above the rooftops. Somebody cries, "Fire!" Then a huge crash deafens me, and the fairy candles dip in unison to a hot breeze.

Hasso's soon back, out of breath. "Armed men. Must be the west! Come on: to the Spire!" He seizes my arm.

But I resist. "My dear boy, I couldn't climb that Spire to save my life."

"That's exactly what—! Nelliam, I'll help you. I'll carry you up."

"No, you must go on your own. I'd burden you; rob you of your chance. But promise me something. Promise that you'll be true, up there."

"True?"

"Observe! Stay aloof! Record whatever happens. Now *go*. Go! Or I'll get angry with you."

He dithers. Of course. But ruin and terror are racing closer every moment.

So then he leaves me. Though not before, absurdly, passionately, he kisses my wizened brow.

I refill my glass from the beaker. Such a shame to waste good wine. I sip, and I wait.

Though death, when it comes, is by no means as blithe and quick as I expected.

Nor yet so final, either. . . .

At about this time I begin to detect something. For some reason my attention isn't being distracted by my sojourn in the *Ka*-store, so much as sharpened. Maybe that's because I have just been Nelliam, who is no one's fool. Maybe it's because the real significance of events shows clearly—luminously—through these lives, as never was during life itself.

From the corner of my mind's eye I catch a glimpse of what the Worm is doing with me while the "entertainments" are going on. It's using me as a kind of shuttle in a loom, to weave weft and warp together into a new design, a different and superior pattern.

It occurs to me that this might make me instrumental in what

197

sort of God it becomes. I might gain some kind of influence over it.

So, during my next slice of life, as a fisherwoman of Spangle-stream, I do my best to ignore the pageant. This isn't easy. As soon ignore your own life while you're busy living it! The proprietor of the life I'm reliving suspects she's being snubbed. But then she cottons on (I think).

Time and again, I present a certain image to myself. I make this image the fiery centre of my attention.

And this image is . . . But wait; not yet.

One day while I'm out in the fishing smack hauling in nets heavy with hoke, a hand reaches into my life. The hand hangs in mid-air like a fillet of white fish, fading off at the wrist. . . .

When I grasped that hand, sky and stream and fishing smack all dissolved at once into a foamy violet fog.

I sat up in the luminous chalice. It was Raf, my blanched zombi, who held my hand.

He helped me up, though I didn't feel particularly weak. On the contrary: quite perky! Perching on the lip of the basin, I decided that the Worm must have nourished me well and kept my limbs toned up while I'd been resting in the bowl. Unless my period of dream-life had seemed far longer than it really was.

"How long did I spend in the *Ka*-store, Raf? Hours? Days? Weeks?"

He shrugged. "I've been away dreaming again."

"And is the current a God now?"

"I'm not sure. It's . . . different. Maybe when a God's born, it's only a baby God to start with, and needs to grow up?"

That special image was still rooted in the heart of me. I concentrated intently on it.

Worm, I thought, *how goes the war?*

Faint images flickered before my eyes; I couldn't make much sense of them.

Worm! I presented that special image to it.

With my inward ear I heard a groan of acquiescence. Victory! I *had* succeeded in printing that special pattern in the new fabric, in one corner at least.

I hopped down from the lip. "Okay," I told Raf, "I'll be on my way." I hoisted the bottles.

"What do you want those for?"

"Mustn't leave litter! Especially not in a God!"

"Oh, it can absorb them. Dump them."

Yes, when its body thinned out again . . . He was right. So I dropped the bottles, which would only get in the way. Let the guild dock my pay, if they dared.

Raf and I parted at Opal Island. The tunnel end of the cavern was still shrunken, but no more so than before. The fronds kept out of my way.

I regained the dark exit. The helmet lay where I had abandoned it, but of the rope there was no sign; and the tunnel was pitch-black. I fiddled with the lamp to no effect, then cursed myself for a fool. The solution was simple.

Worm: light up the tunnel!

And presently the walls glowed faintly blue. Grudgingly; but enough to light my way. That I should be able to reach the mouth was a precondition of that special image I'd fed the Worm. Thirty paces along, I spotted the rope.

Maybe it had been jerked along when the Worm's jaws clamped shut. Or maybe the crew of the *Yaleen* had begun to haul it in . . . I tugged the rope experimentally three times, but nothing happened. *Was the boat still waiting?* I laughed. Because it didn't matter; didn't matter in the slightest.

Before long I reached the end of the tunnel, where the rope led over the ledge and angled down a dark hole.

Worm, light your throat!

Light glowed faintly, and I rather wished it hadn't. Originally I had rushed right through the Worm's gullet in darkness, arriving almost before I knew I'd left. Now that I could see what faced me, claustrophobia loomed. I would have to dive head-first down the hole. Suppose I got stuck, would the Worm obligingly hiccup me out?

No point in brooding. Down I went. Fast, for the sides were slippery. I writhed round the bend, and hauled rope hand over hand.

199

Up. Up. Above me in the dim light I could see the rope sprouting from the lid of the tube like a tap-root. I couldn't see any sign of a seam. Squirming tight up against the lid, I prised. In vain. And maybe when the lid did split open the rope would run free and I would slide back down again.

An image appeared in my mind: of a trapdoor which only opened one way—and only when a weight bore down on it.

Now you tell me! I hung in despair, punching feebly overhead.

A second image blossomed: of the Worm's chin ducking underwater; its jaw cracking open while one corner of its mouth continued to clench the rope (in an askew grin, which seemed directed at me); then tons of river water pouring in.

If that was the only way. . . .

I braced myself as best I could. Clutching the rope in both hands, I shut my eyes, held my breath. *Okay, do it!*

The tube tipped forward. Squelchings and gluggings, offstage. A few preliminary drops dripped down my face, then suddenly a deluge drenched and battered me. I was nearly swept away.

Somehow, *somehow* I clawed hand over hand up through that waterfall . . . And I was still underwater. Why, oh why, hadn't I brought that bloody helmet? If I didn't get some air soon I was going to explode.

Dizzyingly my world tilted upwards. Higher and higher. I hung on for grim death as the river drained down past my eyes and nose. I spluttered, gulped air, blinked—and I could see a great wedge of daylight.

The throat had closed up tight again, leaving a shallow slop of water on the floor of the mouth. It was lucky for me no stingers were flapping about, but none had entered with the flood. (Maybe the Worm could control them?)

Lying hunched where I was in one corner of its jaws, I spied river. Sky and clouds. A chunk of boat—with one welcoming saffron word: my name.

I jerked my head about a few times to knock the water out of my ears. I heard no familiar voices outside, but this hardly surprised me. Given the muting effect of our anchorage, any cries of alarm would have been quickly stifled.

Okay, Worm. Open wide!

As the jaws unglued, I staggered erect. I tore strands of drool out of my way and stepped forward to the lip. The rope, still dripping from its sudden dunking, sagged over the gap of water to the capstan. Since I had stood here last, the boat had ridden back more than twenty spans, dragging its anchor, and half-turned.

The crew were all lined up, staring at me.

"Hi there!" I shouted. "What date is it?"

After goodness knows how many days of whispers, now at my shout a dam of pent-up noise broke open. Laudia, Delli, Sparki and Sal began to babble questions; but Peli bellowed, "Shut up!" louder than any of them, and answered me.

Seven days had passed since I'd gone inside.

A week of war.

"Right," I called, "I'm going to stop the war! And here's how—"

I told them; and they gasped. But I think Peli and Sal believed me, at least.

"I'd like some food and drink sent over. Just in case I get peckish!"

"How about bedding?" shouted Peli.

Hardly. I'd slept in bushes, up trees, on mud and moss, on Spanglestream quayside, and most recently in a chalice of fog.

"No, but I could use a change of clothes and a towel—I'm drenched! And when you've sent everything over, unhitch this rope. Haul your anchor up. Sail the old *Yaleen* well clear!"

Because the boat was already well out of gangplank reach, some debate ensued as to the best method of supplying me; then a wooden laundry tub was dropped in the water, a canvas bag full of my requirements lowered into this, and a line tossed to me to pull the tub across. After emptying the tub, I cast it adrift.

"Hey!" cried Maranda indignantly.

Ignoring her, I stripped off—all but the bodice, which I had to tolerate. Fortunately it was fairly water-resistant. I towelled myself as dry as I could and donned new boots, breeches and a jacket.

201

"Oh, and you must signal downstream! Beach any 'jacks who are on the river!"

"Will do!" Peli unhitched the rope. I dragged it through the water and coiled it behind me in the mouth, leaving myself a loop to hang on to. Most of the rope was held tight in the gullet trap, of course. So now I had the Worm harnessed, after a fashion.

The crew soon upped anchor, upped sails, and stood off. Sparki was already signalling downstream. I stood there in the mouth, my chest braced against the rope.

Worm! And I presented that special image to it.

I met unexpected resistance. An image of majesty. Puissance. *But I'm a God*, this seemed to say.

So blast me with lightning! I retorted. *If you don't like it.*

There actually *was* a mild rumble, though it came from deep within the Precipices. I guessed the Worm was readjusting itself internally, since this rumbling went on for a while. The noise was more like flatulence, a grumbling of the guts, than thunder. After a while, it stopped. That cavern where I'd been must have deflated by now.

Nothing else happened, but I stood firm, still insisting on that image. This Worm wasn't going to make a fool of me now! Actually, the Worm was already obeying; that was what the thunder meant.

Yaleen. Its voice came clearly in my head. *I shall help, because you helped me.*

Nonsense, you've no other choice. And anyway it's your duty to help people, if you're a God.

Duty? Is it? My duty is . . . to know what I am. To know what the other God-being is.

Why not leave well alone, Worm? Look after your women and your waterway.

The other God has eyes and ears here, girl! I need to gather the Kas of its servants.

You'll collect enough of those, as we clear up the mess you caused.

Afterwards, we'll be quits? You and I? It was almost an appeal. The Worm was beginning to sound a bit more human. Less of that solemn "Worm of the World I am" business! Was that the secret of its change: that in becoming a God, it had become a bit more human at the same time? Less of a great big sponge for soaking up minds; more of a person in its own right? A person with a hint of me in it?

Well, I'm not one to bully a God; in future I'll just ask politely.

Ask . . . what?

Oh, of Kas and God-Minds and other things. Of stars and worlds and Eeden.

I'll be sure to let you know, when I know, myself.

Good. If that's all settled, let's move! I waved a warning to the *Yaleen*, then I jerked the rope.

Presently the Worm's head surged out of the Precipice. Propelling itself, I guess, by sucking water into its underside then jetting it out. Or maybe it used the energy it got from burning water. I glanced aside: old Nothing-Bothers-Me was really gawping. Peli was openly weeping with joy. Sal was cheering. I kissed my diamond ring to the two of them. This was the pattern, this the special image: myself riding downriver in the Worm's jaws.

As we swept past Port Barbra a couple of hours later, we weren't of course close enough to shore for me to spot any crowds lining the bank. Nor were any boats likely to sail out and maybe get in our way. However, I still stood grandly at the helm as though steering. Signals were flashing far off, and no doubt numerous spyglasses were trained on me. There are times when one should enjoy one's moments of glory, not shrug them off modestly.

Another four hours, and it would be night. By then we ought to be between Jangali and Croakers' Bayou, and I might as well get some rest. (I wasn't *actually* steering the current.) By dawn we would be approaching Gangee, and getting near the war zone.

I had a choice to make. A decision before me.

For in my eagerness I'd neglected something fairly basic: namely, how I was going to disembark. Perhaps I ought to have hung on to that laundry tub after all! First the diving helmet, now the tub; I seemed to have developed a habit lately of throwing

203

away things that I might need. If only I'd asked for a mirror, too! And not only to tidy myself. Come to think of it, I could probably use one of those bottles my friends had sent over, to flash a signal. . . .

My choice? It wasn't just a question of how I would disembark; though that little problem did rub home the nub of the matter. And the nub was this: I could halt the Worm at Umdala. I could wait for a boat to put out and take me off. Then I could despatch the Worm's head onward into the wild ocean. By so doing I would have restored the current to the whole length of the river, and our world to itself. By and large. Give or take weeks of warfare to liberate Verrino.

But ought I?

I thought of how "conserver"-minded my own guild was at heart; yet how much freer and finer women's lives were as a consequence compared with life in the west. And on account of the fact that men hadn't been able to sail the river. Surely everyone's life in the east, man and woman, boy and girl, was better as a result?

But then I thought of the frustration and resentment the 'jacks would feel after they had tasted travel to distant ports, and sacrificed lives in the process; unless they were all supremely glad to march home . . . three hundred leagues on foot. (For they certainly couldn't sail the river, with the current back in place.)

I thought of the madness of Josep, who had yearned to journey far, only to see his dreams first drowned then parched to death. And I thought of that boy destroyed for a dare on the ice at Melonby. I thought of Kish caught in a spider-web of domestic bliss in Jangali.

I thought of my own brother, destroyed by restless curiosity—because there was only one outlet for it. I thought of my parents, and Narya. I weighed and I balanced.

The Worm could come just *part way* out of its lair. It could stop near Aladalia, say—leaving a further hundred and eighty leagues of northern water free for men and women voyagers, both. True, that was only one quarter of the river's length. But it might be a start, a promise . . . On the other hand, this would leave a long stretch of river-border open between east and west. The Westerners would be wise to assume we could close it if we wished. Though were they wise? And would they refrain from raiding and piracy? Would the towns from Aladalia to Umdala thank me for leaving their shores unprotected?

Ultimately, the wisdom or otherwise of stopping short did rather depend on what the Worm might learn of that distant power in Eeden which had sent us all here in the first place. It hung, too, on what the Worm might learn of itself (God or not). I didn't think the Worm quite knew what a God was; did anyone? Maybe a God was just an idea, waiting for an embodiment—like any other invention, such as the mysterious vessel which had brought our seeds here long ago. Which brought me back to the puzzle of the Big Intelligence, born of men, which ruled in Eeden.

Basically, had I the right to decide to stop short? Had I won this right by restoring the current? Or had I only redeemed the mess I had provoked? In future years would I be seen as a heroine or a criminal idiot?

How could I know the answer to that, till it was far too late to choose a different option? And did this matter? Maybe no one can be a heroine if they set out to be one. And if someone does set out to be one, *distrust* them.

Questions, questions. At least I had a choice. A free choice, for once. On behalf of everyone living, and quite a few who were dead.

The bow-wave rolled foaming away equally towards east and west. I laid down my harness rope and burrowed in the canvas bag, unpacking dried fish, sweetcakes, fruit, a bottle of water, a bottle of wine.

I drank some water then scoffed a few cakes and chewed on a fish-stick. The wine I would reserve to toast Jangali when we passed. A swig or several would help me get to sleep that night; to sleep upon my little problem.

By the time we reached Verrino next day, I would certainly have made my mind up. That's what choices are for. To savour them while you can, and then to seize one. Or the other.

*   *   *

So here ends *The Book of the River*.

My Book of the River, that's to say! The book that the river guild asked me to write, here in Aladalia, even while the war was being fought and won a hundred leagues away. I guess they felt it necessary to explain to everyone from Umdala to Tambimatu exactly what had happened, even if this meant spilling secrets in the process (and perhaps bruising a few egos!). Otherwise, who knows what scare stories and wild rumours would have been flying about for ever more?

Before this book is printed up Ajelobo way they'll probably change the title, though. And maybe some committee of guild-mistresses will go through it first with a pot of black ink . . . And then again, maybe not.

At first I imagined that writing a book might be as daunting a task as swimming the river or walking to Manhome South. But once begun, I found to my relief (then delight) that my story flowed easily enough. My reading of all those Ajelobo romances came in handy at long last! I think I even got better at it as I went along. In fact, I can hardly bear to put down my pen.

What else?

Oh yes: I have nutbrown hair and hazel eyes. I'm slim, rather than skinny (except when on my way to Manhome South); and in bare feet I stand just over five spans tall—or short. I have a chocolate mole on the side of my neck. I forgot those little details. That proves I'm modest. Obviously. (Should I add them in? No. . . .)

But of course there's *more*; which is what these last few private words are really about—for my eyes only.

This part doesn't belong in the book, but I'd better write it down in case I get struck by lightning or something.

For the Worm has kept its promise—just last night. (As if it had watched and waited till I'd finished my whole writing task.) Last night I dreamed I was out alone upon the river in a row-boat; when the grim head (which is actually loitering south of here) rose from the depths. Suddenly I was wide awake in my dream, and in my head I heard these words:

Yaleen, I was made, *aeons ago, to keep this world empty of mature minds. I was put here as a destroyer.*

Recently I brushed against the God-Mind of Eeden and it cried, "Wretch! On six worlds since this one, I found your likeness. Habitable worlds, with no high life on them. You aborted intelligence on them, you kept them lying fallow. You injured my people when they came! What made you, *Demon? Name your Master! War will go on between us till I own you and can use you, to find what made you lie in wait a million years, as a trap and barrier.*

But Yaleen, I think I've found how to enter Eeden. I believe I can send a suitable human agent along the psylink. To fabled Eeden, Yaleen! And back again!

Even in a dream I was able to figure this one out. And retort, *Don't look at me! I* like *it here.*

Come, come, Yaleen, chided the Worm. *One fine day you'll die, then your* Ka *will be with me to send wherever I wish.* Its long white eyes winked, and its head sank back beneath the water.

Me, travel to Eeden along the psylink? As an agent in a war of the Gods?

In the words of some sensible lads of Melonby: not likely! And, no fear! I've some items of human business to attend to.

I *still* haven't seen my parents, to bring them up to date. Maybe I ought to wait till my book is printed and send them a copy first? But that would be churlish. We've been strangers too long. I still haven't bounced Narya on my knee; Narya my sister, not of the river but of flesh.

I'll certainly go to Verrino to begin with. Not merely because it's on the route to Pecawar—nor to gawp at the damage or the prisoners, or to collect horror stories. I very much want to find out if Hasso is alive. I want him to know how much Nelliam appreciated his final kiss. And maybe repay him in kind.

I might stay in Verrino a while, maybe help a bit with reconstruction. But then I'll head on home for sure; back to Pecawar.

Before leaving home again . . . to go where?

I do fear that there's a big "where" waiting for me. And *that* may well be another tale, just as long as this *Book of the River* (new version, by Yaleen of Pecawar). If there is another tale, it may be longer than the river itself—for maybe it will stretch all the way from here to the stars.

I can always hope I'm wrong.

Right now, I just can't tell.